Praise for *Death in a*

"For fans of cozy mysteries in Southwestern settings."
Library Journal

"Marty Eberhardt creates a tale full of endearing characters, alluring landscapes, and local flavor... Seeded with native plant lore, *Death in a Desert Garden* had me guessing right to the end. If you can't get enough of good mysteries with southwest settings, make *Death in a Desert Garden* the very next book on your reading list."
Vicky Ramakka, Author, *The Cactus Plot*

"The lush descriptions of the plants and the ecological considerations involved in running a desert garden are the canvas on which the investigation unfolds. You'll keep turning the pages until the totally unexpected conclusion."
Carolyn Niethammer, award-winning author of eleven books on the food and people of the Southwest.

"Combining a determined sleuth who skillfully navigates all levels of Tucson society, with such a vivid sense of the Southwest... with a mystery that will keep you guessing until the final pages—makes Marty Eberhardt's *Death in a Desert Garden* a first-rate addition to the ranks of debut mystery novels. Brava!"
Kris Neri, Award-winning author of *Hopscotch Life*

"Marty Eberhardt expertly draws the reader into the beauty and danger of the desert, weaving elements of the traditional mystery into the story along the way. The result is a great read!"
Marty Wingate, author of the *Potting Shed* mysteries

Advance Praise for *Bones in the Back Forty*

"Marty Eberhardt has penned another winner."
Kris Neri, Award-winning author of *Hopscotch Life*

"This gripping story intertwines Eberhardt's deep knowledge of the desert landscape with characters whose social and ethical leanings invite readers to pause and consider the impacts each of us has on our fragile environment."
Betsy Randolph, 2021-2022 President, Women Writing the West

"Marty Eberhardt crafts the perfect picture of life as a public garden professional. She skillfully creates characters both as charming as the garden itself and as complicated as the history of the Southwest... filled with twists and turns, making it a great read!"
Michelle Conklin, Screenwriter and Executive Director, Tucson Botanical Gardens

"Eberhardt has skillfully created a world of characters we all want to know, so that we root for Bea as she digs her way into this second harrowing "garden" adventure. We shiver as not only Bea, but her loved ones face threats from a diabolical mind."
Mary Coley, author of *Blood on the Mother Road*, 2022 fiction winner, Oklahoma Book Awards

Other books by Marty Eberhardt

Death in a Desert Garden

Bones in the Back Forty

A Bea Rivers Mystery

By

Marty Eberhardt

Artemesia
Publishing

ISBN: 9781951122454 (paperback) / 9781951122539 (ebook)
LCCN: 2022941801
Copyright © 2023 by Marty Eberhardt
Cover illustration copyright © 2023 by Bill Singleton

Printed in the United States of America.

Names, characters, places, and incidents depicted in this book are products of the author's imagination or are used fictitiously. Any resemblance to actual events, locales, organizations, or persons, living or dead, is entirely coincidental and beyond the intent of the author or the publisher.

All rights reserved. No part of this book may be reproduced or transmitted in any form or by any means, electronic or mechanical, including photocopying, recording or by any information storage or retrieval system without written permission of the publisher, except for the inclusion of brief quotations in a review.

Artemesia Publishing
9 Mockingbird Hill Rd
Tijeras, New Mexico 87059
info@artemesiapublishing.com
www.apbooks.net

Dedicated to those who have lived in and loved
the Gila region of New Mexico.

Acknowledgments

I'm grateful for the landscapes of the Sonoran Desert and the Gila region. Without their endless vistas, and of course their lovely plants, I would not have been inspired to write this mystery series. I'm grateful, too, for the people who have made these habitats their homes, from the ancient Mimbres and Hohokam to present-day readers, writers, scientists and other appreciators. I'd like to mention several in particular.

Marilyn Markel reviewed the archaeology in this book, and made some needed corrections. Wendy Sutton, of the U.S. Forest Service, enlightened me about the Native American Graves and Repatriation Act, as well as other important regulations. Any mistakes I've made about Mimbres archaeology are mine, not theirs. I'd also like to thank the Grant County Archaeology Society and the SiteWatch Program of the New Mexico Historic Preservation Division for providing me with extraordinary experiences in Mimbres archaeological sites.

Dr. Charles Merbs, Professor Emeritus at Arizona State University, gave me the idea of using a button osteoma to identify the bones. Susan Berry provided plenty of helpful insights into 1960s southwest New Mexico.

Bill Singleton once again created a terrific cover. His work is such a good match for this series.

So many people read versions of this book. So many people had so much patience. My wonderful editor/publisher, Geoff Habiger of Artemesia Publishing, continued to provide excellent advice. Liz Trupin-Pulli improved the manuscript enormously, and I'm so thankful for her professionalism and friendship. Early versions of the book were read by Carolyn Niethammer, Margaret Harmon, Bette Pegas, Anne McEnany, Ann Hedlund, Betty Spence, Karen Reichhardt, Jim Heard, and Sam Schramski. My Women Writing the West mystery critique group, Betsy Randolph, Laura Alderson, and Mary Coley, helped immensely with a later version. Seasoned writers Kris Neri and Carolyn Niethammer gave me practical advice. And of course my husband Phil Hastings read and helped with everything all the time.

To all of these, and to hundreds more whose influence led to this particular book, I thank you.

Chapter One

If you work in a public botanical garden, and you're having a bad day, you can walk out the door and your equilibrium is restored. That's what Bea was telling herself, as she went past the traveled part of Shandley Gardens, with its manicured paths and themed, planted beds. She wasn't in a mood to linger in the tropical greenhouse, where things were blooming despite last night's January freeze. She stopped for a moment in the native plant garden, admiring the sun on the long silvery spikes of deer grass, cascading over some sharp-spined agaves, and then she strode out to the wild desert area. The garden's founder, Alan Shandley, had laid out some primitive paths back there, in an area populated by jackrabbits, deer mice, and giant saguaro cacti which stretched like a huge dance troupe all the way to the Rincon Mountains. Bea always found that walking caused her brain to engage.

She was trying to resolve a dispute between two absolutely dedicated volunteers who were also quite dedicated to their own points of view about how meetings should be run. She found herself in this umpire position upon occasion, as her title was education director/ volunteer coordinator. Nothing that a refreshing walk couldn't make clear, she thought as she headed to a particular tree, a big green-barked palo verde that would mark her turn-around point. But she was surprised to see her colleague Javier working in this remote part of

Shandley Gardens. He'd clearly been fixing the old, sagging barbed-wire fence that marked their property line with the national park. When he turned towards her, she didn't even look at the shovel he was holding out, because her eyes were caught by his expression. The lines in his kind, sun-weathered face were screwed into a grimace. He looked down at the shovel. She followed his eyes. There were a couple of ribs lying there, and Bea wondered for a moment why Javier, of all people, would be so disconcerted by an old deer skeleton. Then she noticed the bone at the back of the shovel. "It's human, Bea," Javier said, as she stared at what must be a lower jaw.

"It can't be!" she said, automatically, and then she was silent as Javier carefully put the bone back on the ground and shoveled up a new one. It was the rest of the skull. He held it out to her again, and she stepped back.

Not again, was her first reaction. Business had finally returned to normal at Shandley Gardens after a different body had been found on the grounds last summer. *That was only six months ago.* Liz Shandley, Alan's wife, had been hit by a falling eucalyptus branch. When it turned out that the woman's death was no accident, the entire board and staff had been possible suspects. *It would be utterly horrible if we had to go through all that again. This is not happening.*

"I guess I'd better stop now and tell the cops," Javier said. His mind seemed to be working considerably more clearly than Bea's, which was in full-fledged denial.

"I doubt it has anything to do with the Gardens. It's probably somebody from ages ago. Maybe an ancient Hohokam, or an Apache, or a miner, or something. This place has had a long parade of inhabitants," Bea said, and then stopped herself. "Sorry."

She knew perfectly well that Javier's family had been

part of that "long parade." They'd owned the ranch that was now Shandley Gardens but had been cheated out of their property in the early part of the twentieth century by a wily Anglo rancher. Alan Shandley had bought the place some years later when the unscrupulous rancher went bankrupt. Alan had created beautiful gardens, but when he died, his wife had been quite happy to move into town and turn the place into a nonprofit botanical garden.

"I just hope this has nothing to do with Alan," said Javier. He placed the bones back carefully into the hole he'd been digging and leaned the shovel against one of the sagging fence posts. The barbed wire was loose enough so that any coyote, or human, could get through. That had probably been the case for many years.

"How long has that park service road been there?" Bea asked. Javier knew more about Shandley's recent history than anybody. He'd worked as Alan's gardener for years when the gardens had been Alan's private hobby.

"I don't know. I started working for Alan in eighty-one and the road was here then." That meant Javier had been working on this property for twenty-eight years. No wonder he knew every inch of the place.

"We'd better walk back and call this in," Bea said. She'd purposefully left her cell phone in her office, but Javier had his.

He pulled it out of his pocket and waved it at her. "I'll let Ethan know." As he started punching in their boss's number, Bea thought he'd regained some of the bedrock composure that she so appreciated. The grimace was gone.

It was time for her to get back to the office; this stress-releasing walk had been neither as quick nor as calming as she'd intended. On the other hand, the issue that had caused her to walk out the door now seemed awfully petty.

Back at her desk, she'd just managed to concentrate on the email she was sending to the feuding volunteers when she heard a familiar, heavy footfall approaching her office. Javier stood in the doorway. "The Tucson PD is sending somebody out here right away to tape the spot off. And to talk to me. And to look things over." He swallowed. "I feel like I'm in a plane that's gaining speed and about to take off. Guess I ought to find something constructive to do until they show up."

"Buckle up," Bea said. As he left, she told herself she ought to find something constructive to do, too. She sent off her email and was creating a PowerPoint entitled "Lose the Lawn! Water-Conserving Options." She'd managed to create a decent-looking title slide, plus a couple more, but she kept thinking about Javier out there with the cops. Maybe she should take another walk, not all the way to the palo verde tree, but close... She created a few more slides. She was putting on her jacket when she heard Javier's boots in the hall again. She'd been hoping for that sound. He walked straight through the door and dropped into the chair in front of her desk.

"The bad news is I have to head down to police headquarters for another interview with the cops. That last one was just 'preliminary.' Not with the primary investigator." Javier had had a time of it during the crisis six months ago. "The good news is your friend Marcia is in charge again. I guess I'll see her downtown."

This *was* good news. Bea and Marcia had been friends since elementary school, and their trust in each other was rock-solid. They'd taken each other's measure back in junior high, when a teacher had been sexually aggressive on a school field trip, and the girls had given each other the courage to report the abuse, at the ripe old age of twelve. Marcia and Bea had worked together on Liz's case at Shandley Gardens six months ago. If Marcia was in charge of this latest incident, Bea could unclench her hands, which she'd just noticed were tight in her lap. Also, she reflected, she could give those tight shoulders a roll.

"Well, let's hope Marcia wraps this up soon," Javier said, as he walked out.

Bea had to interrupt her less-than-cheerful thoughts to conduct the weekly newcomer class, which she'd entitled "Arizona is Not Michigan... What and How to Plant in the Sonoran Desert." The usual suspects were there—refugees from dark and endless winters, folks who'd bought homes in Tucson and then were completely flummoxed about how to deal with so little rainfall, mandatory conservation measures, hard-as-rock caliche soil, and totally unfamiliar plants. Bea wasn't on her game, though. When one of the newbies protested that too many desert plants were "skeletal," Bea found herself shivering.

"Are you ill?" asked a woman who'd said she wasn't from Michigan. Bea's class was still aptly titled, since the woman was from neighboring Wisconsin.

"Oh, no, I'm fine, thanks. I probably should put on my sweater. We keep the heat low to save energy, but it can get chilly, don't you think?" Bea wasn't sure if this should be considered diplomacy or outright falsehood, but it turned out to be a useful dodge, because another woman, quite thin and frail-looking, said she'd appreciate it if Bea turned up the heat.

When her class was nearly over, Bea saw Javier pull into the parking lot. The classroom, which was also the board room, was the former dining area of the Shandley home. Its windows looked out onto what had once been an attractive front yard. The yard was still appealing, but it was considerably smaller than it had been to make way for a public parking lot. Javier was getting out of his white pickup, well within Bea's sightline. As she distributed helpful planting handouts and Shandley Gardens membership applications, she saw Javier striding towards the door that led to their boss's office. Ethan Preston, Shandley's Executive Director, had an office that was once the master bedroom, and it had a door that opened onto a side courtyard, where Javier was clearly headed. Bea would have loved to be in on their meeting, but somebody wanted more information on the benefits of membership, and the chairs and tables needed to be put back into committee formation, so there was no hope of hearing what Javier had to say.

Bea went past Ethan's doorway on the way to her office, but it was shut, of course. She couldn't make out anything Ethan and Javier were saying, although she lingered in the hall, pretending to read an important message on her cell phone. Her ruse was useless. She went back to her office and shut the door, determined to concentrate on her volunteer staffing chart.

Javier's steady heavy-booted walk stopped at her door and he knocked. Bea said "Come in!" before he'd gotten in a second knock.

"I don't suppose you're curious."

"Not a chance," she said, rolling her eyes.

"Of course not." Javier plopped down again in the chair that faced Bea's desk. "Ethan told me I'd better stop off here before I got back to my 'actual job.' So... Ethan called Marcia and asked her to have the cops drive to the site via the park service road. That way visitors aren't freaked out by a bunch of cop cars in the main parking lot. I guess they were okay with that... they're down there digging up the poor guy and doing whatever they do to look for clues. Hopefully no tourists will venture out that way this afternoon. The cops will probably send the bones over to the medical examiner. He has a forensic anthropologist on staff. He's my cousin, Bea," Javier said with a little laugh. "Marcia said he will brief Ethan a bit about what he finds before the ME report is done. As a courtesy."

Bea had ceased to be surprised at the people Javier was related to. These relationships had often benefited Shandley Gardens in the past, but a forensic anthropologist was a first.

"So right now we don't know how old the skeleton is. I'm hoping it's really old, like you said. Putting all of us out of the picture."

"Well, I hope we didn't just dig up an archaeological site. That wouldn't be so good, either."

Javier threw his hands up in a "Who knows?" gesture, and left Bea to her computer. But after reading the same sentence over three times, she decided to pack up for the day. It would be good to spend a nice, normal evening with her kids.

As she walked by Ethan's office, he called her in. Her boss was an athletic-looking guy, not much older than Bea, which meant he was fortyish. His shirts were pressed and so, too, were his slacks. Every time Bea registered his immaculate appearance, she thought about how his schedule gave him the time to cultivate it. In her harried single-parent world, there were not enough minutes in the day to become impeccably neat. But now Ethan's hair was sticking up on the left side, where he'd clearly run his hands through it. "I just got a call from the *Tucson Post.* That same reporter from the last time we had a... controversy here. Somebody reported the police digging in the Gardens. I told her I had no information, and that whatever happened probably occurred long before any of us were here. They'd already talked to

Officer Samuelson—Marcia—and of course she told them they don't comment on ongoing investigations. So, in the absence of facts, count on speculation. I just thought you'd want a heads-up."

It would have been easier to go home without this to ponder.

Chapter Two

Bea supposed that Ethan's parting words meant she'd need to discuss the skeleton with her seven-year-old son Andy and his little sister Jessie. Bea definitely didn't want their classmates to beat her to it.

Over baked yams, steamed chard, and turkey burgers, she let her kids know that their classmates might be talking about some old bones that were found at the Gardens, but "the person died a long time ago, and our friend Marcia will do a good job of figuring out what happened."

She hadn't finished that last sentence before Andy yelled, "Oh, *no!* Kids are going to be really mean about this, Mom. Jason Hanson already teases me that my mom works in a 'murder zone.' I guess he gets to watch a TV show called that."

Bea accepted the implied rebuke about her strict TV policies, but she was steamed about this bullying. "You can tell Jason Hanson that he should bring his family out for a nice day at the Gardens. They'll have a great time."

Andy rolled his eyes, a gesture he'd just perfected. Bea let go of the smile she was forcing and gave her son a hug, burying her face in his red hair. Jessie had been coloring a jungle scene during the entire discussion. Not for the first time, Bea wished a little of her kindergartener's carefree temperament would rub off on her brother.

After she tucked the kids into bed, Bea decided to forget the damned bones. The discovery was none of her concern. In the worst of scenarios, the press would be an annoyance for a few days before they went away. In the best, the publicity would bring even more visitors to Shandley. The Gardens had gone from being the "best kept secret in town," a moniker that nobody wanted, to a well-known attraction. Instead of thinking about the bones, she could focus on something positive. She smiled to herself. That would be her boyfriend, Frank. He'd be flying in the next morning...

"Boyfriend" was such an adolescent word for a thirty-five-year-old man dating a thirty-eight-year-old woman. Even though he'd kept his shabby studio apartment in Tucson in the two months he'd been on the East Coast, he'd be spending quite a bit of time in her detached, ground-level "unit" at Palo Verde Acres. And to celebrate their reunion, Bea and Frank were going to spend MLK Day weekend at a B & B in the little mountain town of Copperton, New Mexico. Bea's ex-husband was taking care of the kids for the entire weekend. This was the most time he'd ever offered to be with their children, probably because his mother was visiting, and Bea aimed to take full advantage of the weekend. Who knew when there would be another one?

Her mind went back to Frank. He was almost too good to be true. He was considerate, good to her kids, and sexy to boot. And he was also considerate of his ailing mother, who needed him in Washington, D.C. He hadn't had a stable job in Tucson, just piece work writing freelance stories and doing grant writing, which was his bread-and-butter... and which he could do anywhere. They'd had only a few months together before he'd gone back to the East Coast. She suspected, from his phone calls, that he felt pulled in both directions. In her darker moments, she also remembered that there had been a woman named Sherry in Virginia, not so very far back in his past. Clearly, she'd have a lot to discuss with him, but she was going to have a good time for however long he was here, or however long the good time lasted. Once you had been married and divorced you had to think this way.

***

The next morning Bea had managed to rouse both of her grumpy children at six a.m. and pack them into the car to pick up Frank at the airport after his red-eye flight back to Tucson. Bea's heart quickened when she caught sight of him as she waited at the "Arrivals" curb and she wasn't sure she could afford that kind of reaction.

The children leapt on Frank, their grumpiness gone. Maybe it wasn't only her heart she'd need to watch. They were even more enthusiastic about the promise of hot chocolate once they got home. Back at the apartment, sitting around the breakfast table, the whole situation began to feel shockingly comfortable, as the kids acquired chocolate mustaches and Bea and Frank sipped some very strong coffee.

She began to catch him up on the skeleton story. "So far, we don't know whose bones they are, but I'm hoping maybe we'll know more today. We're all hoping the skeleton's too old to implicate Alan or Liz Shandley, much less any of us at the Gardens now."

Bea was savoring her second cup of coffee, a French roast that Frank had brought from D.C., but then she looked at her watch. Time to get the kids to school.

As Andy put on his jacket, he asked, "Frank, are you going to stay in Tucson or go back to Virginia?" Her son was not one to mess around.

"Your mom and I are going to have some long talks about that this weekend." Andy pulled on his ear, a bad sign. "I'd like to keep hanging out with you guys." Andy looked away, but Bea wasn't fooled. He was listening. "I'll see you when we get back from Copperton, buddy."

Bea's five-year-old daughter gave Frank a big hug goodbye, right after she threw herself at her mom. Then Frank reached for Andy, who gave him a tiny squeeze and wriggled away. He hugged his mother, but then gave his ear a long pull as he got in the car. "Mom, Dad said he wants to spend more time with us, too. But he doesn't."

"Well, you'll be with him for three whole days this weekend, him and Granny Bertha."

"Uh-huh." Andy silently looked out the window the rest of the way to the bus.

Bea was going to have to put her worry about Andy out of her mind for the weekend, too. That would be harder than forgetting the damned bones.

Bea and Frank planned to put in a few hours of work; Bea at Shandley, and Frank at his computer in Palo Verde Acres. Bea had figured on a return to routine, but that Friday was anything but normal. There was a note on her door from Ethan telling her to come to an "urgent staff meeting" at 8:30. That meant Javier, Ethan and Bea, since Angus, the chief horticulturist, was happily snorkeling in the Caribbean, not checking email since he was truly on vacation.

Did Ethan have news about the skeleton?

Her boss wasn't acting relieved when Bea and Javier slid into two chairs facing his big oak desk. His hair was most definitely combed into place this morning, and he looked at the two of them in silence for a couple of moments, with pursed lips. He kept tapping his pencil on a legal pad. Bea's attention wandered from the pencil to Ethan's wooden file cabinet, behind him and partially obscured by his desk. It looked like he had been searching for something desperately. Drawers were open, files were hanging out. Ethan followed Bea's gaze to the cabinet, turned all the way around and looked at it, and said, "Yes, let's do discuss that."

He got up and walked to the filing cabinet, motioning for them to follow him, which they did. *What a mess.* Papers were scattered on the floor. Bea and Javier exchanged what they hoped was a barely noticeable, expressionless look, and waited.

"I pride myself on hiring people I can trust, and then trusting them to do their jobs," Ethan said, marking the word *trusting* with a pencil thrust.

This time, Bea and Javier exchanged a blatant look of shock.

Somebody had to reply. "What is your concern, Ethan?" Bea asked.

Her boss nodded toward the cabinet, and then returned his penetrating look at both of them.

"I don't think either of us understands," said Javier.

"Don't you." It was not a question.

"No, we don't," said Bea, with quite a bit more warmth than Ethan was showing.

"Well, let me enlighten you. Somebody broke into my file cabinet, and rifled through the personnel files."

"Ethan, I did not do that," Bea said.

"Neither did I," Javier rejoined quickly.

"And if either one of us had, do you think we'd leave our handiwork that obvious to you?" Bea asked.

"That did occur to me," Ethan said, and Bea thought the ice cubes in his voice had melted slightly.

"I don't think either one of us has anything to worry about in there, anyway, right?" Bea asked. *There can't be any dirt in there that Javier would want to see. Besides, he'd never break into a file cabinet. It was somebody else.*

Ethan seemed to have been thinking along the same lines. "That's the odd thing. I don't see why either one of you would have cause to do this. But on the other hand, who else would care?"

"Well, the only other person who's ever worked here is Angus, and he's on vacation," Bea said. "Probably somebody thought you had valuables in there, Ethan."

Ethan went back to his desk and sat down. "I'd prefer to be able to trust my staff. Nothing was taken from the file cabinet or anywhere else in my office, as far as I can tell. Check your own offices. I'll tell Marcia about it. Let's all get back to work."

Bea and Javier raised their eyebrows at each other, but not until they were safely in the hall.

But Ethan called them back together an hour later.

"Marcia was kind enough to send me the forensic anthropologist's report. That is, your cousin's report," he said, looking at Javier. He pulled up something on his computer. "The skeleton is an adult male, thirty-five to forty-five years old. He's not an ancient man, given the relatively modern bits of clothing they found, not to mention a Mickey Mouse watch. They dated that to 1968. He was wearing a vintage Summer of Love tee shirt. It helps that things don't disintegrate in the desert very fast. The cause of death *appears* to have been a blow to the back of the head with a blunt object." He continued to read from the monitor, "'Fracture lines reached suture lines because of the bone sinking down into the cranium.' The man's head was hit *around* the time of death, although he can't be sure that it caused his death."

Ethan stopped this recitation and looked away for a moment, then held their eyes. "I'm afraid the medical examiner will probably say that he was murdered."

Bea sucked in her breath and Javier croaked "No!" at

the same instant. Then he looked down at his hands.

"Do the police have any idea who this person is?" Bea asked.

"No," said Ethan coolly. "But there's one more thing. Something that should help identify the skeleton. The man had a very dense bone formation right in the center of his forehead. It's called a 'button osteoma.' About the size of a nickel." Ethan formed a nickel-sized circle with his thumb and forefinger. "It would've looked like the guy had a bad... a really bad bump on the head, except that it would be normal skin color, and it wouldn't go away." Ethan stopped talking and looked at them.

"Well, that should help identify the guy," Bea said, in what she hoped was a level tone of voice. Why was Ethan acting as though they knew something about this already?

Her boss continued. "The police haven't found any records of a missing person with a button osteoma, but they're just starting to look."

"Well," Javier began, keeping Ethan's gaze. "I started working for Alan about twenty-eight years ago in the early eighties. That was a long time after the Summer of Love."

"That was 1967. I wasn't sure how long you'd worked for Alan," Ethan said. He let go of the pencil he'd been gripping.

"But Alan and Liz *were* here forty years ago," Bea said. She immediately wished she'd kept her mouth shut. A scandal involving their founders was *not* anything Ethan wanted to think about.

"I can't believe that Alan had anything to do with this," Javier said. He stopped and looked at his hands again. Maybe he was thinking about how much gardening those hands had done with Alan Shandley. They were big, callused hands, competent hands, hands you could trust to do things well.

"Let's hope not," Ethan said. "Okay, let's really get back to work this time."

"You remember that I have the afternoon off, right Ethan?" Bea asked.

"Lucky you," he said. She wasn't going to let his negativity or even another possible murder spoil her weekend, damn it.

Chapter Three

By 2:00 in the afternoon, Bea and Frank were on the interstate headed east in her aged Toyota Corolla. Bea hoped the kids would be picked up in a timely way at school, and then reassured herself that her former mother-in-law was in charge, and she'd managed a houseful of boys and a randy husband.

Bea explained her morning session in Ethan's office.

"Well, it's disturbing, all right. Bea, how hard is it to break into the Shandley Admin Building?"

"Probably not all that difficult," Bea conceded. The money was in a safe in a part of the building with an alarm system, but Ethan's office wasn't protected. It hadn't needed to be, they'd thought.

"No offense, but that sounds like the kind of rose-colored glasses that get nonprofits into trouble," Frank said.

"Our windows are pretty old. They don't really lock."

Frank gave her a look.

After two hours, the saguaros of the Sonoran Desert gave way to the yuccas of the Chihuahuan. As they turned north at San Marcos, Bea wondered if she'd made a mistake in booking their weekend in neighboring Copperton. San Marcos's main strip was now a succession of boarded-up gas stations, graffiti-strewn motel skeletons, and empty stretches of desert where the native plants had not grown back, and the tumbleweeds were decorated by blowing plastic bags.

"We always used to stop here when I was little, on the way to El Paso to see my grandmother. There was this great drug store with a soda fountain and the best root beer floats."

"Another casualty of the interstate system, I'll bet." said Frank.

"Yeah. Well at least Copperton is not an interstate stop. It's in the middle of more than three million acres of forest."

"A lot of places now in '09 are not what they were before the recession."

Frank looked over at Bea and took pity on her pained look. "Bea. We have the weekend off. The forest won't have changed, the hiking will be great. Don't worry."

Bea's spirits soared as they headed up to the Continental Divide. Copperton was nearly 4,000 feet higher than Tucson and a couple of thousand feet higher than San Marcos. The spare, thin shapes of the yuccas and sotols of the flat Chihuahuan Desert began to yield to the fullness of piñon pines and junipers on undulating hills. The higher they drove, the greener and wilder it seemed to get. There were bits of snow along the road, and she could see white in the mountains to her left. They cranked up the heat. The car thermometer registered twenty-nine degrees outside. There was a Continental Divide Trail sign with a tall peak behind it, so Bea told Frank she was going to pull over.

"I don't think we have time to walk much. The sun will be setting soon," he said.

"I just want to get out and smell the pines." They stopped at the base of the mountain, and Bea pulled on her wool hat and gloves, novelty items that she kept in a corner of the coat closet in Tucson, to be used once a year or so. They ranged around the trailhead that went all the way to Canada. About an inch of old snow sprinkled the bases of the pines and alligator junipers. Bea couldn't hear a car, nor a plane, nor a person. She did, however, hear a cow, and began to notice their evidence. Frank pointed out the fresh dung, amused at her excitement about winter, which he'd just left behind in suburban Washington. "Okay, then, let's go on to the B & B. Maybe we can take a moonlight walk from there," she said.

They didn't end up hiking after they checked in. It was, after all, the first time they'd been together for several months without the kids in the next room. The artist/owners had created an altogether wonderful space, full of photographs of the Salvaje National Forest, oil paintings of the Salvaje River, and sculptures of the ravens, hawks, deer, and trout of the region. They also had high-thread-count sheets and a down comforter.

They had to ask where to find a late dinner in the little mountain town, and were directed up to the Continental Divide again, at another junction, to a bar built well over a hundred years before. It was populated with characters who looked like they'd walked right out of the gold mining days, too. Bea had never seen so many chest-length white beards in one place.

One of the Bearded Ones took up a harmonica at the microphone and Bea dropped any of her preconceptions. The guy could play blues harmonica like she'd heard in New Orleans. She went up to him during the break. "That was fantastic! I never expected to hear blues harmonica like that here!"

"Where are you from?" He had wrinkles everywhere, but especially by his eyes, which shrank to slits when he smiled. He had a basketball player's build and Bea found herself craning her neck to talk to the guy.

"We're from Tucson," she said, nodding her head

towards Frank, who was still at their table, looking amused.

"I've done some gigs there. Come sit with us awhile. I'm Ed." He eased into a seat at the front table with a young woman who said she'd be singing with him in the next set. She was wearing a blue floor-length, tie-dyed skirt, a purple tie-dyed tee shirt covered by a flowing white cape, and red knee-high boots. Her blonde dreadlocks were randomly bound with orange, green, and yellow ribbons.

"Trust me, Rainbow can sing the blues," said their new friend.

"What do you do in Tucson?" Rainbow asked, after a few minutes.

"Oh, I work at Shandley Gardens, it's a botanical garden. It's kind of new; you probably haven't heard of it."

"No," Rainbow conceded. Ed looked at her closely, and seemed like he was going to say something, but he didn't.

"And you?" Rainbow asked Frank.

"Oh, I'm struggling writer," he said.

"Lots of those around here," Ed said. "Break's over. See you later. Stay at our table!"

Rainbow belted out "Love Has No Pride" and "Nobody Loves You When You're Down and Out." Bea and Frank thought their chiles rellenos were good, but the reason to be here was clearly the music. After the set, Ed came back to the table, and Rainbow wandered over to some friends at the bar who looked like they'd come straight out of 1970, minus the bellbottoms.

Ed settled down to a pale ale from an Albuquerque-based brewery. He took a long sip, bent his head down a bit, and focused his narrow, clear eyes on Bea's. "Did you say you worked at a place called Shandley Gardens? I knew a man called Shandley once, from Tucson. And he sure loved gardens. He was trying to grow all kinds of fruit trees and grapes and stuff on some property he bought up on the road to Hoodoo National Monument. He pulled out real quick, though."

"Yeah?" Frank prodded.

"Yeah. I heard the local real estate guys didn't much like him coming in, thought he was kind of a snob. Maybe they forced him out, I don't know. Always thought it was peculiar, he seemed to love it here so much. He used to come in here all the time. I remember talking about Tucson with him, places where I could get a gig, stuff like that."

Bea had been sweating a bit from the chiles rellenos— New Mexico rarely messed around with mild chiles—but she suddenly shivered.

"You feelin' sick?" asked Ed.

"No, no," she said, looking at Frank, who was watching her very carefully, giving nothing away. Bea gave a false little laugh. "Guess I'm just a desert dweller not used to the Continental Divide. I'm fine. So, I'm thinking the guy who founded our gardens was the same guy you're talking about. Was his name Alan?"

"Yes, I believe it was, ma'am. And he had a wife who was beautiful. Very blonde." He hesitated for just a moment. "She was a pistol, too."

"That sounds like Alan's wife Liz," Bea said. Was this woman destined to haunt her? She thought she was getting away from all this, from Liz and Alan and all the complications they'd brought to her life last year. She wasn't about to tell this guy that Liz had been murdered at Shandley Gardens, if he somehow didn't know about it.

"Liz, that's it. They still around?"

"Nope, they both passed away." Bea was relieved that she didn't have to have that conversation.

Ed finished his beer and headed back up onstage to tune up his guitar for the next set. The minute he left the table, Frank turned to Bea and said, "It would be so cool to find that property. Let's see who owns it now. Maybe there's still an orchard, remnants of Alan's garden. Hey, maybe Shandley Gardens can have a branch in the mountains up here and the staff can get away from the desert in summer!"

Bea took a swig of her beer. "Yeah, maybe."

"Bea, what's the matter? Don't you want to know why he left so suddenly?"

"Well, yeah, I wouldn't mind locating the property. But Frank, we do have another issue we've got to resolve this weekend, one that's a lot more important than why Alan and Liz pulled out of some real estate deal God knows how many years ago. I know you had a job interview in D.C. We've been dancing around discussing that. I don't even know if it's something you're serious about."

"Do you want to talk about this here?" he asked quietly.

"Might as well."

"Well. I was offered the job in D.C. Communications Officer for the U.S. Land Preservation Trust."

"Are you going to take it?" Bea was affecting that light, false tone again. She sounded like her mother.

"That's what we have to discuss. I could take it, and we could have a long-distance relationship. That has some obvious drawbacks. I could refuse it and stay here. The drawbacks to *that* are that I'm not really making a living freelancing, and I'm going to need to fly to D.C. a lot to help my mother. I don't know if I have the money to do that right. Or..." he paused and gave Bea a hopeful look, "you could find a job in D.C. There are a lot more jobs there than there are in Tucson."

"Oh." She was still back in the beginning of this new information. "How long have you been thinking about this job? When did you apply for it? You didn't mention it." She gave him a little smile to soften her bluntness.

"It all happened very fast. An old friend at the Trust recommended me, and my park service and journalism backgrounds fit their criteria. I haven't accepted it, Bea. I have a couple of weeks to make the decision."

"Oh. What do you want to do?"

"I love Tucson, love the desert, but it makes sense for me to take the job, given what's going on with my mom and my finances. What would make me *want* to take it is if you were willing to look for a job out there and move with me. We could always come back west when... well, you know they don't give ALS patients that long. Three to five years, usually. Horrible to be so blunt, but I'm trying to be realistic and think this through."

"Frank, this is feeling a little like a marriage proposal. I am not ready to make a three-to-five-year commitment to you, to uproot my kids, to leave Tucson. It's too much."

"I get that, Bea. I expected that's what you'd say. So. My cards are on the table. The other two options are real. I *didn't* mention breaking up as an option, you know. Let's enjoy the weekend. We don't have to decide anything right away."

That made more sense than anything he'd said yet.

They both ordered another beer and listened to Ed, who'd switched from blues to honky tonk. He had Hank Williams down. They'd paid the check and were just about ready to leave when he ended the set on "I'm So Lonesome I Could Cry" and mouthed "Wait a minute!" in their direction. Bea thought it would take her more than a minute to put on all these layers of unfamiliar winter clothing, anyway. She'd forgotten how quickly the temperature dropped in the mountains at night. It was probably in the teens out there.

"If y'all are interested in what *was* the Shandley place,

you might want to talk to my wife. She used to be in the country club with them. Me, I didn't go there much. I'll tell her about you. She likes to talk about the old days here, and she can tell you who bought the place in case you want to try to visit."

He scribbled a number on the back of their check. "My wife Lila's cell phone. I don't believe in the things."

It was easily as cold as Bea expected out in the bar parking lot. It was icy, too, probably because snow had melted and refrozen a time or two. The ice was less of a hazard than the wildlife, however; Frank had taken the wheel, and he just missed colliding with a large buck that appeared out of nowhere. Bea had visions of a totaled car and a long visit to the county hospital, but Frank managed to avoid both the buck and an oncoming driver who veered into their lane.

"Thank God you're driving," Bea said, and she left her hand on his knee until they got back to the B and B. She'd just let all the uncertainty go for now.

She was more than ready to crawl under the comforter in their room and to seek further comfort in Frank's arms.

Chapter Four

They made it to breakfast about five minutes before the kitchen closed down. They sat in the light-filled dining room, savoring huge mugs of coffee and *huevos revueltos,* scrambled eggs with green chiles, tomatoes, onions, cilantro, and cheese.

Bea caught Frank's eye. "I have to admit I'm curious about Alan's mountain garden. I was thinking... maybe I could even run tours to Copperton for Shandley Gardens members in the summertime. Everybody's dying to get out of the heat then, right? Maybe I could find this and some other places for a Garden tour. I bet it'd be popular."

"Well, I don't think you need to have a work reason to check the place out. I'm just plain curious."

So, she gave Ed's wife a call. As soon as Bea said her name, Lila said, "Oh, yes, Ed said you'd be calling."

"So... Ed said you might be able to tell us something about the property that Alan Shandley used to own. Alan started the public garden I work in."

"Certainly. Can you meet me at four at the Take a Break Coffee Shop? I can catch you up on the place."

People were so friendly in this little town. So far, anyway. "We'd love to do that," Bea said.

"See you soon." Lila's diction conjured up images of a country clubber, a neat little woman with grey hair fashioned into an expensive haircut, tasteful jewelry, and shoes that matched her slacks. Somebody who might be on the board of directors of Shandley Gardens. Except that this person couldn't really be married to laid-back Ed, could she? Bea would find out soon enough. Meanwhile, they had plenty of time to take a hike north of town. The snow was several inches deep, despite the abundant sunshine. The trail dipped into thick ponderosa pine forest, and then rose to provide views into a deep canyon with walls broken into oddly shaped columns of volcanic tuff.

"I read they're called 'hoodoos,'" Frank said.

"Excellent name for them. Jessie would like it. And she'd like the one shaped like a bear. I'll take a picture for her." He snapped one quickly. "Are you going to call the kids tonight?"

Bea sighed. "Pat asked me not to call, because they got all teary the last time I called when he had them for the weekend."

"That might be easier if you didn't live in Tucson. Dealing with your ex-husband, I mean."

"I think that Pat would make it very difficult for me to move. We have joint custody."

"But not really."

"Yes, not really, but I'm not sure I want that fight. The divorce was just eighteen months ago, remember." Frank had been in Tucson for about that amount of time, but she'd known him just the past few months. Too much was happening too fast. Time to change the subject.

"We'd better turn around now if we want to meet Lila in the coffee shop at four."

They walked into the coffee shop at 4:05, and Bea looked around for the owner of the country club voice she'd heard on the phone.

"Bea?" asked a large woman with unbound, waist-length wavy grey hair, a beautiful teal-and-purple hand-knit sweater, jeans, and hiking boots. Clearly, Bea was going to have to readjust her assumptions.

"You must be Lila. This is my friend Frank."

Lila's handshake was very firm indeed. She worked with her hands.

"Yeah, all the years of gardening and sculpting don't make for very soft hands," she said, causing Bea to shake her head quickly, as if she didn't mean to insult her, but she hadn't said anything, had she?

"Get some tea if you want it. I recommend the rooibos. It's the best I've had outside of South Africa."

Bea tried the rooibos, and Frank had an espresso. Bea had always thought rooibos tasted like straw, but this stuff had a rich, almost carob-like taste.

"So, you work at some public garden that Alan Shandley planted. Was it his home first?"

"Exactly. After he died, his wife Liz moved into town and started a nonprofit to run the place."

"That sounds like something she'd do. I'll bet she got a lot of kudos for it, and she didn't have to take care of the property by herself anymore."

"You don't sound like you cared much for Liz."

"Oh, nobody here did." She looked more closely at Bea to see if she was offended, decided she wasn't, and went on. "Alan was fine—courteous to locals—but Liz was a different story. I used to sell real estate, and so I was a Chamber of Commerce member, a country club type, the whole nine yards." So Bea'd been right about her voice. "I grew up with folks like that, in Pennsylvania, so it came easily to me here. But Liz! She hated the country club décor, she thought the food was 'appalling,' and she told Alan, in the hearing of many of us, that no one in our town could speak in words of more than one syllable. I have an English degree from the University of New Mexico, for God's sake, and I'm hardly the only one in Copperton who can parse a sentence, or who could in the 1960s, when they were here. But I digress. You wanted to know about his property, right?" Bea nodded, and she went on.

"He had this place up the highway to the national monument. They'd just paved that road when the Shandleys got to town, so there was a lot of buzz about tourism. Plus, the mines had just changed from underground to open pit, and Copperton was in a boom economy. It was a good investment. And as you know, Alan Shandley made lots of money on real estate in Tucson, so he thought maybe he'd start a summer home community up here for all those Tucsonans suffering the summer heat. The richest Tucson folks went to La Jolla and Carmel for the summer, but those places are pretty far away. Alan's idea was that his little complex would be perfect for families whose working dads could pop over for the weekend in the summer, and the whole family could drive over any weekend they wanted the rest of the year. It was a good idea; I told him so at the time."

"So, what happened?"

"Bea, to be quite honest, I've always been curious about that. Alan built a lovely adobe for himself and Liz. He bulldozed the way for a big lodge up there, but he did a good job of leaving a lot of the pines around the place. More expensive that way, but nicer. Then he made this "common area" with apple and pear and peach and apricot trees, and grapes, and he was trying out all kinds of flowers. I could tell that was the part he liked the most. Next thing I knew, he'd sold the whole thing at a loss."

Bea looked at Frank, then back to Lila and asked, "Why would he do that?"

"I have no idea why, it didn't make any sense at the time." She shifted in her chair and took a sip of tea. "Of course, I have my own theory."

"What's that?"

"Well, it had to be Liz. She probably went on about how primitive we are here, and how none of *her* friends would want to spend the summer here, and I think Alan just threw up his hands and pulled out."

Frank had been watching Lila intently. He broke in and said, "I'm thinking that Alan could have found folks who liked his plan even if his wife didn't. Alan was such a good businessman, I'm kind of surprised he left so abruptly."

"I don't know, Frank, she could be pretty insistent," said Bea. "We saw that at the Gardens. And we think she may have had something to bludgeon him with." She turned to Lila. "Metaphorically, of course."

"Wait. Somebody in Tucson got murdered in a garden. I only half registered it. But that was Liz Shandley, wasn't it?" Lila asked.

"Yes, unfortunately," said Bea. This murder was *never* going to be out of the picture.

"Alan didn't knock her off?"

"No, no, he died a few years before... it happened."

"Well, I think he had reason to get rid of her, if not violently. But anyway, Eddy said you'd probably like to visit the place Alan owned. Is that right?"

Bea and Frank looked at each other. "If we can," he said.

"If it makes sense," Bea said at the same time.

"Well, I can't tell you if it makes sense or not. But I can tell you who owns the property. It's a pretty eccentric couple."

Eccentric for Copperton? But Bea didn't say this out loud.

"They're quite reclusive and not particularly welcoming to visitors. But it so happens that they like me because I helped them with their fruit trees. So, I could probably take you up there. Alan had a great gardener, for sure, but these owners did all the work themselves. Eventually, they needed some horticultural advice, so I helped them out several years ago. Frankly, I'd like to see the place again myself," said Lila.

Bea was intrigued. "Can we go tomorrow or Monday? We have to leave by noon on Monday," she said.

"I'll see what I can work out. Sorry, I've got to run, somebody's coming by my studio at 5:00 to pick out a sculpture for their yard. At least I hope so." Lila put a ten-dollar bill on the table and waved off Bea's protestations. "See you again soon, if all goes well."

Bea and Frank had learned their lesson about how early restaurants closed in Copperton. They found some tasty enchiladas and were back in the room by 7:30, when Lila called. "Well, my friends complained they're 'not in the business of being a tourist attraction,' so I told them I'd be looking at their trees again, for free this time. They caved and said to bring you tourists up to the property at eleven tomorrow. I'll pick you up at the Lodge at 10:30. It's on the way."

This worked well for a romantic morning and a breakfast of blue corn muffins with ginger/red chile jam and green chile and cheese omelets. Bea was starting to regret bringing Gardens business along on this romantic retreat. It would have been a much better idea to go on a long hike, just the two of them, maybe up higher in the mountains again. It looked to be a beautiful-blue-skies sort of day, and the snow would soon be gone up high, turning paths to mud. They would hit it just right. But they'd made a commitment, and Frank seemed intrigued by the chase.

Lila showed up right on time Sunday morning in a well-used pickup. It turned out that they were heading deeper into the mountains to see this eccentric couple, although not quite as high up as in Bea's imagined hike. The place was beyond the bar/restaurant by the Continental Divide, and about the same elevation, around 7,000 feet. It was down a bumpy dirt road that followed a little frozen watercourse; there wasn't much water in it in January, but Bea pointed out the huge logjam in the creek.

"A summer monsoon storm probably loosened up some of the vegetation in the burned area up in the high mountains, right, Lila? I remember hearing about a big fire up there last summer," Frank said.

"Yeah, you're right. Too many years of drought. Bark beetles in the trees. Everything's following climate change predictions to a tee, including worse wildfires," Lila said.

Fortunately, before they could spend too much time on this gloomy subject, the house came into view.

It was still a charming adobe home, although the time for repainting and treating the wood had long gone by. It was low and square, the kind of place that probably had several bedrooms and an inner courtyard. The front porch was covered with trellises, which held some dried-out brown vines that might have produced grapes. In front of the house were two abandoned sedans and an old pickup. As they pulled up, the front door opened, and a hunched-up white-haired woman came out with a broom.

"Kind of the definition of a witch," muttered Frank.

Lila said, "Exactly."

Bea's thinking ran towards cancelling her imagined Copperton Garden Tour.

Lila introduced them. "Bea, Frank, this is Gert." Bea held out her hand in greeting.

"Well, come in, said the woman." She gave a distasteful look to Bea's hand. "I don't shake hands with folks from the city. Who knows what diseases you're bringing."

"Okay," said Bea brightly, in that tone she seemed to

have picked up from her mother.

Bea was only halfway through the door before she registered the chaos of the living room. There were magazines on practically every surface. Bea spotted old issues of *Field and Stream*, *Arizona Highways*, *New Mexico*, *Outdoor Life*, *Archaeology*, and *Earth*. There wasn't much evidence of Gert using the broom she'd come outdoors with. Bea was no neatnik, but she wanted to pick up a dust rag. She looked up on the mantelpiece, made from a pine log, where several geodes and large crystalline rocks were interspersed with fossils and painted Native American pots all covered with several years' worth of New Mexico dust. Gert gestured for them to sit, and Bea did so, emitting a dust cloud that briefly curtained her vision, and then made her pull out her bandanna to wipe her eyes. Frank sneezed beside her.

Gert was not fazed, and said, "Sorry, Lila, but Mack's over in Tucson. We gotta make a living somehow, and if you want to sell antiques, you gotta have a shop in a city. Poor man, he spends more time there than I do. So thought I could answer these folks' questions myself."

"I'm sure you can."

The ball was in Bea's court.

"So, Gert, I work at Shandley Gardens. It used to be Alan and Liz Shandley's home. I just found out that Alan owned this property, and planted gardens, and had some idea for a development here, and I'm just interested in seeing what he was up to. Just curiosity about our founder, and his other gardening projects."

"He wasn't up to much, I'd say. He built this house and that's all. But it worked out for us."

"Would it... would you mind showing us around? I guess I'm not so interested in the house," Bea was thinking she was afraid to see the rest of the rooms, "but I'd love to see the gardens."

"I could do that. Though you picked a funny time of year to look at gardens. But I can show you what little there is out there. We wouldn't have as much left if it weren't for your friend Lila."

Bea realized that she'd been labeled as Lila's friend, and she liked that.

Her friend said, "Oh, I just told Gert and Mack the obvious. With the way the climate's changing, they needed to mulch, mulch, mulch to keep the trees alive as long as possible. And prune off all the dead wood. Which, in the case of the apricots and peaches, would be only a Hail Mary pass. Because those trees don't usually last thirty-five years, like these had when I last saw them. I guess Alan, or that gardener of his, found some really good heritage trees that live an exceptionally long time."

"Yeah, right. Well, out we go," Gert ordered. She threw on a serape, and they tromped back out the front door and followed the little creek to a place where the banks flattened into big meadows on either side. "Those apple trees are still going strong!" said Lila approvingly. Then she added, "But the peaches are gone, and the apricots, too. Forty years was too much to ask. Are the pears still producing?"

"Little bitty things," said Gert. "I don't think even you can help us with anything but the apples anymore. Guess it's time to turn the others into firewood."

"You're doing all the right things, Gert. Keep up the mulching and pruning."

"That's it for the professional advice, huh? Okay, seen enough?" She was quite a hostess.

"I think that's all there is to see of Alan's gardens right now. He put in the Tombstone rose and wild grapes on the front of the house, and the irises in the courtyard, but they're not much to look at right now," said Lila.

Frank hadn't been paying attention to the conversation. He'd wandered away from them, to a flat area on a terrace above them. In a minute, he came down with a questioning look.

"Hey, Gert. What are those big holes in the ground up there? About four feet across. Did you pull some trees out of there?"

"That's where Alan's big, fancy guest lodge was supposed to be. But you really aren't from around here. Those holes are where we dug pots, of course. Alan, too. He found the first batch, him and that weird-looking gardener of his. We all dug, you know, in those days."

Bea knew that there had been lots of illegal artifact hunting in the national park next to Shandley Gardens, but she was fuzzy on what was legal and what wasn't. But that wasn't what she was curious about right now.

"So... what was so weird-looking about the gardener?" She thought she'd found a casual tone.

"Oh, he had this bump on his forehead. You would have thought he'd been in a fight, except it never went away. But he was weird in other ways, too."

Bea was suddenly breathless, but she managed to say, in a voice that was a little too high-pitched, "How was he weird in other ways?"

"Oh, he was one of those hippies that think they have God on their side, that they know how everybody else should live. Disappeared. Probably went to some commune and died of drugs. He wasn't popular here. Always telling people how they should act."

"I see," said Frank.

Bea didn't see at all. But she did note that the gardener, like Liz Shandley, was not popular in Copperton because he was an outsider "telling people how they should act."

"So he left when Alan did?" Bea asked, in what she hoped was a mildly interested tone.

Gert stared at her. Lila cocked an eyebrow. "What's it to you?" Gert asked.

"Well, I... you know I'm just interested in our founder's life here, that's all."

Frank's look said, "Thanks for curbing your usual candor."

"I think you've seen all there is to see here," said Gert. "And Lila says we're doing everything right with the apple trees, and it wasn't our fault the rest died. Old age. It gets us all. Alan's dead, I guess. How about that snotty wife of his?"

"She passed away last year."

"Good riddance."

Bea tried hard to show no emotion at this rudeness. She hadn't liked Liz, either, but Gert seemed to have few filters. Bea smiled at the woman. "Thank you so much for the tour." Gert gestured with her chin at the front door. They hustled into Lila's truck.

As they headed down the mountain, Lila said, "I'm not at all sure that was worth your time."

"Oh, but it was." Bea took a breath. "The most interesting part was about that gardener. Did you know him?"

"Oh, I met him. He was a talented gardener, I'll say that for him. He was way ahead of his time in seeking out those heritage fruit trees that did so well here. And he planted this "monsoon garden" with all the late summer wildflowers. It just keeps reseeding. People park on the highway in a good rain year and walk down the driveway to get a peek, until Gert chases them off with that broom. I think she likes cultivating her witchy image. But that gardener... I don't remember his name, but he was terribly self-righteous. He would tell people that God didn't approve of what they were doing, that they were hurting Mother Earth and her people, that sort of thing. He just kind of drifted in here, and then I guess he drifted out when Alan sold the property. Alan was more tolerant than Gert and Mack; they wouldn't have put up with that guy. He probably would have told them they were defiling their Mother, that they were bound for hell."

"Why would they be bound for hell?" asked Bea.

"Oh, any number of things, I'd guess. Things a hippie of that era would hate. They had a couple of mining claims and mined Mother Earth. I know he wasn't happy with them digging up Indian bones and leaving them unburied."

When Bea and Frank exchanged a glance, Lila said, "Please don't get me wrong. Of course, I don't think you should dig up bones, either. Thank God you can't do that now, legally. You know, the pots people wanted were buried with the dead. They'd destroy ancient Native American pueblos when they dug. A lot of that went on in the old days, unfortunately. You'd find bones along with pottery. You know, the Mimbres Indians were around here a thousand years ago or so, and during their classic period, they made those beautiful bowls. Have you seen them? There are some in the downtown museum you should check out."

"Yes," Bea said, "there are three of them in Ethan's office at Shandley Gardens. They're beautiful. White background and black designs. There's one with geometric designs, and one with birds, and one that looks like a horned lizard."

"Those sound exactly like what I'm talking about, Bea. Maybe your founders would be going to hell in that guy's book, too," said Lila.

Bea and Frank exchanged another thoughtful look and were silent. Frank pulled Bea close.

"I love seeing you two lovebirds together. Been dating long?"

"Oh, a few months," Bea said.

"Got any kids?"

"She does."

"Ah. Single parenting's tough, isn't it. I did it for ten years," Lila said.

They chatted a bit about how old Bea's kids were, and how old Lila's were when she was a single parent, and Lila said she'd love to meet Andy and Jessie some time, and she and Ed had two empty bedrooms; maybe Bea could bring her kids for a visit. Bea couldn't imagine anybody in a big city being so welcoming so fast. She told Lila that, and she just laughed.

"Welcome to Copperton, warts and all."

Just before she climbed out of the car, Bea made a decision.

"Lila, it would be interesting to talk to somebody about the archaeological sites on Alan's property. And I've always been interested in ceramics." This was sort of true. "Is there anybody who'd be good to talk to about all this?"

"Well, I have a friend who works for the Forest Service who might help you. But probably not before you leave at noon tomorrow." said Lila.

"If you think of it, email me the person's name," said Bea. "And, Lila, thanks for everything."

"Well, wait a minute. I do have an idea for tomorrow morning, if you're interested. Some of the old guys who used to know Alan meet at ten at the downtown doughnut shop on Monday mornings. They might enjoy reminiscing about him. And trust me, some of them pot hunted themselves in those days. All over the place. You might drop in there. They'd love a new audience."

Bea looked at Frank. He seemed okay with this idea

for their last morning together.

    "Thanks again, Lila. You've been wonderful."

Chapter Five

The doughnut shop was a species common any-where in America since the 1950s, which may have been the selling point for the old men in the corner. Two of the three sported felt ten-gallon hats, shirts with pearl snaps, thick jeans and worn cowboy boots. Their stomachs poured over their tooled leather belts in a way they probably didn't in Alan's Copperton days. One of these two actually had a handlebar mustache. The third guy was bald and bareheaded, with a similar stomach hanging over his jeans, but he wore hiking boots and a fleece vest. They all looked to be in their seventies or eighties; if Alan were alive, he'd be in his mid-eighties, Bea knew.

"Would you get us some coffee and doughnuts? I'll talk to them," Bea said.

"I don't exactly feel like a doughnut after that break-fast at the B & B," grumbled Frank. Bea ignored him and walked over to the table.

"Good morning, gentlemen," she said. They looked surprised, but not unhappy to be greeted by a young, trim, small, fine-featured blonde woman several decades younger than they.

"Hi, pleased to meet all of you. I'm Bea Rivers, and I work at Shandley Gardens in Tucson. It used to be Alan Shandley's home." The mustache guy and the bald man stared at her a little harder. "My friend Lila mentioned that Alan almost started a garden and resort here in

Copperton, and I heard that maybe you guys knew him. We're always interested in stories about our founder. If you have any, could my friend Frank and I impose on you and talk for a bit?"

All of them looked over towards Frank at the counter, and Bea's eyes followed theirs. Frank was wearing hiking pants, not jeans, with fairly new hiking boots and a black fleece jacket that matched his curly black hair. He was shorter than all of the other men, but even in winter clothes, you could tell he worked out.

The cowboy with no mustache, the one who hadn't reacted when she mentioned Alan's name, was the first to speak. "You're welcome to join us, ma'am." He had a voice like a 1940s radio announcer.

As she sat down, the bald man said, "I think I heard Alan Shandley turned his home into a botanical garden. Didn't his wife get murdered or something over there?"

"We're forgettin' our manners. I'm Buzz Winters," said the cowboy with the radio voice. He was still handsome, Bea thought, in an octogenarian way. Very much the tall, rugged, outdoorsman, with bright blue eyes. She revised her original opinion about overhanging stomachs. His didn't... not much anyway. "This here's Rob Chance..." The mustached guy mumbled, "Pleased to meet you." Buzz turned to the bald guy. "And this is Tom Franzen." Tom nodded to her.

"Great to meet you" She turned to Frank, who was setting some small mugs on the table. The coffee couldn't possibly be as weak as it looked, Bea thought. One sip changed that assessment. Frank's lips twitched with a suppressed laugh before he announced, "I'm Frank Ferguson. Pleased to meet you all."

As he went back for the jelly doughnuts, Buzz said, in that deep voice, "I didn't really know Alan Shandley, ma'am, but I reckon these two did, and there's probably a story or two to be told."

Bea noticed that Tom and Rob exchanged a glance. She couldn't read it.

"Weeelll," said Rob, stretching out his long legs, "Tom and I didn't know Shandley well, understand. In those days, we thought he was crazy to be buildin' a resort way out there on the highway to the Cave Houses. And out of adobe, too. We were tryin' to modernize the town, not take it backwards. So we weren't close, you'd say. Thing is, we were all in the archaeological society, in those days. It's changed a lot. But we all found stuff on our property, and we'd get together and compare our metates, arrowheads, bowls, you know. And Alan had some fine stuff, I'll say that."

"His wife thought so, too. She was a piece of work," the bald one, Tom, added.

"How so?" asked Bea.

"Oh, she was always pushing him to do stuff, like make that place more upscale. She wanted to get in some chef from back East for the guests there. She told him they shouldn't allow locals in the bar. *That* didn't win her any popularity contests."

"Matter of fact, I think she cared more about this project than he did," said Rob. "But she got murdered, right? You didn't answer that question."

"Yes, she did."

"Well, she was one bossy woman. Never knew for sure why Shandley pulled out, but I doubt he woulda made money off that resort of his, especially with *her* ideas. He didn't really fit in here, him and Liz," Tom said.

"And that's about all we knew about him," said Rob. He pulled his legs back under the table.

"Yup, that's pretty much it," said Tom. He looked down

at his coffee and took a sip, keeping his eyes on the coffee after he put it down.

It seemed their invasion of the Monday morning coffee club was supposed to be over.

"I'm very interested in the heritage fruit trees Alan Shandley planted here. They seem to live so long. Lila tells me that he had a gardener who found them. You wouldn't know how to contact him, would you?" Bea asked.

"You're a curious one!" said Buzz. *Maybe he'd been a country western singer. The voice would fit.* He continued, "But I wasn't around then. I left home in the Sixties. Went out of state. I came back, though, to retire. No place better."

"Yup, said Tom, without much expression. "I didn't know any gardener."

"Me, neither," said Rob. "Nice talkin' to you." Bea knew she'd been dismissed a second time.

"Thanks so much. Great to meet you all," said Bea. "We've got to get back to Tucson." The three men nodded goodbye. "We'll just take our doughnuts with us," she added.

"Didn't like' em much, did you?" said Rob, the one with the mustache.

"We're just full from breakfast. My kids will love them."

"Have a good trip," said Buzz. He seemed to be the only one who was friendly, and the only one who didn't know Alan. Was there a coincidence here?

Bea and Frank were silent until they were out of sight of the plate glass doughnut shop windows.

"I'll drive," said Bea. "Sometimes it helps me to think."

They drove up and over the Continental Divide again, and the snow patches disappeared as the desert below began to reveal itself. The sky was huge and ringed everywhere with small mountain ranges.

"I have to call Marcia," Bea said.

"Yeah, it looks like we may know whose bones were buried by your back fence. It also looks like a lot of people here didn't like Liz, and some people didn't like Alan, and the people who knew the gardener thought he was a weirdo. But people usually aren't killed just for being obnoxious. Also, you can't help but wonder why Alan left Copperton so abruptly."

"That about sums it up," said Bea. "Except that Gert is not the most savory character. And we haven't even met her husband."

As they pulled into the gas station in San Marcos, Bea added, "You know what else? We don't even know this gardener's name."

Just then her phone rang. It was her ex-husband Pat. "Are you getting back soon?" he asked as soon as she answered.

"In another couple of hours."

"Well, Jessie's got a fever of a hundred and two, and my mom thinks she may need to go to urgent care. I have a meeting, but Mom will wait till you get here to decide if you should take her in."

"Pat, what are her other symptoms?"

"She says her ear hurts."

"Damn! Another ear infection. She's been on too many antibiotics for those at this young age."

"Well, I'll tell Mom you'll take over in a couple of hours."

Back to my real life.

"So, Jessie's been on a lot of antibiotics?" Frank asked when Bea was off the phone. He looked over to check her expression. She could feel her jaw tightening. She moved it around a bit.

"Yes, a lot of antibiotics, for sure. I've been reading that doctors overprescribe them for children's ear infections. But Pat's mother Bertha is a retired nurse, and I'm sure she'll think Jessie should have them. Of course, the fever could be something else entirely. I may need to spend the rest of the afternoon and half the evening in urgent care. I've been through this a lot. Ear infections don't send you to the top of the waiting list. Any way you look at it, I'm going to need to be home with Jessie tomorrow."

"Your ex's mother, the nurse, couldn't take care of her?"

"There's a radical idea. Pat's mom might like to do that, if she's still in town."

Frank took another glance over at her and began to talk about a story he had written for an outdoor magazine about a hermit in the Arizona mountains they'd just sped by. The guy had made a fortune selling hard apple cider during Prohibition. The entire surrounding community had kept his secret, in an unusual show of solidarity across all social barriers.

"You know that's what Johnny Appleseed was spreading, right?" he asked. "Seeds to make hard cider. It's been said that frontiersmen lived in an 'alcoholic haze.' Lots of the hard cider trees were chopped down during prohibition, by the FBI, but old Sloane Barker's orchards were a little out of the way, out here in rural Arizona. There's a monument to him in the town. His epitaph was "A friend to all, to all good cheer.""

Bea's jaw was loose and so were her spirits, thank to Frank's little diversion. Then they had to stop by Pat's. His mother Bertha had called to say that she'd gotten a doctor friend to prescribe amoxicillin, so nobody would be spending the night waiting in urgent care. Pat was out filling the prescription. "I told him that was the least he could do. I can take care of Jessie tomorrow; she probably needs to stay home from school at least a day. Why don't you bring her over in the morning?"

"Thank you, Bertha. I so much appreciate your help."

It was a relief that Pat wasn't home to meet Frank, but Bea felt Bertha's appraising eyes on her boyfriend. Bertha blinked when Jessie ran to give him a big hug, and Andy high-fived him. She doubted that Bertha would want Frank to do sick child duty, and Bea wasn't sure she would have asked him to, anyway.

"Pat will drop the medicine off at your house," said Bertha, all efficiency. "He'll put it on the doorstep if you're not back yet when he gets there."

Bea was startled to see an attractive blonde woman emerge from the back room. Bertha sniffed. "I don't know if you've met Frank's friend Suzie." Bea hadn't met Suzie, but she was not the girlfriend Bea had met last October. They were the same physical type, though. Younger than Pat—fit, tall, with long blonde hair. There had probably been a couple of others she didn't know about, too. *Stop it, Bea.*

"Hello," she said, in an upbeat tone, "I'm Bea, Andy and Jessie's mom, and this is Frank." Bea studied the woman. Pat was definitely going the trophy-girlfriend route. Suzie was in Lycra workout clothes that showed off a nearly perfect figure. She removed some headphones to shake Bea's hand; Suzie apparently wasn't interacting with her children while Pat was out. Which was fine with Bea. Suzie ruffled Andy's hair, and he ducked. Unfazed, Suzie blew Jessie a kiss, and Jessie pulled her unruly dirty-blonde hair over her eyes. Suzie headed back to Pat's bedroom, plugging in her headphones.

Bertha had looked critically at Frank, but her glance at the retreating Suzie was positively withering. She said nothing, except, "You might want to look into getting tubes in Jessie's ears. The antibiotics are necessary this time, but I wouldn't want you to have to keep doing this."

"Too bad Bertha doesn't live in Tucson,' Frank, said on the drive home.

"Yes." She didn't say it was even more too bad that Frank didn't live in Tucson.

Chapter Six

After the usual breakneck pace of getting-ready-for work-and-school Tuesday morning, Bea dropped Jessie at Pat's house. He'd already left for work, and there was no sign of Suzie, but Jessie was glad to spend another day with her grandmother. Frank left Bea's place to do some computer work at his opld apartment, which he'd sublet to a friend, who was conveniently out of town. Maybe this was good, Bea thought; she wasn't ready for him to live with her family for several days. Or anyway she didn't think she should be ready for that; it bespoke commitment. She needed to proceed carefully, since he was dating a package deal involving three people. "Careful, Bea," she said aloud. She had to warn the self that didn't want to proceed with caution one bit.

Bea sat down at her desk, closed the door, took a couple of deep breaths, and called Marcia Samuelson on her cell phone. The fact that she picked up right away might have been that the call was from an old friend, but more likely because Bea was calling from Shandley Gardens, and Marcia was in charge of the investigation there.

"Marcia, you're not going to believe this, but I may have found a clue to the identity of our... bones."

"On your romantic weekend?"

"Yep."

"Hang on. I'm near Shandley right now. Let's talk about this in person."

Sure enough, in a matter of minutes, Marcia was in the chair facing Bea's desk. "You just can't stay out of trouble, can you?" Marcia asked, with a smile.

Bea gave her a full report, including descriptions of witchy Gert, the pot hunting that both she and Alan had done on the property, the gardener's disapproval of it, and the less-than-forthcoming Coffee Club bunch. She said, "So this guy... I wish we had a name!... could have been hit on the head in Tucson, or in Copperton, where he probably had enemies. They could have transported him to Tucson."

"And it looks like your founders are once again smack dab in a murder investigation, albeit from their graves. Luckily, I have an old friend who left the Tucson Police Department for the one in Copperton, to escape the heat and the traffic. She grew up in Copperton, in fact, and still has family there. Anyway, I'll give her a call about all this. Maybe she and I can work together."

"Marcia, here's what I think we need to know. Somebody needs to figure out why Alan left Copperton so abruptly. It seems like that has something to do with this story. Also, those old guys said they didn't know the gardener, but they were a little too definite about that. And oh, my Lord, Gert might be capable of anything. Or nothing. It would be good to understand her better. She's not someone you can discount."

"It sounds like you're pretty interested in this saga, Bea."

"How can I help it? Murders keep lassoing my life, whether I want to be involved or not."

Marcia laughed. "Do you think that boss of yours would give you a day with pay to head over to Copperton and talk to folks? If we left early and came back late, we could put in a good day's work. Maybe we can divide up and get more done, and you know I value your insights."

Bea nodded. She and Marcia had been each other's most trusted friends up until their paths diverged in high school. They'd been the only girls in their neighborhood who'd played with the boys in the arroyos, catching horned lizards and looking for potsherds. Then there'd been that incident in junior high, when they'd given each other the courage to tell the principal about the teacher who should not have been taking girls on camping trips. In high school, Marcia had been Student Council President, and Bea had been a rebel. But she still campaigned for Marcia, despite her own clique's cynicism. They didn't spend much time together these days, but Bea was always glad when they did.

"Well... maybe I could get Frank to take the kids to school and do the evening stuff."

"Good practice for him. I'll let you know if I set something up. Day after tomorrow."

"Okay, Marcia. Wait a sec..." she pulled the slip of paper with the Copperton archaeologist's name out of her purse. "Lila, the singer's wife, the former Chamber-of- Commerce-person-slash-sculptor-slash-horticulturist, gave me the name of the Forest Service archaeologist who can tell us about pot hunting in southwest New Mexico. That could be good stuff to know."

"It could. If the gardener's screeds against pot hunting got him in deep trouble, which is possible."

"It sounds like it made him unpopular."

"I need to head back to the station. I'll make a few calls and get back to you."

Bea barely had time to catch up with her emails before Marcia called. "Okay, my friend, it's all set up. We leave at six a.m. day after tomorrow, if you can go. Back by nine that night."

Bea called Bertha, to get an update on her Jessie. She

was much better, which was great, because Bertha was leaving town, and Bea felt pretty uncomfortable about asking Frank to watch a sick child... Bea's parents now lived in California, though she'd grown up in Tucson. Bea was an only child, so she had no siblings delighted to mind their niece and nephew. Her ex-husband claimed he was far too busy to take the children without several days' notice. Bea's good friends Barb and John Rice would probably do what needed to be done, but she'd rather save their kindheartedness for emergencies. She probably would have to tell Marcia she couldn't go unless Frank was willing to take care of her kids.

She took another couple of deep breaths and called Frank.

"Marcia has asked me to go on a little fact-finding trip to Copperton day after tomorrow. If I did go, how would you feel about watching the kids?'

"Sure." Was that hesitation she heard in his voice? "I can come over that night."

"Frank, you'll have to get them on the school bus, and pick them up at the bus stop, and feed them dinner. It's a lot."

"We'll see how I do," he said with a laugh. *Was that resentment in his voice?* "What time do I need to be there in the morning, Bea?"

She could get used to this, she had to admit.

"Is Jessie okay?"

"Jessie's much better. Her fever's gone, but so is Granny Bertha, as of tomorrow morning."

So far, everything was going smoothly. But her boss Ethan was less than accommodating about this field trip.

"Well, I really can't see what it has to do with your job duties here. Explain that to me."

"Wouldn't it benefit all of us at Shandley if this thing

got solved soon?"

"Is there anything we need to be worried about, in terms of the Gardens' reputation?"

Bea explained that Alan had had a gardener in Copperton who sounded like he had a button osteoma.

"Oh, my God. Please, let's keep this out of the paper, not to mention out of the claws of that big-haired woman on Channel Two who pursued us last time. *If* the skeleton really is Alan's gardener, somebody over in Copperton had it in for him. That's what I'm going to believe. Maybe you can find something out to validate that theory. Go ahead, take the day with pay."

"I hope your theory's right."

"Better than if our founders committed murder? Yes." He sighed. "You bet it would. Alan's a legend in the plant world, and not just locally. We need to keep him a *positive* legend."

"I know that's important to you." Her eyes settled on a table at the back of Ethan's office. "Um, Ethan, I was wondering about something. I think those pots on your back table are Mimbres pots. At least they look like pictures I saw when I looked them up a few days ago. Were they Alan's?"

"They came with the house, like a lot of the artwork. I know absolutely nothing about them. I doubt they have anything to do with anything, Bea. But okay, you have my blessing. The sooner this is solved, the sooner we can get back to what we're supposed to be doing."

Bea got volunteers to cover her school tours on Wednesday. She headed home and managed to scrape together some veggies and fried rice, which both kids said was "yucky." As she was bribing them with popsicles for dessert, Frank called and asked her to put Jessie and Andy on the line, together.

"What do you want me to make for dinner Thursday night?"

"I don't know," said Andy, just as Jessie was shouting "Lasagna!" Jessie could always be counted on to have an opinion.

"Lasagna it is," he said. Was Frank being so nice because he wanted her to move to Washington? Or was he just a good guy?

Wednesday passed without drama, at work *or* at home. Bea could have used more Wednesdays in her life.

Chapter Seven

Marcia picked her up at 6 a.m. sharp on Thursday morning in an unmarked police car. It felt good, riding in this car. Bea felt childish thinking this, but here she was in a symbol of power and authority, and she felt powerful and authoritative in a way that wasn't familiar. "Power tends to corrupt, and absolute power corrupts absolutely," her father, a gentle insect biologist, was fond of quoting. In her teenaged years, she challenged him: "So, in our quest for personal purity, should we always cede power to others, then?" It occurred to her that this is just what she'd done, with her ex-husband, letting his career be more important than hers. She'd chosen a low-key profession where she didn't have to challenge others much, either.

She realized Marcia was talking to her, and she pulled herself out of her thought trench. "So, my friend in the Copperton P.D.—Sandra Ramirez—has been doing some investigating. And just so you know, here's what she's found out: first of all, the gardener's name was Crow Johnson. I would be surprised if Crow was his given name, but he told people that crows were his totem.

"Aren't crows symbols of bad luck and tricksterism?" Bea asked.

"Depending on the culture. They can also mean good luck, and access to the magical and mystical. We should assume he picked the totem for those latter meanings."

Bea knew Marcia had always been a pragmatist, and she wouldn't be too impressed with a name change like this.

Marcia continued, "Sandra found out he had a reputation as a drifter. She found an old hippie friend of his whom she's interviewing as we speak. Should be interesting."

"So what's on the agenda today?"

"We're going to talk to your contact in the Forest Service, the archaeologist, so that we can understand what the world of archaeological remains was like in the late Sixties, as opposed to now. Sandra also wants to discuss your chats with people last weekend. Then we'll interview one of those old guys you met at the doughnut shop. Her old hippie informant told her that Crow got into a shouting match with that guy."

"Which guy was that?"

"Rob Somebody. I have to look at my notes."

"Rob was the guy with the handlebar mustache."

"So you and I will talk to him. Then we'll split up and you can do some library research, if you will." Bea nodded. "Then we'll talk to Gert and her husband Mack, who's back from his shop, Curry's Collectibles, in Tucson. One of my plain clothes colleagues went by the place yesterday; it looks pretty dusty. It's hard to imagine that he can make much of a living off of it... just some old cider presses and farm tools in the windows. So, anyway, we'll have a little time then before we go back, and we'll see what comes up next."

"It sounds like a full day."

"Always." Marcia leaned over and patted Bea's knee. "Good to have you along."

***

Bea found herself in a cramped room at the Copperton

Police Department with two competent women. She'd been aware of Marcia's competence ever since she'd been the eight-year-old Chief Fort Engineer, bossing the neighborhood boys around to create the perfect hideaway in the Tucson Mountains. Sandra Ramirez, who'd worked with Marcia at the TPD, was short and small-boned like Bea, and she cut a trim figure in her Copperton Police Department uniform. Like Bea, she had a short haircut that showed off her fine features, though Sandra's hair was dark, and Bea's was quite blonde. Sandra was about Bea and Marcia's age—pushing forty. Sandra immediately took charge.

"Glad you can help us out, Bea. So, I got a lot of good information from an old hippie buddy of Crow's. Apparently, Alan hired Crow shortly after he bought the property, and they got along well at first."

"At first?" Marcia asked.

"Yeah. But then, Crow told Alan he'd better do the right thing when his bulldozer ran into some bones... and pots, which Alan removed from the site, and which Liz was very impressed with."

"Oh. What did Crow think Alan should do?" Marcia asked.

"Well, Alan should smoke some datura and ask the spirits what he should do. Crow offered to broker the conversation. Lord knows what the Mimbres would have thought about Crow claiming that kind of connection to them. So apparently, Alan called his friend at the University of Arizona Anthropology Department instead. That's all the hippie guy knew. So I looked back through U of A current and former faculty, and I'm pretty sure I found who Alan would've called. He's retired by now, of course, but still alive, so maybe he can shed some light on what Alan did with the bones. The bones on his Copperton property,

I mean. Maybe it will provide a connection to those bones on your Tucson property!"

"I actually hope they're not related," Bea said.

Sandra laughed and continued her story. "The old hippie said Crow had a sister in Wisconsin, so we're trying to follow up on his background. But we may never be able to completely place him, if no one reported him missing. He went from town to town, state to state, and people weren't surprised when he moved on. Hard to trace him back to his roots."

"Do we know if Crow had any enemies in Copperton?" Marcia asked.

"Apparently Liz Shandley did not like the way he inserted himself into the matter of their private property. Archaeological artifacts were considered just that in the Sixties."

"I'm sure that Liz wouldn't like anyone messing with her private property." Bea had had a number of interactions with Liz before her death. She tended to insert herself into things.

Sandra continued, "And Crow came to a meeting of the archaeological society and told them all they'd burn in hell for their sins of collecting the artifacts. He was not a popular character. One of those classic cases of someone who had some validity to his message, but whose delivery would always turn people the other way. Apparently, he claimed to be both a 'true Christian' as well as a 'Native American in a past life, who could channel all tribes.' He probably just smoked too much pot."

"And datura. We've had some kids get really sick from that in Tucson, as you remember," Marcia said.

"I'm more and more convinced that those old guys I met who'd been in the archaeological society probably lied when they said they didn't remember Crow," Bea said.

"Yes, we should definitely talk about that. But the Forest Service archaeologist, Ramona Alvarez, will be here momentarily. Let's see," Sandra said, consulting her notes. "We also discovered that Alan bought the property in May 1968 and sold it in October 1969. Any questions before Ms. Alvarez gets here?"

"Was he really a good gardener, I wonder?" Bea asked. "Alan had such high standards. He seems like such a flake, it doesn't make sense that Alan hired him."

"Maybe gardening is the only place he was really grounded. Literally, I guess. Sorry for that. Anyway, it seems like nobody disputes his gardening skills," Sandra said.

The receptionist knocked on the door. "Ramona Alvarez to see you," she said.

Ramona came into the room and gave each of them a firm handshake as they introduced themselves. Ramona had a candid, open face, and didn't seem fazed by being interviewed by several people at police headquarters. She was nearly six feet tall, and older than the rest of them... mid-fifties probably, with greying hair pulled into a loose ponytail. She wasn't in uniform today... she'd already been in the field, given the mud around the bottoms of her jeans.

After an explanation about the bones found in Tucson, Sandra said that they needed to understand what someone would do if they found artifacts on their property in the late Sixties.

"The laws were very different then," Ramona said. "There were laws that applied to the discovery of 'antiquities' on *public* lands as early as 1906—that's the Antiquities Act. You probably have heard it invoked at the end of presidents' terms, when they use it to create national monuments," Ramona told them.

"That's what Clinton used to create the Grand Canyon-

Parashant one. The one that's a million acres on the North Rim," said Bea.

"Exactly. So, much later, the National Historic Preservation Act was passed, just before Alan bought his property. It preserved all kinds of important sites, some of them on private property. A small Mimbres site like Alan's with intact walls and the possibility of data collection would have been eligible, but the Shandleys would make that decision."

"Well, it sounds like Liz would have been against that if she considered the artifacts her private property, like you mentioned, Sandra," Bea said.

Ramona raised an eyebrow, and continued, "In 1990, with the Native American Graves Repatriation Act— which we shorten to NAGPRA because it's such a mouthful—human remains on public lands were protected. At the same time, state laws went into effect protecting unmarked burials everywhere, on state land and on private lands, too. The affected tribes must be contacted when something is found."

"I guess that's what Crow was trying to do," said Marcia. "He was trying to have a séance with the ancestors."

"His instincts were good, but his methodology, not so much," said Ramona. "The Mimbres classic period, the period when they created the amazing pottery, was from about 1000 to 1150. There was a terrible drought after that, and the Mimbres went on the move, as did a lot of groups in the Southwest. We don't definitively know what happened to all of the Mimbres, but it seems some went north, and many went south. We know this from DNA testing and cultural similarities. These days, the Acoma, Zuni, and Hopi tribes are notified about Mimbres human remains, and they decide what to do with them."

"And in the late Sixties?" asked Sandra.

"You could do most anything. You could parade down Main Street with a Mimbres skeleton on the Fourth of July," Ramona responded. She added, quickly, "Of course, now you couldn't possibly."

Sandra's phone buzzed, and she checked it. "Hold on, I have Dr. Ramsey Peasely, that University of Arizona archaeologist, on the line."

"Must be the one that Alan contacted, all right," Marcia said, as Sandra murmured into her phone at the far end of the room."

"Thank you so much, Dr. Peasely. You've been an enormous help," they heard her say. She hung up and gave them a thumbs up.

"All right, Sandra!" Marcia said.

"So. Here's the deal. Alan felt uncomfortable with the bones. Dr. Peasely remembers this, all these years later. Alan said he wanted to be able to keep the pots, but he hated how he found them. He told Peasely that he found the pots on the heads of the skeletons, who were in the fetal position."

"Yes, that's the way they often were buried," said Ramona. And there was often a 'kill hole' in the pots, which may have been drilled to free the spirit of the pot, allowing it to accompany the deceased on his or her journey. Sometimes people patched up the 'kill holes' before sales."

"I don't remember any 'kill holes' on the pots in Ethan's office, at the Gardens," Bea said.

"Ah, so the Shandleys kept at least some of their pots?" asked Sandra.

"I don't really know where the Shandleys got them. But Ethan says they 'came with the house.'"

"Because my informant tells me that he heard the Shandleys had a good business in the markets in Santa Fe. But that could well be a rumor. There was a lot of resentment about them as outsiders, according to Peasely."

"I could certainly imagine that," said Ramona. "Outsiders coming in to develop a guest lodge and then breaking into the antiquities market."

"And Liz was easy to resent, even when she was dealing with people in her own town," said Bea.

"I'd like to talk to you about your discussion in the doughnut shop when you were here, Bea," said Sandra. "Ramona, you've been a huge help."

But Ramona wasn't ready to be dismissed. "There's something else you should know. People in town are a little touchy about their pot-hunting days. Even now, folks get it that they shouldn't be digging stuff up, but unfortunately some think it's fine to take home any "surface" artifacts... you know, sherds or arrowheads or whatever that are lying in plain sight on public land. Pot-hunting was a family Sunday picnic activity until just a few decades ago. They even talked about 'skeleton picnics' sometimes. You're touching some tender places, especially with the old-timers, just FYI," said Ramona. "On the other hand, the current archaeological society members do a great job of educating the public about leaving all artifacts in place, unless the sites are excavated by professionals. Kids around here are learning proper respect for these sites, and they're talking about it with their families, including their grandparents. That part is terrific."

"Got it," said Sandra.

"I'll do whatever I can to help. I have to get back and figure out how to deal with the budget cuts," Ramona said.

"You, too, huh?" said Sandra sympathetically.

"Yeah. With climate change, the fire season's getting longer and more dangerous. Firefighting's the one thing we can't cut. But everything else, well... we'll see."

"Anybody for some coffee?" Sandra asked after

Ramona left. I've got more to tell."

Bea and Marcia definitely wanted coffee, which Sandra brought to them, with sugar and a half pint of half and half that she said she provided to the department on a weekly basis. "I can't stand that chemically stuff," she said. Bea noted that the coffee was considerably stronger than the doughnut's shop's fare.

"Okay, so, according to Dr. Peasely, Alan said he didn't have any idea he was digging a site. It had some rocks that formed kind of a border, but Alan didn't think much of them. So, he hired a bulldozer to flatten that site for his lodge, up there above their home site. Peasely said if Alan *had* known anything about the Mimbres, he would have recognized that a nice, flat area above the flood plain would be a perfect Mimbres site. But the one Alan found wasn't really big, not like some of those along the Salvaje and Piedras Rivers. So Peasely said that U of A wouldn't have the resources to excavate it fully, and he told Alan he had a right to the pots, but he ought to cover the bones back up. Alan said he'd do that, and Peasely had no reason to doubt him."

"So where does this leave us?" said Marcia. "What's your take?"

"Well, as far as *your* suspects go, the Tucsonans, I'm not sure that Alan had a motive—yet—to knock Crow off. Not sure Liz had a motive either."

"My boss will be glad to hear that," Bea said.

"I'll bet. Bea, would you mind waiting in the car for just a few minutes? Sandra and I have a couple of things to go over," Marcia said.

Marcia came out to the car in ten minutes or so, and they headed for a place Sandra had recommended for green chile stew. They decided it was a good choice: there was a ten-minute wait. They finally got seated at a little table with Mexican oilcloth with hummingbirds on it. When they got their iced teas, Marcia said, "Sandra told me something that may or may not have anything to do with this case. Lila got a threatening note in the mail yesterday, one with letters cut from a newspaper. With a Copperton postmark. It said not to be such an interfering bitch."

"Oh, no." Bea's first thought was that she'd brought this on Lila. Maybe it was crazy Gert. But Marcia was still talking. "Lila discounted the note—she said she'd gotten some pretty nasty reactions from locals for her stand on gun control, through the years—I guess she's the town's most prominent gun control advocate. She seemed to think that this note was just more of the same. Just talk."

"But it was mailed just after we went to see Gert."

"She says it was a friendly visit, and she wouldn't expect something like that from Gert. It was also just after you and Frank met those old guys in the doughnut shop."

"And I told them Lila mentioned the gardener to me."

"I mentioned that to Sandra. I hope she can figure out who sent it, political enemy or otherwise. She also told Lila about the investigation, which I guess you didn't mention to her."

Bea suddenly felt like she didn't deserve to be called Lila's friend. "Maybe I should just bow out of this whole thing. I hate to think that I brought trouble to Lila's door."

"Lila could be right. She recently wrote an op-ed in the local paper that may have gained her some enemies. But I'm telling you this because it *may* have something to do with this investigation."

They got their green chile stews, but Bea left quite a bit in the bowl. "It's a little spicy for me," she said, when Marcia pointed to it with a questioning look.

"That hasn't stopped you before." Marcia didn't need to explain that she wasn't talking about peppers.

They headed out to Rob Chance's place along the Piedras River east of town. Marcia wanted to "see him in his habitat."

Bea was ready to move in. Even in winter, it was stunning. The leafless cottonwoods formed a thick grey-brown phalanx down at the river. Pear and apple trees filled out the terrace above, and a modern ranch-style home stood higher than the trees, flanked by an old adobe barn with a new red metal roof. Behind it all, the juniper and piñon strewn hills rolled out as far as Bea could see.

Rob greeted them from a swinging love seat on his front porch. "Would you like a glass of homemade cider from my trees down yonder?"

Marcia demurred, but Bea saw no reason to pass it up. She assumed it wasn't the hard cider Frank had been talking about, after all.

They sat down at a little wooden table flanked by a couple of wooden chairs painted with apple trees. "My former wife's artistic efforts," Rob said, when Bea complimented him on the chairs. The little twist he made with his mouth warned Bea to drop the subject.

It was cold on the porch, but not quite uncomfortable in their winter coats. Rob excused himself and returned back with a tall mug of hot cider that had a deep, sweet, heady smell even before Bea picked it up.

"This tastes even better than it smells," she said, and took a long draught. Marcia caught her eye, and she put the cup down.

"Thank you." Rob sat down again in the cushioned swing, crossed his legs, and asked, "So what brings you charming women to my house? And in a Tucson Police Department cruiser? Last time I was in Tucson was about five years ago."

"Official business, sir," said Marcia. "We are investigating an unnatural death, and we have reason to believe it has something to do with events in Copperton... I'm Marcia Samuelson, a detective with the Tucson Police Department, and this is Bea Rivers, whom I believe you've met. She works at Shandley Gardens."

"I see," Rob said, narrowing his eyes.

"An old skeleton was found on what was then Alan Shandley's property. We know you knew Alan once, and we're hoping we can get some information from you that will help us. There was a possible murder, but of course you don't have to talk with us if you don't want to."

"Well, now, I'm mighty curious, and I can't see how I could possibly incriminate myself, seein' as how I haven't done anything incriminatin'. So, ask away."

"Thank you," said Marcia. "Do you mind if I record this?"

Rob shifted his posture in the swing, leaning forward a bit, and then sitting back again. "Guess not, ma'am."

She put a small recorder on the table, and, after identifying herself and Rob, and other relevant information, she asked, "So you were in the local archaeology club in the late Sixties?"

"Yes, ma'am, I was. I ran the Ford dealership for a livin', and I was President of the Arc Soc for about ten years."

"Was Alan Shandley a member of the archaeology society?"

"Well yes he was, Ma'am, Alan and that wife of his came a few times. So hell's bells, what does the Copperton Arch Soc have to do with a possible murder in Tucson?" Bea hadn't understood the abbreviation for Archaeological Society the first time, since he pronounced it "arc sock."

"Well, Mr. Chance, we honestly don't know. We're just exploring things here. We're trying to understand what was going on in Copperton forty years ago. We're just gathering information."

"Any idea who the skeleton was? Did it have somethin' to do with Copperton, then?" Rob twirled his impressive mustache.

"We don't know much about him. It's possible it was a man named Crow."

Bea thought he flinched, but maybe she was imagining it.

"He came to the archaeological society and told you to quit digging up bones," Marcia prodded.

"Oh, there was some guy like that. How am I supposed to remember all the fruits and nuts who come through town? Yeah, I remember him lecturing me, telling me that Jesus Christ and the spirits of all the people who went before would find me. Looks like I'm still here, hale and hearty and eight-five."

"Someone at an archaeological society meeting said you got into a pretty public fight with him. Does that bring back any memories?"

"Miss... Samuelson, is it? I don't take kindly to being suspected of murderin' some crazy hippie forty years ago. Bea here asked me if I knew the gardener when she and that boyfriend were here a few days back, which I can now see was a trap. You can't expect me to think he was that idiot who came bargin' into our monthly meeting! But I didn't kill him for his rudeness, even if he deserved it. Seems to me you're bein' rude yourselves, ladies." He was turning red, and his breath was coming fast. Bea hoped he wasn't going to have a heart attack.

"We're sorry to offend you, sir," said Marcia, but she didn't sound all that sorry. Her face was a mask. "Here's my card. Call me if you think of anything."

"Thanks for the cider, Mr. Chance," said Bea, wishing she hadn't accepted the offer. The sweetness suddenly felt sour in her mouth.

Rob Chance didn't reply that she was welcome.

"Thanks for your help, sir," Marcia said, and she and Bea walked toward the car.

"I think I know why you didn't have any cider, Marcia," Bea said. "Better not to be in his debt," she said, sliding into the police cruiser. "But I'm learning. Did we get anywhere, do you think?"

"Let's see what happens the rest of the day. We're not meeting Sandra until four o'clock, up at your buddy Gert's place. Let's divide up. There's a small university here; how about if you search the old newspaper records for 1968 and 1969 for any mention of Crow Johnson or Alan or Liz Shandley. Or Gert or Mack Curry, or any of those cowboys you met at the doughnut shop. That should keep you busy."

"No kidding. What are you going to do?"

"I'm gonna sit in my vehicle, where it's warm and private, and try to take care of some business around another case in Tucson—involving some people who are still very much alive. If I have time, I'm gonna talk to your friend Lila to see if I can get some background on Mack and Gert Curry. And whatever else she thinks of. I'll call you after that and check in."

"Ten-four, Officer." Bea saluted.

"Sorry, Bea. Thanks for your help."

"*De nada*. I'm enjoying myself."

Chapter Eight

Bea walked into a comfortable university library with huge picture windows overlooking Copperton and its surrounding mountains. The place was nearly empty; Bea supposed that students didn't use actual paper books much these days. She needed help with an even less common library tool. She found the file cabinets with microfilms of old copies of the *Copperton News,* and asked the student librarian to help her set up July, 1968 through July 1969 in the spooling film reader. The student rushed to find her supervisor, a woman who looked to be in her sixties, who threaded the film expertly, and left Bea to it.

Bea found herself fascinated by 1960s Copperton. The newspapers were full of Vietnam War news, while international news was a very small proportion of the local paper's contents. But now people were getting all of that online, and on cable TV. She scrolled through issue after issue, filled with half-page advertisements for tomato soups, 3 for 39 cents, a ten-pound bag of potatoes for 59 cents, a quart of Russian dressing for 28 cents.

Then Bea discovered an article on May 15, 1968 about Alan.

Tucson Real Estate Magnate Hits Copperton
Alan Shandley, the developer of such

iconic Tucson properties as the Mesquite Mall and the Sixth Street Shops, has found a new and potentially lucrative opportunity in Copperton. He plans to develop the old Blackwell property off of Highway 24 as a "lodge and gardens that will beckon Tucsonans and others from the Sonoran Desert to Copperton's wonderful year-round climate." Mr. Shandley sees this as a "rustic resort" that will "give folks in the big city a way to let go of it all" and enjoy our region's attractions, including the hoodoos in the national monument, which are right up the road. Shandley, a dedicated gardener, plans to install gardens that will add to the ambiance and relaxation of his guests. Prominent businessman Rob Chance remarked, "This is exactly the kind of development our town needs."

Bea remembered the hoodoo Frank had taken a picture of for Jessie. She loved this word. She continued scrolling through.

She also found several mentions of Tom Franzen as the President of the Chamber of Commerce during this period, but she doubted there was anything the Chamber did that had any bearing on the case. She kept spooling through the newspapers, getting a little bored, but she found a story dated January 21, 1969 that made her sit up.

Disturbance at Copperton Archaeological Society

Robert Chance, President of the

Copperton Archaeological Society, reported a significant disturbance at the Monday,
January 20 meeting. According to Mr.
Chance, an individual named Crow, last
name unknown, wandered in and was ver-
bally abusive of the members, and even
engaged in a physical confrontation with
President Chance. Mr. Buzz Winters, visiting from Hollywood, escorted Crow out
of the meeting.

Archaeological Society member Nina
Purdue described the incident: "This
long-haired hippie barged in and started shouting that we were dishonoring the
ancestors and God Himself with our col-
lections. His eyes were all bloodshot,
so we knew he was drunk or on some drug.
Rob told him to leave and when he started
shouting again, Rob punched him, and the
guy kicked him you know where. It went on
from there until Buzz broke them up and
threw the guy out the door."

Mr. Chance reported that the club proceeded to vote that Crow was barred from
all future meetings, and that the police
would be called should he attempt to
attend another.

And Rob Chance said he barely remembered anyone
named Crow. It now seemed awfully unlikely that Rob
Chance didn't remember this incident.

Bea had a hard time staying alert as she paged through
more ads. Stories like "Tonkin Gulf Crash Kills 26" were
interspersed with descriptions of Ladies' Club fundrais-

ers. She did wake up when she read about Woodstock. 1969 was *that* year, the year her parents said so many things had changed.

Then, in an article dated October 14, 1969, she discovered something about the Shandleys:

Shandley Lodge Property Sold

Alan and Elizabeth Shandley have sold their property on Highway 24, designated as Shandley Lodge and Gardens, to Mackenzie and Gertrude Curry, of Albuquerque. Mr. Shandley, a noted Tucson real estate developer, had planned to operate a rustic vacation property at the site. He built a residence for himself and his wife, but has not yet begun construction on the lodge. He cites "changes in our priorities" as the reason for his sale. Tom Franzen, President of the Chamber of Commerce, said, "There probably never was a market in Copperton for a project like this. We at the Chamber wish Alan and Liz all the best in their Tucson endeavors."

Mr. and Mrs. Curry run Curry's Collectibles on Main Street. They plan to live in the residence, but will not build on the lodge site.

Bea also found a quarter-page ad with a large photo of Rob Chance's smiling face, as yet unlined, but with the same handlebar mustache. "Come on down for the best deals in town. Buy American. Buy Chance Ford," it said.

All in all, it had been a reasonably instructive afternoon. As Bea was copying the relevant articles, her phone buzzed with a call from Marcia. She went outdoors to take the call, which, it turned out, was a highly uncomfortable thing to do, as it had begun to sleet.

"Got anything good?"

"Yeah, maybe. No smoking guns, but a lot of confirmation of stuff we've heard."

"I look forward to hearing about it. Well, in Tucson a repeat offender has just repeatedly offended. But I've got local news, too. We need to head up the hill to meet with the Currys. I'll pick you up in fifteen outside the library."

"I'll be there with copies of some articles."

"Bueno."

Fortunately, as they climbed up to the Continental Divide, the sleet turned to big flakes of snow. It wasn't sticking yet, though. "So, what'd you find out?" Bea asked.

"Lila was very helpful. It seems that the Currys used to have a shop in Copperton."

"Yes, I discovered that in the newspaper."

"Good for you! Lila said that they moved the shop to Tucson in the seventies, *after* the period you were researching. Guess why?"

"Because they were run out of town."

"Yep, for a pretty interesting reason. They were charging admission for a mummy that they said was a Chinese railroad worker. Some high school kids suspected it was bogus, and they sawed off a finger. It was paper mâché. Folks had been paying $1.00 admission, and the town claimed it as a tourist attraction. The Currys found it was better to do business in a big city, and moved their store out of state. Interesting that they didn't go back to Albuquerque, where they lived for many years. Lila said that she'd heard 'through the grapevine' that the Currys had been investigated for selling stolen pots, but the case was inconclusive. Bottom line: as you suspected, they're not the most savory characters. Also, interestingly, there is the Tucson connection.

"Lila had a little more to tell me. She was in the Chamber of Commerce when Tom Franzen was President. He was building a tourist hotel in town at the same time Alan was building his place out here, and Franzen was quite hostile to the competition."

"Aha. Then you'll be interested to know what I found." She read Marcia the articles she'd copied, and finished just before they pulled off the highway into the Currys' driveway. The snow was dusting the ponderosa pines.

"Well, there's some food for thought with those articles. We can talk about them with Sandra before we leave. It doesn't look like she's here yet," Marcia commented. "I told her to go ahead and do the interview, since we're on her turf."

Mack Curry opened the heavy mesquite door, decorated with ornately carved flowers. Bea suspected that Alan and Liz had found it in Mexico. She'd been too distracted by Gert's presence, complete with broom, to notice a beautiful door on the last trip here. Gert was on the couch, broomless. Mack held her attention this time, though. He was stocky, with a shock of thick white hair that fell across his eyes. "I thought there were three of you cops coming!" he said in a voice louder than she expected in a man of his age, which she guessed to be about 75.

"Yes, Officer Ramirez should be here any minute."

"You never said you was a cop, when you came up here with Lila!" Gert yelled.

"Lila brought a cop up here?" asked Mack. He wasn't happy. This was not going well.

"I am not a police officer. I do education and volunteer coordination at Shandley Gardens in Tucson, just like I told you," Bea said. Gert's look of disbelief was interrupted by the doorbell, and Gert shuffled to the hall to admit Sandra, while Mack stared at Marcia and Bea with open hostility.

Sandra was diplomatic and composed. "Thank you so much for meeting with us on such short notice. We'd appreciate your help on a case we're working on in both Tucson and Copperton," she said.

Bea decided she'd study Sandra and try to emulate her. Small women who held their own were her heroes.

Mack looked slightly less hostile, and Gert just gestured toward the couch. None of them had sat down yet. Bea remembered the wheeze of dust from the couch on her earlier visit, and she selected a cushionless chair. Sandra and Marcia sat on the couch, which, predictively, emitted a dust cloud expansive enough that it made Bea cough.

Both Currys ignored her cough. Gert demanded, in a crackly voice, "So what's the case?" Bea looked hard at her for the first time since they'd come inside. Gert was wearing what used to be called a "house dress," but which hardly anyone wore anymore. She had tights on underneath it, and fraying slippers. On top was both a pink cardigan and a purple shawl. The room *was* chilly.

Sandra answered Gert's question. "Alan Shandley had a gardener named Crow Johnson. Crow had something called a button osteoma in the middle of his forehead; it looked like a big bump." Bea noticed that the Currys exchanged a look at this point.

"A skeleton with this same bone formation was recently found in Tucson. The police have determined that the person was killed about forty years ago, about when Crow worked for Mr. Shandley. Since both of you knew the Shandleys and Crow Johnson, we wanted to ask you a few questions. We have no reason to believe that you were involved in what looks to be an unnatural death, but since you bought this property from Alan Shandley, and may have run into Crow Johnson, we wanted to ask you some questions. If you don't mind, I'd really like to be able to record you to make sure we don't get your words wrong," Sandra added with a smile.

Gert looked over at Mack. He nodded.

"We got nothin' to hide, lady," she said. "I always wondered what happened to that crackpot gardener."

"Okay, great." Sandra cleared a place among the archaeology and history magazines on the coffee table. Something that seemed to be a bill of sale surfaced below one stack, and Gert snatched it up before Bea could get a look. Sandra smiled again, in a friendly way, set the tape recorder in a non-dusty spot left by a magazine heap, and began with setting the scene for the recording.

"So, can you tell us what you knew of Crow Johnson, Mr. MacKenzie?" she asked.

"Well now," Mack began. "That Crow—what a name! I'll bet it's not the one he was born with. That Crow was more trouble than he was worth. I don't know why Shandley kept him on after he left here."

"He kept him on?" Marcia asked.

"Yeah, I heard that guy went back to Tucson with Shandley."

Bea looked at Marcia, who looked at Sandra, all with tiny turns of their heads. Mack didn't seem to notice, and he steamed on.

"Anyway, we only met him a couple of times, long enough to know *we* didn't want him around here. He thought he was the Second Coming of Christ or something. Told us to rebury our arrowheads. Alan had already gotten the good pots out of this property, him and Liz. All that was left was some nice pot sherds, and some arrowheads, manos, metates, that kind of thing. Heard that guy got into fights in town, too, with some of the town's big shots. Not a good idea. Anyhow, Alan was welcome to him."

"But don't you go thinkin' we killed him over a goldarned arrowhead!" Gert yelled in her raspy voice.

"Did he give you a hard time about the bones that were unearthed, too?" Marcia asked, in a sympathetic tone.

"Well, Shandley did most of that diggin'. Like I said, he got most of the good stuff out, and you know there's bones around it. Shandley buried them right back in there. We just got the surface stuff. He bulldozed the place good," said Mack.

"And that's about it," Gert added.

They waited to see if Mack had more to say. He didn't.

"When did you meet Alan Shandley?"

"Well, now, not 'til he put the place on the market. I was up in Albuquerque, lookin' for a place down here, maybe. Was lookin' to live out here in the boonies, then maybe set up shop in Tucson, where I thought I might do better business. So, yeah, I met him in '69."

"Was there anything that struck you about Mr. Shandley that we should know?"

"No, ma'am. Well, I guess I wondered why he was so all-fired ready to get out of here that he'd sell the property at a loss. He was only here a few months, him and Crow, too. But since we did okay on the deal, who cares?" Mack said.

"Mrs. Curry, do you have anything to add to that?"

"No," Gert said, and folded her arms.

"Do either of you have anything at all that you could tell us about Crow Johnson that might help us?" Sandra asked.

"Hell, no," Gert said.

"Haven't thought about him in years. Can't help you

there," Mack said.

"Yep, we can't help you any more than we already have," Gert said, tightening the arms folded across her chest."

Sandra and Marcia exchanged a glance. Marcia nodded her head just a little.

"Thanks so much. Here's my card," said Sandra.

"And mine," said Marcia. "Feel free to give either of us a call if you think of something that might help us."

"Ain't you gonna give us your card?" Gert asked Bea.

"Of course," she said, fishing one out of her wallet. "But I'm not an official investigator. I'll make sure Marcia and Sandra know anything you tell me."

Mack looked over his wife's shoulder at the card. "You really ain't a cop, you were tellin' the truth."

Gert chortled and dropped the card on the pile of magazines on the table. "That's it, then," she said, walking towards the front door." She did like to keep things brief.

"Thanks so much for your help," Sandra said, extending her hand when she got to the door. Gert didn't take her hand, and Mack had stayed seated.

"So pleased to meet you," said Marcia, extending her hand into nothingness.

"Thanks for meeting with us," Bea said. She just smiled at them, keeping her hands by her sides.

Gert grunted and opened the door. The women waved goodbye and exited.

"They were more hospitable than they were the first time I came," Bea commented.

"They didn't have to talk with us at all," Sandra said.

"True enough. We have to get back to Tucson, but is there some place we can debrief today before Bea and I get on the road?" Marcia asked.

"It's a small town. Probably best to just meet at the

station," Sandra responded. Bea remembered the close quarters of the doughnut shop and the restaurant she'd been to at lunch and was glad of a non-public location.

They sat in front of Sandra's desk and compared notes. Bea gave Sandra the articles to read, and she made copies.

"Things don't look so good for your Tucson folks," said Sandra. "Crow went back to Tucson with the Shandleys."

"Yes," Bea said. "He probably harassed Alan and Liz about their pot hunting, just like he harassed everybody else. But Alan seemed to like him, even if nobody else did."

"For sure Rob Chance didn't, or Gert or Mack. Rob was violent with him and Gert and Mack had nothing nice to say about him," Marcia added.

"Also," Sandra said, "we don't know yet who sent Lila that threatening note. It could have nothing to do with this case."

"But if it does, it sure isn't from Alan or Liz Shandley," Bea said. "It seems like it's probably from a local..."

Marcia and Sandra nodded. Sandra had more to say. "My first informant said he thought Crow was from a little town in northern Wsconsin. He thought it was called Raspberry or something like that. Well, we found some Johnsons in a town called Strawberry, way up there, just inland from Lake Superior. I hope to talk to them to see if they lost a family member in 1969 or so. I'll let you know what I find out."

"Great. Well, we all have some things to check," said Marcia. "But Bea and I need to get back. It'll be nine o'clock easy before we get home. Is there a good takeout place we can stop by?"

Sandra suggested a drive-through burrito place on the way out of town. She recommended the pork/green chile or chicken/green chile specials, and they picked up one of each before climbing up to the Continental Divide again, this time south of town. The snow had stopped, leaving barely an inch on the ground at 7,000 feet. The two old friends were mostly quiet on the way back. Bea had started to think about Frank's two-week deadline. In a little over a week, he had to accept or reject the job in D.C.

The kids should be asleep by the time she got back, and she wanted to go in and watch their stomachs rise and fall.

Chapter Nine

Frank had let the kids stay up far too late watching a movie; they'd just fallen asleep when she got home. He said they'd all gotten along famously. Bea was so grateful everything had worked out that she gave him only a half-hearted reprimand for his permissiveness.

After exchanging information about the day—Bea's debrief being considerably more eventful than Frank's, which consisted of solitary writing and the child care routines that Bea knew so well—Frank asked her the question she'd been dreading. "Have you thought more about the job offer?"

"You really want to take it, don't you?"

"It's a good opportunity with benefits. I've been kidding myself about making a living as a freelancer. It's a bird in hand. And it's near Mother. Those are big positives... for me."

"Not so much for me. My job is a bird in hand here, and I like it a lot."

"We don't have to decide yet."

They didn't have any difficulty making the decision that he should spend the night at Bea's apartment instead of his own, however. They watched a bit of a Katherine Hepburn movie before they were sure the kids really were asleep. "This is so normal," Bea said to Frank, her mouth full of toothpaste.

"Well, then, let's shake things up a bit," said Frank,

removing her toothbrush and kissing her Colgate-full mouth. They shook things up until well after midnight.

The alarm clock went off all too soon, ending Bea's luxurious dreams. "You stay in bed," she told Frank, touching his cheek. There was no reason for both of them to be sleep-deprived. He smiled and closed his eyes. For her, it was wake-the-kids/find-the-socks/find-the-box-of-the-new-cereal-Jessie-wanted/pack-peanut-butter-but-*not*-with-peach-jam-sandwiches/get-to-the-schoolbus-in the nick-of-time.

When she got to work, she slowed her pace as she walked into the office, remembering the night before. Javier was just outside her office door and caught her dreamy look. He didn't say anything, but she was embarrassed. *I'd better snap out of this reverie.* Ethan came into the hall and called her into his office, to get an account of the Copperton trip he'd permitted her to take. She returned to thinking about unpleasant things, and gave him the lowdown. He frowned at the news that Alan and/or Liz were not off the hook for this supposed murder. "It's fortunate for the Gardens that this hasn't leaked to the media. We can hope that since the crime scene tape is so far away from our pathways, nobody will notice it."

"Unless one of our birdwatcher visitors brings their binoculars. Or unless somebody other than the park service folks uses their access road by the back fence. Or unless somebody from the park service has a big mouth."

"You're starting to exhibit a policeman's mind!" he said. When she looked at him to try to figure out how to take this, he continued, "I prefer to think of it that way rather than that you are being realistic, which, of course, is the case. But let's get to what I want to talk with you about. The board Events Center committee meets this afternoon at five. I'd like you to come." He saw her hesitation. "Would you have trouble with babysitting?"

Did he actually understand that she had another full-time job? "I'll work on it... if you really need me."

"Yes, I think I do. You're aware that the building designs call for LEED certification, platinum or at least gold status. Green technology, a green roof, every water conservation measure we can find, etc."

Bea nodded cautiously, knowing that Ethan was referring to the Leadership in Energy and Environmental Design designation for a "green" building.

"And you know that our major donor wanted it that way."

Yes, I remember that well. It was all part of last summer's mess. Bea nodded again.

"Well, the additional donations are not flowing in the way that the board had hoped when they voted to expand the original footprint of the center. Which is not surprising, given the recession. Anyway, this committee meeting is key; they will come up with a recommendation to forget green building leading to LEED certification *or* shrink the building footprint to cut costs."

"We can't back out on LEED! That's exactly what will distinguish us from every other wedding and party rental in town. That, and the beautiful gardens. Plus, it will attract younger people. Plus, it's the right thing to do and we have to be a model."

Ethan nodded, "Which is exactly why I need you to tell them all this, in your own words."

"I'll be there," Bea said, resolved to make it work.

"Thank you, Bea. I appreciate it."

Ethan had once told her that he'd never "have the courage" to have children. When she asked him what he meant, he said, "Let's just say I didn't learn much about good parenting, growing up. And I wouldn't want to deal with all the logistics. They've gotten in the way of many of my friends' dreams." As far as Bea could tell, Ethan didn't even let serious relationships get in the way of his career. But still, given all this, he was a decent boss.

She thought about asking Frank to get the kids after school, but this was starting to feel a little too easy. She shouldn't rely on him this way. She called her friend Barb Rice, who came through, as always.

"I owe you so many times over, Barb."

"You'd do the same for me if you were a stay-at-home mom." This was true.

Bea wasn't going to be able to manage a trip home to put on more professional clothes for the committee meeting. A denim skirt and clogs would have to do. She worked on what she'd say for a while, dealt with a couple of minor volunteer corps crises, led a tour group of ten-year-olds and another of retirees. At 4:45, she actually put on some makeup, which she wasn't very good at, since she did it so infrequently. She checked her email to make sure there weren't any last-minute messages about the board meeting, and noticed one from Lila. The subject line read, "Caution: nasty person at large."

Bea decided to read it even though the meeting was starting soon. "Somebody sent me one of those nasty notes with the letters cut out from a newspaper. It called me an interfering bitch. The odds are that it's one of my not-so-good friends on the other side of the gun argument. I've circulated petitions for background checks and bans on assault weapons. But who knows? I suppose it *could* be somebody who doesn't like me aiding the cops in investigating an ancient murder. So, friend to friend, watch yourself."

This wasn't new information, but hearing it again made Bea sit up straight. This was starting to feel like quite a bit more than an intriguing puzzle she needed to solve to get things back to normal at work. But *work was what she needed to focus on right now.* Bea took three deep breaths and walked into the board room a little before five o'clock.

The Board President, Alicia Vargas, smiled when she came in. Bea knew that Alicia wouldn't want to waive the LEED certification. Neither would Armando Ramos, the university botanist, although Bea couldn't say she was glad he was still on the committee. "You're looking fine today, Bea," he said. She thanked him without making eye contact. He gave her the creeps.

Ethan's problem was no doubt the new board member, Margaret Rhodes an octogenarian who was the third person on this committee, and one of the two new people on the board since last summer's exodus. The other was John Nelson, a mild-mannered nurseryman.

Bea had driven by Margaret's mega-mansion surrounded by an enormous well-watered lawn. Why was Mrs. Rhodes on the governing board of a public garden which tried to show people how to live sustainably in the desert? Bea doubted that the woman cared much about the environmental features of their proposed building, and she probably didn't like the idea of shrinking its original size, either. *Well, she obviously hasn't found the money for the grander version of the Events Center,* Bea thought. *Ethan and the others probably figured she would. That must be why they asked her to join the board.*

Early in the meeting, Ethan asked Bea to state her thoughts about the Events Center. She explained that younger people would care about getting married in a place that was a model for environmentally conscious living. It was a good business investment for that reason.

"Well said, Bea." Armando Ramos tapped her on the

shoulder to emphasize his point. She pulled her shoulder back.

"I tend to agree with you," said Alicia Vargas.

Margaret Rhodes took a drink from her thermos. "Cold." She made a face, and then said, "Well, I do see the business argument."

Bea's boss gave her a grateful look.

The committee voted to recommend the scaled-down, environmentally-friendly version of the Events Center to the full board. This meant that the measure would pass, because there was only one other board member who wasn't on the committee. Bea knew that Ethan was trying to build up the board; they'd lost three members in the aftermath of last summer's murder.

It was time to go home. Back in her office, Bea turned on her phone, and discovered that she was supposed to call Marcia. Something about Gert or Rob... anything but bad news about Lila. Bea wasn't ready to deal with whatever it was until she'd fed, read to, and lullabied the children. She took a few hours to do just this, and thought about how great it would be to end her evening with a good book. But the kids were in bed, and she had no more excuses. She took three deep breaths (this was becoming a habit), and started to dial Marcia, when her phone announced a call from Frank.

"I was waiting until the kids were in bed. I need to talk to you," he said.

"Frank, Marcia called me a while ago, and I'm really overdue to call her back. I want to give you some time. Can this wait a bit?"

"Sure," he said, but he didn't sound convinced.

Marcia was all business. "Okay, so Lila's husband Ed gave me a call. I wanted to update you. He said that he'd always figured that Alan left Copperton because he had enemies on the Chamber of Commerce, or at least Liz did. But with all this talk about bodies and pot hunting, he wanted to let us know about another fight, besides the Chamber of Commerce drama.

"Apparently, Alan just wanted to keep the nice pots he'd found, bury everything else, and move on. He told Liz that Crow Johnson had a point about respecting the dead. She tore into him about missing business opportunities in Copperton; she thought they should sell the pots up in Santa Fe, and she'd heard there were a couple of other properties on the market that they could buy, and bull-doze, and sell the stuff, and then develop. Alan said abso-lutely not and was pretty worked up about it. Liz walked out on him 'very dramatically,' according to Ed. Alan went out after her, slamming the door, but she'd taken the car. Ed gave him a ride home, and he heard Alan had to borrow a truck for the next few days, probably because Liz high-tailed it back to Tucson in their car."

"Wow, where did all this happen?"

"In a bar. Ed was at the next table. They were sitting up front, and he was taking a break from singing, right up front, too."

"So, Alan was pretty much willing to do what Crow thought was right, but Liz wasn't, and she was angry about it. Angry enough to kill Crow? That seems like a stretch."

"A stretch, yes, but a possibility. Also, Sandra talked to Tom Franzen, who was furious that she might be implying he was a suspect. He said the antipathy between him and Alan was 'pure, red-blooded market competition,' and he felt 'what any normal person would think about that nut.' Like Rob Chance, he said he didn't connect the crazy fanatic Crow with the person you were asking about back in the doughnut shop."

"I don't believe either of them about that. It's too small

a town for them not to make that connection."

"I agree with you," said Marcia. "Also, I am trying to figure out when Crow came to Tucson, and how long he was here. If we can trust Gert and Mack on that piece of information about him moving on to Tucson with Alan. I have a call in to Myron."

"Good idea!" Myron had moved to New York City, after his mother's murder, and no one at the Gardens had heard from him since.

"I haven't heard back from him, but I'm hoping he remembers Crow."

"So… in 1969, Myron would have been about twenty, right?" Bea sensed Marcia nodding. "He went away to college in the East somewhere. I'm sure Liz and Alan insisted that he do that, but that's neither here nor there. So, Myron might have missed the guy entirely."

"That's certainly true. Alicia or Juan Vargas might have some good information. We know your board president and her husband can be helpful, and we know they were acquainted with Alan in the Sixties. They've been central to the Tucson business community for decades, right? If you have a moment with her, you might ask her what she remembers, if anything, about Alan's gardener. She probably needs to know Alan and Liz are suspects in this investigation, too."

"Yeah, she'll want to know that. She'll be at the Gardens tomorrow for her weekly meeting with Ethan. I could try to talk to her then." *I certainly hope Ethan has already clued her in.*

"He's still okay with you spending time on all this, right?"

"I think he gets it that the faster we clean this up, the better it is for Shandley Gardens." Bea paused for a moment, recalling Lila's email. "I assume Lila hasn't gotten any more nasty notes?"

"No. Sandra's still not sure who sent the one she got. She's on it. Get a good night's sleep, Bea."

"First I have to call Frank. It sounds like it might be... something I don't want to hear."

"That's just what the doctor ordered. More urgency in your life. Sleep tight."

Bea approached the call with Frank with a bit of resentment, given her old friend's comment. But, like a lot of things lately, Frank's concern did deserve her attention.

"Bea, I have some bad news. I'm really sorry."

Wow, he wants to break up? I thought we were getting along great.

"My mother's caregiver called me today in tears. Mom is getting depressed. She had a serious choking incident at lunch. She's been saying stuff like 'What's the use of going on if I can't even eat without an IV?' The caregiver wants me to come back right away and raise her spirits. Even though Mom said that her only child has better things to do than be there, I feel like I have to go back."

"I understand, Frank."

Then there was silence.

"I really wish this weren't happening, Bea."

"We both have to do what we have to do. Go help your mother." That sounded harsher than she meant it to be. "I'd do the same thing in your place." That sentiment sealed the deal.

"My flight leaves in an hour and a half. Looks like we won't see each other before I go. Bea, I'm sorry."

"It's okay, Frank." Of course, it wasn't okay, but she had no right to feel otherwise. She could feel D.C. pulling Frank closer. Maybe permanently? She had to allow for that possibility. She had to be rational about this,

She tried to read a magazine, to think about something other than the possibility of breaking up with Frank or the killing of a dogmatic hippie in 1969. But this effort was hardly soothing; the news was full of the recession. She turned off the light and willed herself to sleep. She succeeded for an hour or so until she felt herself being shaken awake. She was about to snap at Frank that she needed her sleep, didn't he understand that, when she realized it was a very small hand on her shoulder. She opened her eyes to Andy's pale freckled face framed by red hair sticking out every which way, his right ear lobe red from pulling.

"Mommy, I dreamed I was falling down a well." Bea stroked his forehead and whispered that he was all right, he was so safe and so ready for sleep. He dozed off quickly, but of course she didn't.

Frank sent her an email in the morning. "Miss you all, but it was important to come back. Let's talk tonight. I need to let the Land Trust know in a week."

Chapter Ten

It was raining in Tucson. A slow, cold rain. Consistent winter rains meant a good spring wildflower season. Bea had to agree with the tourists—March and April in the Sonoran Desert were the most glorious months, if the winter had given them several long, slow, wet, chilly days. "I sure wish it would snow instead of rain," said Andy, and Jessie started jumping around the house yelling, "I want to see snow!" so that Bea barely got them bundled into their raincoats and onto the school bus. She realized that Jessie didn't even remember seeing snow, although Bea and her ex-husband had taken the kids to Flagstaff and they'd all played in the stuff in their friends' back yard up there. But that was three years ago, when Jessie was only two, and Andy was four, and she had begun to feel that Pat was acting out some sit-com role of a family man. He hadn't learned good parenting from his own father, who had been better friends with the bottle than his wife and children. Pat had learned only half the lesson he could have drawn from trying to be different from his despised father, she thought—only the one about working hard at a job you cared about. He hadn't learned that being a husband and father took just as much effort and was more important.

That winter weekend in Flagstaff, he'd been good for one snowman and one sled ride, and then he'd retreated to their guest room, claiming work issues. Even then,

Bea had wondered if all those phone calls were about his green products business. They'd dragged the marriage through another year, with Pat claiming that work called him away, even on Christmas Eve. Of course, he'd been calling a woman from Flagstaff, and he'd spent Christmas Eve day with her, too. She made no demands on him, certainly not the kinds of demands the mother of two young children is likely to make.

Now, Bea was a divorcée no longer acting out the charade of the ideal four-person family. She'd kept the show going longer than she should have, probably, but she hadn't been able to conceive of breaking up with the father of her children. Pat had had a lot easier time with that concept.

Alicia Vargas's car was already in the parking lot when Bea pulled in. She and Ethan must have scheduled an early meeting. Bea knocked on Ethan's door. He told her to come in but looked annoyed that a staff member was interrupting his meeting with the board president.

"Marcia wanted me to ask Alicia a question." Ethan looked at her sharply. Alicia smiled in an encouraging way. "I'll be in my office if it's convenient to stop by when you're done with this meeting." Bea looked at Alicia as she said this, and then ducked out.

A few minutes later, Alicia and Ethan both walked into her office. Ethan was making sure she wasn't going around his back in some way; usually anything she'd say to the board president would go through him.

"Mind if I sit in?" he asked.

"Of course not." Bea answered.

"Great job at the committee meeting, Bea," Alicia said smoothly, settling into a chair. Ethan followed her lead. Alicia Vargas did everything smoothly. Her black hair was swept up into a neat bun, her black slacks fit her slim legs perfectly, her black cashmere sweater offset the heavy silver beads so that they shone. Ethan looked just as professional, in his khakis and Oxford cloth shirt, both of which probably got professionally cleaned after each use. Bea was conscious that the pants she'd bought at Target were a little baggy.

"Marcia wanted me to ask you something that might help with the mystery of the skeleton on the back forty," Bea explained.

"Fire away," Alicia said. "I'm curious to know how I could possibly help. Ethan's filled me in with what you know so far, I believe."

"Yes. Well, the thing is, you knew Alan and Liz in the Sixties, and we… well, Detective Samuelson… was wondering if you ever met a gardener named Crow Johnson, or if you ever heard or saw anything about him."

Alicia burst out laughing. "Bea, you know that we were hardly best of friends with the Shandleys in those days. Liz never considered people with my heritage to be her social equals, let's face it. The last thing I'd know about is some gardener they had for a project that never got off the ground in New Mexico. I did hear about the project. It was in the news, briefly."

"The thing is," Bea heard herself repeating this phrase and thought she needed to clean up her speaking skills if she was going to be talking in board committee meetings, "someone in Copperton thought Crow came back here with Alan when he pulled out of New Mexico. So, you might have heard something then."

"Well, I suppose it was worth asking, but we just weren't on those sorts of terms," Alicia said. "Sorry." She looked like she was going to get up, but then she stopped herself. "But there's something that Juan and I were remembering. It probably has no bearing on this situation, Lord knows, but it did happen in the middle or late Sixties, shortly after we were married. We were talking about it last night."

Ethan had already risen to take his leave, but he sat back down.

"Liz was really excited about an opportunity to offer the Shandley property in Copperton as a location for some cowboy movie. Alan vetoed the idea, apparently, saying he didn't want the place overrun by Hollywood types, with all their demands and all their equipment messing up his garden. He was the my-home-is-my-castle kind of guy. Liz was publicly furious about this, as only Liz could be." Alicia pursed her lips at Liz's unseemly behavior. "Anyway, I guess they filmed the scene they wanted in Copperton, because after Liz goaded Alan—at a cocktail party— about how he was missing an opportunity for Hollywood fame and fortune, Alan said something like, 'Why don't you just hire yourself out for the movie, in Copperton, Liz. You could be a star.'

"'Maybe I'll just do that,' she said, and she walked out. Liz was good at dramatic exits. I don't know if this has anything to do with anything, but it does feature our founders and Copperton. Unfortunately."

"Well, thanks, Alicia. I'll be sure to tell Marcia this."

"You're welcome." She checked her watch. "I'm gonna be late to talk with a new café supplier." Alicia ran the Native Foods Café, among her many business enterprises. As she went out the door, leaving behind a pleasant scent, Bea realized that Alicia's perfume was one of the reasons she trusted her. It had a hint of sage. It wasn't from Paris; Bea had asked her about it. It was made in Tucson, from local plants.

"How's the Spring Fair coming?" her boss asked. She turned her head from the door to him. Clearly, she'd better focus on some more traditional job tasks. He might not be too pleased with her new status with his own boss.

She got back to her job, until Marcia called. She'd had a little more success in her inquiries than Bea. Myron Shandley had returned Marcia's calls. He'd become a Manhattanite since leaving Tucson after his mother's death. He'd told Marcia he was trying to forget Tucson and forget his parents. He was just starting to figure out who he was at age sixty, something he "should have done forty years ago," he told Marcia, "so talking to you about another traumatic incident down there is the last thing I want to do."

He did remember Crow. Myron had come home from college at Christmas, and he figured the year was 1969. He said, "This wild nut case had set up a tipi in the back forty, over by the Park Service road."

Marcia said, "I asked him if there was any way to identify the spot. He said it was by a palo verde big enough to sit under and read, because he saw the guy with a book there."

"There's a palo verde that big right where the skeleton was found," Bea responded. She knew it because it was one of the biggest of these green-barked trees she'd ever seen outside of a wash or other riparian area, and *she'd* thought of bringing a book to read under that same tree at lunch one day. It was often her turnaround point for desert walks; that had been her goal when she'd come upon Javier with the shovelful of bones.

"Myron said more," Marcia added. "He didn't remember the gardener's name, but he remembered the bump on his forehead. He said that during the Christmas break when the gardener was there, his parents fought so much he couldn't stand being home. He said he'd blocked out what they were saying. When he came back in the summer, to intern in Alan's business as he knew he was expected to, he said the gardener and the tipi were gone. His parents were much more civil to each other, he said, although, and I quote, 'mere civility was the highest level of affection I ever saw between them that summer.' One day, he asked them what had happened to the crazy gardener, and he remembered the incident because things got frosty after that. 'No fire, just frost,' was the way he put it. He said, 'Dad told me the guy just disappeared one day, and he left no note.' He told me his father looked really sad. But Liz lit into Alan, saying something like, 'You never should have hired the guy, he was crazy and WAY too nosy.' His dad just walked out of the room. Myron remembered the incident because his parents had been decent to each other and then there was a deep freeze for the rest of the summer. He couldn't wait to get back to college.

"Also, oddly, he said that Alan gave him something Crow wrote, and asked him to keep it. Myron thought that it was such a weird request that he did keep the paper, somewhere in a box of stuff from his dad. He's sending us a copy. Myron said the guy could not spell 'worth beans' but that it was some poem dedicated to Alan Shandley."

"Whew! That's a lot to digest. Well, good, because Alicia didn't remember Crow at all. But she did remember something else." And Bea related Alicia's story. Marcia thanked her and hung up.

The rest of the day, Bea was busy planning for the spring events season, the crazy time when everybody wanted to visit to see the flowers in peak bloom. At the end of the day, the rain had let up, and the desert smells pulled Bea out into the garden. She went out past the cactus garden with its huge barrel cacti massed together, raindrops glistening on yellow spines, past Madagascar pachypodiums, so-called because they looked like elephants' trunks, past the limberbush in the native plant garden, leafless now, red-stemmed and springy, full of a latex-rich sap. In the wildflower garden, she took a sniff of an early-blooming yellow brittlebush flower. The rain-smell propelled her past the fifteen acres of planted gardens to the back forty. The area had always been her pressure valve. Dwarfed by the huge saguaros and the soaring mountains, seeing so little created by humans except for a few narrow paths, her all-too-human concerns assumed their proper proportions. But something sordid had intruded in this spot now, something that was all-too-human, but also undeniably consequential.

There it was—the site. The police had removed the crime scene tape. Javier was standing by the fence, lost in thought. He was usually so aware of his surroundings, but he clearly didn't realize she was coming his way until she called out his name.

"Hey, Javier! Are you trying to solve this one for us?"

He grimaced. "I wish I could. Ethan told me it doesn't look so good for either Alan or Liz. But you have a whole bunch of possible suspects over in Copperton, right? And he could have been killed over there, and brought here, or somebody from Copperton could have made a murderous visit here, right?"

"All true."

"You and Marcia figured out our last mess. Maybe you should go back over there and figure out what's going on." Javier was making circles in the dust with the toe of his boot.

"That's the job of the Copperton P.D. You really don't want this to be Alan or Liz, do you?" Bea asked.

"Of course not. But I'll tell you what's worrying me. Though maybe I shouldn't say."

"What?"

"One time, after I'd just started working for Alan, I heard something break in the living room, and I went to check on it. Liz had obviously just thrown a Native American pot at Alan. It was in pieces on the floor, and she was gasping with anger, and he looked dazed. I kind of backed out of the room and she said, about me, 'At least he minds his own business, unlike that semi-literate Eagle, or Redtail, or Penguin, or whatever his name was.' And Alan said, quietly, 'His name was Crow.'"

"Thanks for telling me, Javier."

"I remember it especially because she added, "Even if he is a Mexican. *Me*, that is. I minded my own business even if I am Mexican. I remembered that. And Alan yelled at her to apologize, and she just walked out. That's why I remember that day."

"Oh, God, Javier, I'm sorry."

"*You* have nothing to be sorry for." He shrugged. "Anyway, I never met Crow. He was long gone when I started working for Alan. He would sometimes make a comment that his 'crazy hippie gardener' had put in a planting, or that he lived in a tipi on the property, or that he loved anything that bore fruit. Alan never told me the guy's name. When I asked where the guy had gone, Alan just shrugged, and said, "I have no idea.""

"I know you don't want Alan to have murdered him."

"Nope, I don't." His boot was drawing bigger circles in the loose desert soil. "I think it must be time to retire from this place, Bea," he said.

"Oh, Javier, how would we get by without you!" She meant it. Javier had been Shandley Gardens' first employee, and as far as Bea was concerned, he was still the most critical one.

"You'll do fine without me, Bea. You and Angus and Ethan and whoever else. Really." Bea gave him a hug. She wasn't so sure.

"I'd better get back to work," Javier said, taking his leather gloves out of his back pocket.

Bea headed back towards her office, and for once the pungent scent of the creosote bushes didn't energize her. She idly pulled a mesquite pod off a small tree—a last-season leftover. She smelled its sweet earthiness and took a little chew as she walked and thought. Back in her office, she left Marcia a voice mail about Javier's disclosure, and Marcia picked up the phone partway through.

"We have a positive identification of the victim. I reached Crow Johnson's sister in Strawberry, Wisconsin. His real name was Robert Johnson, but they called him Bobby."

"I guess he thought 'Crow' was a little more interesting."

"He rebelled against more than that. I got an earful. They threw Bobby out of the family. They are strict religious fundamentalists, and they didn't like his involvement, and I quote, with 'drugs, heathen religions, and other immoral behavior.'"

"It seems to me that he was quite a moral judge in his own right."

"Well, he kept that part of his heritage. And a couple of other pieces of information: He had a button osteoma, although his sister Joanne didn't call it that, and she last heard from him in 1969 in Tucson, Arizona."

"The year Alan sold his Copperton property, the year that Crow moved to Tucson."

"Yes. He sent her a card "with some of those cactus trees on it," which she threw out. She never heard from him again, and she said the family figured he 'probably died in San Francisco with a lot of other folks who left the Lord.' The family chose not to file a Missing Persons

Report."

"So, we know who he was. We just have to figure out who killed him, and why."

"That part's harder. By the way, Bea, I was going to call you."

"Got another assignment?"

"No. Lila's husband Eddy ran into Mack and he went off on a riff about how Ed didn't know how to keep his wife in line, and what was she doing hanging out with cops, like that little girl from Tucson who'd been nosing into their business. He told Eddy he ought to know about cops from his protest days. Eddy asked him point blank if he'd sent Lila an anonymous note, and of course, he denied it. Thought you should know you'd been mentioned."

"Copperton doesn't seem to stay away from my life. But thanks."

Bea didn't have time to think about any of the new developments until after the kids had finally gotten to sleep. She agreed with Javier; the best outcome of this mess would be to find a murderer among the cast of characters in Copperton. She didn't have any warm and fuzzy feeling about Alan really, and certainly not Liz. But she didn't want to see Shandley Gardens hurt by the bad publicity that would ensue if one or both of them had knocked off some poor gardener. And her part in this drama was pretty much over. She needed to get back to focusing on setting up the spring class schedule, organizing the Spring Fair, touring the legions of Midwesterners who had fled the dark and the snows, teaching newbies to Tucson about what to plant in the desert, and, not incidentally, paying attention to her kids. And trying to figure out what to tell Frank about his decision. One thing about that was clear. She didn't need the additional stress of contemplating a move to the East Coast.

That night, as Bea was plumping up her pillow to read a mystery that might temporarily distract her from the complications of her own life, the phone rang. She expected it to be Frank, but it was Lila, calling from Copperton.

"How're things, Bea?"

"They could be better, but I'll survive."

"I have a proposition for you. There's snow in the forecast for this coming weekend. Eddy and I miss playing in the snow, and neither of my girls deigned to give me any grandkids. We'd love for you and Frank to come up for the weekend with your kids. What do you say?"

Bea hesitated for just a moment. If Lila could brush off Mack Curry's (or whoever's) aggression, she could, too. "You are the nicest person I've met in years. Frank's in Virginia, taking care of his mother, but if you'll have the three of us, my children are dying to play in snow! We could just show up around noon on Saturday and leave at noon on Sunday, if you could handle us for that long."

"That sounds perfect. All the better if you're alone for the weekend, as I well know."

"Lila, I hope you're okay about that note. And I heard about Mack's words to Eddy."

"He's a piece of work. Don't let it faze you." And she wouldn't.

Andy and Jessie were *both* jumping around the kitchen when Bea told them of her plan. This was normal behavior for Jessie, but Bea was happy to see that Andy could still be a happy-go-lucky kid. This was only Wednesday. She hoped they could maintain the good cheer until the weekend. The weekend when Frank would have to decide if he was going to accept the job.

Chapter Eleven

Thursday and Friday passed relatively uneventfully, for which Bea was immensely grateful. She decided she'd drive the three hours to Copperton on Saturday morning, because Jessie had a birthday party on Friday afternoon, which gave her mother an excuse not to take the mountain pass in the dark. Just before Bea went home from work on Friday, Marcia sent an email saying there weren't significant new developments in the case, and Bea told her she'd keep her eyes and ears open, but mostly she'd be in Copperton to spend time with her kids and some new friends.

It had snowed in Copperton. On Friday night, four inches had fallen, and the cold temperatures kept it from melting. The highway had been ploughed by the time Bea got to the area around the Continental Divide. Lila greeted them with the news that their timing was perfect; they'd have snow and no mud the whole time. And Eddy proved to have artistic talents beyond the blues harmonica: his snow "zoo" of make-believe animals kept Bea's kids entranced all afternoon. The Saguaro Monster and Mesquite Bean Monster, created by Andy and Jessie respectively, were eating a meal of sticks and stones with an equally unusual six-winged bird, a metal sculpture created by Lila. Bea had noticed it as soon as she pulled up to the big blue Victorian house in the center of town.

Just as the kids' energy flagged, Lila called them all

in for Mexican hot chocolate, redolent with cinnamon, as well as homemade apple bread. Both children asked her about the paintings on the wall, most of which she'd created herself, in colors like a full box of crayons. There were traditional New Mexico landscapes of juniper-studded hills above a flowing river, and sunrises behind pine-clad mountains, but there were just as many of fanciful birds and cats and deer. Andy, who'd been interested in drawing early, but hadn't shown much interest since the divorce, was inspired to draw his own "dog monster," which Lila told him was first rate.

Bea was looking forward to the evening's entertainment. Eddy would be playing the banjo that night, and Rainbow would be singing at a community square dance. Bea wasn't much of an artist, but she did love to dance, and kids weren't welcome at the dances she went to in Tucson. Eddy said there were two other good old boys in their band, as well as a caller, and that kids were absolutely invited, although the protocol was that their partner should be an adult. Lila volunteered to be squired by Andy, so Bea and Jessie could form the second couple.

They arrived early, with Lila, at a cavernous building just off Main Street. Eddy had come even earlier so that he could practice a little before they played. Bea recognized some of Lila's animal paintings for sale on the walls. The two new band members showed up, one with a fiddle and the other, a guitar. They looked like younger versions of Rob, Buzz, and Tom, down to the cowboy boots and tooled leather belts. Bea wasn't sure how well they fit with Rainbow, who was arrayed, again, in tie-dyed splendor, her dreadlocks fully splayed out. But it turned out she could sing old-timey and country music just as well as she sang the blues. The two cowboys played licks and harmonized, but Jessie couldn't stop staring at Rainbow. Bea anticipated loud renditions of "Turkey in the Straw" in imitation of Jessie's new heroine.

The crowd poured in; the dance was a bargain at $5 a head, and $1 for children. There were several parents of Rainbow's generation, with tow-headed kids whose unbrushed hair matched Andy's for wildness. There were also a lot of grey-haired retirees, including several women with waist-length locks and men with equally impressive gray beards, like the ones Bea had seen in the bar on her first visit to Copperton. Hair seemed to be a theme. Plenty of less noticeable people filled up the hall, and they asked Bea if she'd recently moved to Copperton, and told her she had beautiful children. What impressed Bea the most were the age extremes. Not only were there plenty of kids Andy and Jessie's age; there were an equal number of folks who looked to be in their seventies and eighties.

Two old women in particular stood out. They both had complete square-dancing regalia, including full calico skirts and white blouses with bows around their throats. Despite their age, which must have been around eighty, they had trim waists. One of them also had tiny hands and feet, and a cloud of curly white hair. She wore dancing slippers. She had the kind of beauty that defied wrinkles; what would she have looked like at twenty-five? The other woman was bigger, with a square jaw and handsome features framed by a practical short cut. Bea remarked on the women to Lila, who said, "Those ladies used to be married to Buzz Winters and Rob Chance, my dear. Let's see if they'll be in our square. They'll want experienced folks for most of the dances, but they'd be glad to start us out."

The caller kept it simple at first, with plenty of do-si-dos and allemande lefts, and the two graceful older ladies, Doris and Beggie—short for Begonia—were immensely helpful with the kids.

"You've done this before," the tiny one, Doris, said to Bea.

"My mom's a really good dancer," Jessie announced, to her mother's embarrassment.

"Well, she reminds me of myself at that age. I taught my little girl to dance, too," Doris said.

As the steps got more complicated, the kids dropped out. There were video games going on at the far side of the hall, and they went to watch. Bea and Lila teamed up for the next square, which required more concentration than the first few. Every time a couple flubbed the steps, they laughed, and so did everybody else.

Then the band went on break, and Bea found herself in a huddle with Doris and Beggie. Lila wandered off to chat with some of the legions of people she seemed to know.

"You two are marvelous dancers. Thanks so much for your help," Bea said.

"We've been at it for a lot of years. Doris even danced in the movies in the old days."

Doris looked down, blushing. "That was so long ago."

"Where's your husband, honey?' asked Beggie.

"I'm divorced," Bea said with a shrug.

"Is that a blessing or a curse?" asked Beggie.

"Well, I suppose it's a bit of both. I guess that's not too surprising."

"Well, now, in my case it was a blessing, pure and simple. Rob has a temper that I don't miss one bit. But Doris, now, she still carries a torch for Buzz, though I have no idea why."

Doris's face turned as red as her calico skirt.

"Have you been divorced a long time?" asked Bea.

"Oh, honey, not long enough," said Beggie. "About forty years. Both of us."

Doris just nodded.

There sure was a lot happening in Copperton forty years ago, Bea thought.

"Do you and your kids live here now?" Beggie clearly liked to be well informed.

"Oh, no, we live in Tucson. We're just visiting Lila and Ed."

"Old friend of Lila's, are you?"

"Actually no, I just met her."

"She's a sweetheart. Some good old boys in this town don't like her—too liberal, they think. My ex-husband, for one. And yours," she said to Doris, "and plenty of their buddies. They think she ought to keep her mouth shut about 'trying to get their guns taken away.' Stuff like that. I know for a fact that she has a gun, and she brings home venison most every year. She just has common sense about what guns are *for*."

Bea decided to take the conversation in a different direction. "It turns out she knew the guy who started the public garden I work at in Tucson."

Beggie and Doris exchanged a quick look, and Beggie resumed her inquisition. "Now would that be Alan Shandley?"

"Yes, did you know him?"

"Uh, huh, nice man. Nicer than my ex. Word has it you royally pissed Rob off asking about his old pot-hunting days, is that right?"

This really is a small town. "I'm sorry I pissed him off..." It sure sounds like it's easy to do so.

"Don't be. Although I warn you, he's a bad enemy to have. I'm just glad Rob and I never had any kids to keep us tied together. Now Doris, here, had a daughter with old Buzz. But Doris and her daughter Annie did just fine without Buzz bein' around more. He enjoyed cattin' around, like most Hollywood types, right Doris?" At this point, Bea took her eyes off Beggie and turned to glance over at the silent Doris. She was no longer blushing; in fact, she'd turned pale.

"You'll have to excuse me, I have to go to the powder room," she said, and took off, graceful in her dancing slippers, but at a near run.

"Well, I'll be. I put my foot in it. Hope she's all right," said Beggie, and she trotted after her friend, no doubt to get some more information.

"What did you say to those two to drive them off like that?" asked Lila, who appeared hand-in-hand with Jessie. Bea didn't have to answer that question, because Lila went on, "Jessie's agreed to be my partner, and Andy's ensconced with the other kids. It looks like you'd better find yourself a partner for the next set."

Bea looked over at Andy, who was earnestly involved with a girl and boy about his age, both of whom had shoulder-length hair. She shrugged her shoulders and said, "Oh, I'll just watch." She had an eye on the bathroom door, because she wanted to apologize for upsetting the ladies who'd been so generous in their square-dancing instruction, and she had to admit, she was curious about what had happened.

She didn't see the two women leave the bathroom during the next square dance. Then there was a waltz, and a tall, athletic-looking man in an old Patagonia vest and khaki hiking pants asked her to dance. They flowed well together, despite the fact that he was a full foot taller than she. Bea missed dancing. She knew that Frank wasn't comfortable with that kind of public demonstration. *You can't find everything in a person*, she thought. She danced a polka with the man after the waltz, and then she saw that families were heading for the door and Lila was looking at her. Bea made her excuses to her partner, whose name was Jim. He looked sorry to see her go, but his expression changed to "Oh, that's it!" when Andy ran up. His new friends, who seemed to be twins, headed off with their parents.

"Thank you so much for taking us here!" Bea told Lila.

"Yeah!" Andy said.

Lila drove back carefully through the icy streets. Fortunately, the house was only about eight blocks away. *Nothing was very far from anything else in Copperton*, Bea thought.

After the kids had tumbled into bed, Bea sipped a fine dessert wine with her hosts. She gave them the low-down about why she'd wanted to meet the old boys at the doughnut shop. It wasn't a sudden overwhelming interest in pottery, as she'd indicated; it had to do with Crow Johnson.

"You weren't too convincing about loving ceramics. But I figured you'd let me know what that was all about, if you wanted to. I kind of figured it out, when Marcia told me there was an investigation into Crow's death."

"Lila, do you think any of those three guys would kill Crow? Or could Gert or Mack have done it, for that matter?"

"Bea, the guy was annoying, but that's not much of a reason for murder. But if he had evidence that one of them had done some serious grave-robbing on federal or state land, I guess that could be a motive."

"That's what I'm thinking."

"I'm gonna leave you two to gossiping. I'm beat," Ed said.

"More wine?" asked Lila.

"Why not?" Bea said. How nice to be taken care of.

"So, tell me about Frank," Lila said. Bea looked at her

feet. "Well, only if you want to," Lila said.

Why not? She's sympathetic and she knows about being a single parent. Maybe she can give me insights that my old friends can't. Bea went through it: how Frank would probably take a job all the way across the country, how she didn't see how she could keep up a long-distance relationship with two kids.

"Yeah, that's tough. And I can see why you're not dying to move to D.C.—I left the East many years ago with no regrets."

"How did you meet Ed?"

"Oh, he found me. He wasn't afraid of me, like most of the guys around here. You know, I wasn't supposed to have my own life, be successful, make more money than a man. And Ed wasn't even afraid of a woman with two kids and an ex-husband who didn't pay much child support. He didn't care what they said… that I was an out-of-line woman, no wonder my husband left me. Eddy just rolls with things, plays his music, enjoys life. I'm lucky."

"You sure are. So, can you tell me more about Doris and Beggie?"

"Thick as thieves. The used to be tight with Tom Franzen's wife Gloria—he divorced her and took up with a trophy wife from Santa Fe."

"She sounds like my ex's current fling."

"My condolences. Anyway, Gloria surprised everybody by connecting with her high school sweetheart and moving to Oklahoma or someplace like that. Meanwhile, Beggie's a strong one. She left Rob and now runs half the committees in town. Supposedly Doris and Buzz's divorce was mutual. I've always wondered if that wasn't one of his publicity stunts, just one more thing she let him get away with. Although she did tell me she liked to eat raw garlic sandwiches."

"What?"

"One time she told me she used to sneak raw garlic sandwiches, although Buzz didn't approve. 'I'd eat them every time he left town,' she said. I think she's got more spine than people give her credit for."

"But she didn't eat them when he was in town."

"Well, no."

"One other thing, and then we ought to go to bed."

"'Ought to' is overrated."

"Agreed. But Lila, aren't you afraid that the note you got is from someone dangerous?"

Lila stretched her legs out and contemplated her feet.

"I've lived in this town since a couple years after I graduated from UNM. I went to the same Little League games and football games and holiday parties as half the town. People have told me I'm their 'token liberal friend.' Most people would help me out if I were in trouble. If you'd asked me even two years ago, I'd have said that there was no way that note was anything but a nuisance. But there's a subtle change in town. People have less tolerance for my views... on what some people see as 'government regulation', maybe even regulation of archaeology. I don't know. I really don't *want* to think that I have to worry."

"I sure hope you're right."

They hugged and said their good nights.

The next morning, Jessie asked if they could move to Copperton, and Andy, who was old enough to understand that this might not happen easily, told his mother in a serious tone of voice that it was "a good idea, if you can work it out."

Lila explained to them that their mother would need a good job if they moved, and there weren't many of those in a little town. Andy frowned and nodded. Jessie chose to throw a tantrum. "PLEASE! PLEASE! PLEASE!' she shouted.

"Maybe you can look for a job here, Mom," said Andy.

My boyfriend wants me to move to D.C., my children want me to move to Copperton, and my ex-husband wants me to stay in Tucson. I guess I'm most in synch with my ex-husband on this, she thought, surprising herself.

On the drive home, Andy said, conversationally, "Mom, I know we can't really move to Copperton. But it still would be fun."

She had one child who was too old for his years and another who didn't want to give up the power of toddlerhood.

Back in Tucson, she thought about calling Frank. He had to tell the Trust of his decision on Tuesday. She decided to put off that conversation; it had been such a good weekend, that she wasn't going to spoil it by calling him.

Chapter Twelve

This time around, it wasn't a dead body that changed Bea's routine, or even an old skeleton. It was a body in a coma.

Mondays were usually slow at Shandley Gardens. In the old days, six months ago, they'd been closed on Mondays. But Ethan thought they were busy enough to open up on Mondays most of the year now, except for boiling hot summer months. Locals visited on the weekends, and Mondays were for tourists and school groups. Bea was hoping to firm up some more instructors for spring classes, and to get the next volunteer training going. But at 7:30 in the morning, she got a message on her cell phone to call Alicia Vargas, the board president, as soon as possible. She had to wait fifteen minutes until she got the kids on the bus.

"Bea, I'm going to come directly to the point. You're going to need to be the acting executive director for a while."

Bea managed a squawk, which was hardly a directorial response. "What?"

"Ethan was involved in a hit-and-run. On his bicycle. Now he's in a coma. I am recommending you to the board as acting executive director. It'll be the first item of business at tomorrow's board meeting."

Bea found her voice. "What happened?"

"Apparently a car blew through a stop sign over in the

Tucson Mountains and hit Ethan. He has brain injuries; if he hadn't been wearing a helmet, the doctors say he would be dead. He also has a broken leg, a broken shoulder, and three fractured vertebrae. They don't have any idea how long he'll be in a coma, Bea. It could be a few days, it could be much longer. The doctors didn't sound very encouraging, frankly."

Bea managed to get out an "Oh, my God." She swallowed, and said, "I'm having a hard time digesting this." *That was an understatement. This couldn't have anything to do with their other problems, could it?*

"Yes. We've notified his adopted parents, but as you may know, they're not close. I'm glad I insisted on decent health insurance for employees. He should get good treatment. You'll need to tell the staff and volunteers about this, Bea. The media may pick up on it. I have confidence in your ability to rise to this challenge."

"Thank you. I guess. This isn't the way I would choose to become a director."

"No, of course not. You'll have your hands full this morning. At lunch, you and I will meet about Gardens business, and what needs to be done."

"Okay." This was happening far too fast for Bea to make a more cogent response.

Alicia's tone softened. "I'll bring us some goodies from the Native Foods Café. You're the obvious person to step up in this situation, Bea. I'll try to spend time on site here and help you through. You're up to it."

She didn't seem to have any choice about feeling up to it. "Thank you."

Angus still wasn't back from vacation. He'd be out a few more days. She envied him, snorkeling in the Caribbean. She wondered briefly if he would have been made the acting director if he'd been around. There didn't seem to be any reason for him to come back early from his vacation; he was head of horticulture, and he'd arranged for everything to be well taken care of by Javier and volunteers. She knew Javier would never want to be an administrator; he'd made that clear when Angus was hired. So having a staff meeting would consist of her talking to Javier.

She found him in the Rose Garden, doing his winter pruning. "Javier, we'd better sit down."

"Please not another body!"

"Sort of." She explained the situation.

"That's awful," he said. "We need to tell more than those parents of his. I know a couple of Ethan's basketball friends. They probably know some of his jogging buddies. Armando Ramos is one of those; I know you don't like him, so I'll talk to him." Bea grimaced at the mention of her least favorite board member. "Ethan needs some visitors, a support system to stop by even if he's in a coma."

"Thanks, Javier."

"Sure, I'll try to take care of that kind of thing. You're gonna have your hands full with his job and yours. And your kids." Unlike his fellow staff members Ethan and Angus, Javier had had his own children, and knew about how much work kids were.

"Yeah, I'm busy all right, Javier. But you've got grand-kids to take care of!"

"Yes, but they go home at night. Usually. And we both know that Ethan's parents won't be much comfort."

She did know that. It seemed that Ethan had been adopted because his rural Arizona parents thought they ought to have children, not because they actually wanted a child. He'd told Bea once, in a moment of candor, that plants had been his best friends during a lonely child-hood. He'd worked hard academically, and as a nurseryman, as an athlete and now as an executive director. Bea sometimes wondered if he was a happy man beneath the polish and professionalism, but she was his employee, not his friend, and his personal life was none of her business. He was a fair and reasonable boss, and she'd do whatever she could to keep things on an even keel until he could get back to work.

Next, Bea called the volunteer president, Joan Madsen. "Dr. M" was at Shandley at that moment, "playing in the dirt," as she called it. She was a very well-respected retired professor of plant sciences. She ran a tight meeting, but she derived great pleasure from using a trowel instead of a computer. She showed up in Bea's office five minutes after Bea asked her to come by, in dirty-kneed jeans.

"What's the emergency, my dear?" she asked, as her eyebrows disappeared behind thick grey bangs.

"The emergency is that Ethan was in an accident and is in a coma, and I have to be acting director."

"Well, let's start over, from the beginning," said Dr. M, sliding into the chair that faced Bea's desk.

Bea told her what she knew.

"You'll do fine, Bea. But I don't know about poor Ethan."

Bea nodded.

"You don't suppose... you don't suppose this has anything to do with that alleged old murder on the back forty, do you?"

"Oh! No, I don't think so," said Bea. The idea had occurred to her, but she'd thrown it out as paranoia.

"I'm sure you're right. I'm just conflating dire incidents. It just occurred to me that maybe Ethan had been hit on purpose, but there's no hint of that, right?"

"I have no idea." *Okay, you just said out loud what I was trying not to consider.* Joan Madsden made sure she knew everything that was happening at Shandley Gardens; most of the volunteers were probably speculating about the skeleton. It was a miracle that the story hadn't made it into the press. There's no way they'd be that lucky with a hit-and-run.

"I'll call a meeting of the volunteers for tomorrow," Joan said. "You can explain the situation, and answer questions."

"A lot of them won't be able to make it on such short notice. I'll send out an email in advance. I have a feeling that Ethan's accident will be on the evening news," Bea said.

"That's a very good bet. And that awful Stephanie Shores on the morning broadcasts will suck this in and spit it out." Joan started out the door, and then turned around. "Oh! I almost forgot to give you this. We definitely have our work cut out for us."

Joan handed over the latest issues of *Tucson Trends,* a weekly newspaper. It was open to a colorful ad featuring a couple of guys in board shorts surfing a lawn. "Turfin' Tucsonans" the headline proclaimed.

TIRED of being LECTURED TO ABOUT GRASS?
TIRED of CACTUS and GRAVEL?
BREAK OUT!
Rejoin the AMERICAN WAY OF LIFE!
CALL TODAY for an estimate for reclaiming your lawn.
623-TURF

When Bea groaned, Joan told her, "That new volunteer who's an undergrad, you know the one I mean? She interned with Turfin' Tucsonans. She sure has nothing good to say about them." She shrugged and headed out the door.

Bea thought about whether it was completely crazy to "conflate" Crow Johnson's skeleton and Ethan's bike accident. Ethan was not at all involved in the investigation, and probably hadn't even been born when the murder took place. So, Bea threw *that* worry out. Besides, the culprit might just turn himself in (she realized she assumed it was a male, which probably wasn't fair). Maybe he'd see the news broadcast and feel super guilty.

By this time, it was noon, and Alicia Vargas was at the door to her office with mesquite muffins, Three Sisters Soup filled with corn, beans and squash—the Three Sisters of Native American agriculture—and some prickly pear sorbet. Bea took the sorbet to the freezer in the room that once had been the Shandleys' kitchen and tried to compose herself for the load of responsibilities that was about to fall into her lap.

Alicia smiled when she came back in. "I'm sorry I was so abrupt when I called you this morning. I'm afraid I react that way to shock, sometimes."

"No offense taken. I'm still just trying to absorb all this. You haven't heard anything more about Ethan, right?"

"No. I'm afraid we should plan for you to be in this position several weeks, unless we hear otherwise."

Bea took a deep breath. "Okay. So, what should we address first?"

"Tomorrow's board agenda." Alicia put a page in front of Bea. "The first agenda item is a review of the financials; we're on target for this year's budget. I will report on them this time, but this will be your job henceforth." Bea nodded.

"Then, as you can see, we have to vote on you as acting director. Now there's something I need to tell you about that."

Something in her tone made Bea look up to check

her board president's expression. Alicia was quiet for a moment, and she put her hand on her chin as if calculating how to phrase her next words.

"I should tell you that one of our board members, Armando Ramos, does not favor you as the acting executive director."

"Oh?"

"He thinks it ought to be him."

"Oh." Now it was Bea's turn to weigh how to phrase things. "He's been wanting a job here for some time, hasn't he?"

"Yes, and Ethan has not seen fit to create one for him. I have discussed this with the other two board members, Margaret and John."

This was why they needed more than four board members; the vote could be tied.

"Margaret is inclined to follow my lead." *That makes sense. She's from the same social set as Alicia, as well as the Shandleys. Margaret would trust Alicia over Armando Ramos, any day.*

"John Nelson is a nurseryman, of course, and he's inclined to have faith in a fellow plantsman. In fact, Armando pushed to put him on the board. However, I explained to John that the executive director must be able first and foremost to administrate, not dispense plant knowledge, and you've shown great success in building and managing our volunteer corps."

"Thank you." Bea thought that Armando had more negatives than a lack of administrative experience. He was a self-serving and lecherous individual, in her opinion. Now he was also one of her direct bosses.

"Then we have the vote on where we go with the Events Center, and thanks to your convincing words the other day, I think that will also go smoothly." Alicia smiled.

"You'll need to meet with the architect ASAP."

"Thanks again. But what's this next agenda item?"

At this, Alicia's facial muscles tensed. Her high cheek-bones seemed to get higher.

The agenda item said "Additional staff."

"Well, Bea, you haven't had time to think about this, I know, but you are going to need someone to do every-thing you've been doing so that you can do Ethan's job. I am proposing a three-month contract for someone to run our education programs and coordinate volunteers. Do you know someone who could do that?"

"Yes, Joan Madsden would be wonderful. She doesn't want to work full-time, but she might do it to help us out." *Why is Alicia so tense about this?*

"Excellent. I just want to give you a heads-up that Armando is already lobbying us for a research botanist. Again."

"Like him, for instance."

"Like him. I believe this is his fallback position should we not appoint him as acting director. Of course, that would be a conflict of interest, so he would just argue for the position, at a pay rate appropriate for a PhD scientist. If it were approved, he would probably drop off the board and apply. I'm sorry to have to be so blunt with you, but if we are to work together, it's the only way."

"Well, if I am acting director, I should decide if we need any new staff. And I wouldn't do something like that now, behind Ethan's back. I *could* use somebody to help me temporarily until he's back, and the budget looks strong enough for that. But I don't see that this is the time for us to be ramping up our programs or our costs."

"I knew you'd do well at this, Bea. So that's about it for the board meeting, barring anything unexpected under 'New Business.'" Alicia took a look at Bea's empty plate.

Her stress hadn't stopped her from enjoying Alicia's chef's creations.

"Thank you so much… for everything," Bea said.

"Of course. Now let's get some sorbet, and then I'm sure you have plenty to do. As do I."

Bea lingered over each spoonful of the sorbet, but soon enough, she was elbow-deep in Ethan's grants files. She managed to focus on them and little else until she got the kids.

She was able to push everything but them away until bedtime. After the last lullaby, the last goodnight kiss, she sat down on the couch and steeled herself. Her new job changed the equation. She had to call Frank.

As she reached for her phone, it rang.

"I miss you," Frank said.

"I haven't had time to miss you. Life has gotten beyond crazy." He didn't respond, and she realized she'd sounded harsher than she'd meant to. "That's not true. I'm sorry. But let me catch you up with the drama around here."

When she'd finished, he said, "Congratulations, Bea. You'll do great." She thought she heard regret in his voice.

Bea took a deep breath. She had to say what she was going to say. It wasn't fair to try to hold onto him. "Frank, take the job. Take care of your mother. I just can't go anywhere."

"Bea, are you saying you want to break things off… totally?"

"Frank, it's not that I want to. I think it's only fair to you. Your mother needs you. Lord knows I don't want to compete with her; that's just not right. And if you stay in D.C., it's hard to see how a long-distance relationship could possibly work out. It's difficult enough when people are unencumbered, and I'm awash in responsibilities here. And it's not like you're within driving distance."

Now it was Frank's turn to take a deep breath. "I see your logic… but please, Bea, can we leave the door open? Call each other? *Try* to visit each other and see what the next year brings?"

"Is that really what you want?"

"I think so."

"Well, Frank… thank you. One thing you can be sure of. I won't be involved with anybody else. I don't have any interest in it, or the time or energy for it, Lord knows."

"Me either."

Was that true? Could he feel as overwhelmed as she did, with his mother's illness? Maybe. Maybe he would need to seek solace from a woman in D.C. He'd said things were over with Sherry.

Frank continued, "And who knows what will happen in our lives in the next several months? Ethan may recover fully."

"Or not." They were both quiet for a moment.

"Okay, Bea, I will accept the job offer. But do not take this as an end point. Please. It's a waypoint."

"Frank, you have to take the job. I didn't think things would go like this, but if you're up for it, I'm glad to leave the door open for now."

She'd expected to end the phone call in tears, and instead, she was feeling appreciated. There was another silence.

But are we simply taking the easy way out? Like so many couples who are afraid to state the obvious, letting the clock run out so that nobody get hurts in the final moves of the game?

Well, if that does happen, it'll still be nice to have Frank to talk to. Even if it's only for a few weeks or so. I'll definitely miss having him help with the kids. I'm glad I never got used to that.

Oh hell, I'll miss a lot more about him than his child care abilities.

"I miss you, Frank."

"I miss all of you. Call me tomorrow after your board meeting."

He really does care. That makes it harder.

Chapter Thirteen

It was inevitable. The television, radio, and newspaper reporters were like cats crazed by catnip. "Shandley Gardens: Murder and Mayhem in Paradise." Ethan's accident was front-page news, and his story was paired with the discovery of old bones on the back forty. The coverage was followed by a long recounting of Liz's murder the previous summer. Marcia was quoted in the morning paper, saying, as usual, that the Tucson Police could not comment on ongoing investigations.

Bea switched on the morning news, and found the big-haired, low-cleavage reporter who'd followed the events of the summer. The reporter was positively salivating over the "connections between an old murder and a possible new attempted murder." Bea should have known that if Joan Madsden made that connection, the media would be all over it.

"Who needs the supermarket tabloids when we have Shandley Gardens right here in Tucson?" asked a cheery male anchor with astonishingly bright white teeth.

Oh, joy. When Bea pulled into the Gardens parking lot, a live remote truck from Channel Two was already there. Ms. Big Hair, alias Stephanie Shores, was lying in wait for Bea. Last summer, she'd been able to run away from the reporters and let Ethan deal with them. No more.

She let Stephanie hook her up with a mike on her collar. She spelled her name, B-e-a-t-r-i-c-e R-i-v-e-r-s, and saw it posted under her image on the screen beside the photographer. She explained that yes, she would be acting director until Ethan recovered, and yes, some bones of a man who had died about forty years ago had been found on the property, and no, she did not know of any connections between that case and her boss's bicycle accident. These were Tucson Police Department matters. Meanwhile, the Gardens was open for business, and spring was just around the corner!

Stephanie Shores looked disappointed. She took back the microphone, and said that Channel Two would have an update on the noon news about "possible connections between the two murders at Shandley. Some have suggested that there may be a connection with a third murder, of Liz Shandley, also here at the Gardens, last summer."

"Ethan was not murdered," said Bea after Stephanie signed off, pleased with herself. The anchors had said, after her report, "We're waiting to hear more with bated breath. Tune in to the *News at Noon* to hear more about this breaking story!"

"No, he's not dead yet," said Stephanie, with a knowing smile. Bea found her breakfast rising, and she hurried to her desk.

The volunteer meeting was scheduled for 9 a.m., and clearly, she was going to have to think carefully about what to say. These were Shandley Gardens' ambassadors to the community.

Her attempts at diplomatic wording, scratched out multiple times on a yellow legal pad, were interrupted by a phone call from Marcia.

"I saw you on Channel Two," Marcia began.

Bea nodded. "Fun and games."

"You should know that we have no evidence of any link between Ethan's accident and Crow's probable murder. That rumor didn't originate from anything we've learned. Most likely, whoever hit Ethan had been drinking all night and was afraid to face the consequences; the accident occurred early in the morning. We're following up on a couple of leads. There's nothing more on the Crow Johnson case, except that Rob Chance was jailed for drunk and disorderly behavior last night. Sandra's still trying to find out why he knocked a guy out cold in the bar up there on the Continental Divide. And Buzz Winters bailed him out of jail. So, Bea, are you doing okay with all this publicity?"

"Yep. I have to tell the volunteers what on earth is going on and what they should tell people, officially and otherwise. You just helped with that. Not the Rob-and-Buzz part. Just that there are two separate investigations, and nothing is positively known. And there's no connection to last summer, right?"

"Not as far as we know. Good luck."

Bea fielded questions from the volunteers for the better part of an hour. She'd take their questions over Stephanie Shores', any day. They were concerned about Ethan, worried about the Gardens' reputation, sympathetic with Bea's new tribulations. After the meeting, Bea asked Joan Madsden if she'd be willing to be "me for three months or so, until things even out."

"If that's what you and your board think is best, I'm game. But if you need much more than that, you'll have to find somebody who really wants the job."

"Thank heaven for you."

The board meeting was at noon and Bea was ready, she thought. She'd brought her only suit into work, and she changed into it in the staff bathroom. With a little lipstick and makeup, she looked almost corporate—except for her shoes. She wore plain black flats, and whatever else happened, that was not going to change. No painful heels for her—not with bunions. Not even without bunions.

She was the first person into the board room. She took Ethan's seat at the head of the table, arranged her papers in front of her and took a couple of deep breaths. Unfortunately, Armando was the next through the door. "Hello, Bea," he said in a challenging way. *What a jerk.* He wore his trademark Hawaiian shirt and flip-flops.

Alicia was next, and she gave the two of them an appraising look before sitting down next to Bea. She had on her own perfectly tailored suit, with a silk scarf that brought out the turquoise of her earrings and the greens of her suit and blouse. Margaret Rhodes appeared in a skirt and pearls, dressed as Liz Shandley had always been at board meetings. Finally, John Nelson came in, ten minutes late, in gardening clothes, and with dirt beneath his fingernails. Margaret surveyed him and Armando with her nostrils ever so slightly flared.

A motley bunch of bosses, for sure.

After the financial report, they got to the first agenda items, which were updates on Ethan's health and the bones investigation. Alicia covered the former and asked Bea to discuss the latter. Margaret Rhodes sighed deeply as Bea explained that Alan had employed the gardener who had likely been murdered, and that he and Liz might be suspects.

"I would like to mention something else. Please do not put this in the minutes," Margaret said to John Nelson, the board secretary. He looked up in surprise.

"Javier has worked here a very long time," Margaret said. "Also, his family once owned this property and I believe there may have been some resentment about the way they lost it."

Bea felt the need to interject something in Javier's defense. "He has worked here less than thirty years.

The skeleton is about ten years older than that. Also, I know that Detective Samuelson is aware of the history of Shandley Gardens, including Javier's family connection to it." She didn't add that Marcia knew about this because Bea and she had talked about this during last year's murder investigation.

"Very well," said Margaret in a skeptical tone.

It was a somber board that considered the next agenda item, the appointment of an acting director. Armando stepped right in. "Bea has her hands full with the volunteers and the classes. Plus, we need someone with credibility in the botanical community to take this job."

"Would you do it for free?" asked Margaret Rhodes.

"No, of course not. Since I have a PhD, I should be paid accordingly. Ethan has only a Master's."

"Despite our relatively positive financial position, I don't think we can afford to pay both you and Ethan at such a high rate right now. We're looking at hiring a part-time educator at a much lower rate to help Bea," said Alicia. Armando scowled. Alicia called for a vote. Bea became acting executive director on a three to one vote.

The Events Center vote went as planned. Then Alicia brought the part-time educator to a vote. Armando voted for that, and then he said, "If the director is not going to be a plant expert, we really should hire one on staff. With an advanced degree."

John Nelson, the nurseryman, looked at Armando as if he was now beginning to take his measure. Alicia seemed to notice the look, too. "Would you like to make that a motion, Armando?" Once again, he was defeated, three to one. He looked apoplectic.

"Any new business?" Alicia asked.

"Yes," Armando said. Bea steeled herself. "We need a fifth board member to break ties. We've discussed needing somebody with communications expertise. I recommend someone with a huge media presence... Stephanie Shores."

Bea couldn't restrain her gasp. Alicia turned to her. "What occasioned that reaction, Bea?"

She realized she'd better be very careful here. "Well, Stephanie Shores is now trying to link up Liz's murder last year with the bones in the back forty and Ethan's accident. I don't think it's a stretch to say that she cares more about sensationalism—and ratings—than the welfare of the Gardens."

Alicia turned to Armando to see what he'd say. He was nonplussed. "Our experience of last summer clearly shows that bad news can put you on the public radar, and that brings in visitors. Stephanie has a huge following. With good reason," he smirked.

Oh, so that's it. Armando would have a lover to vote with him.

"Armando," said John Nelson, while studying his hands, "it's a bad bet to have someone on the board that doesn't have the organization's best interests at heart." He looked straight at Armando when he'd finished that statement.

"Shall we take a vote?" Alicia asked.

"*No*," Armando said.

"Well then, this meeting is adjourned," said Alicia.

The board meeting took place during Stephanie Shores' noon newscast, which Joan Madsden had watched. She'd left Bea a voice mail about it.

"She's just stringing people along," Joan said. "No facts to report, but a maximum of innuendo."

"We just narrowly avoided putting her on our board."

"Good Lord! You'd better find some more people quickly to neutralize Armando Ramos."

Joan certainly had his number. Bea had never said

anything to her about Armando.

She remembered that Javier was going to talk to Armando about contacting Ethan's jogging buddies. She needed to spend a little time with somebody with his feet firmly on the ground right now, and she needed to get out of the offices and into the gardens. She went out the back door and stopped a moment in the cactus and succulent garden. Nothing was in bloom yet—it was still too early for that—although the spring annuals would be showing themselves soon.

Javier was in the butterfly garden, putting in a few more plants before the butterflies came in droves during spring bloom. He said that he'd been to see Ethan. He'd read people in comas may understand what's being said, so he told Ethan about the new plants he was putting in, and he read him an article about attracting pollinators. Ethan's adopted parents didn't seem to be around. Also, he'd brought him a couple of healing herbs in pots. He said that Armando was spreading the word among Ethan's work-out friends. Then Javier said something that made Bea step back in surprise, right into an aptly named cat-claw acacia. "I hate to say this, Bea, but you don't think Armando had anything to do with Ethan's accident, do you?"

"Why do you ask?"

"We both know he wants Ethan's job. Let me guess. He made a play for it today." Bea nodded. "And he was... I don't know, he sounded kind of false about 'making sure people know about this terrible thing.' It's an awful thought to have. Forget I said it."

"I'm going to have trouble forgetting that. So, Javier, do I remember that Stephanie Shores did a TV segment with Armando here, a few weeks ago?"

"Yes." He grimaced and turned to look at her full on.

"He taught her how to plant a one-gallon salvia. She acted like he was letting her in on the secrets of the universe. It was stiff competition for the *telenovelas*."

"So, we now have to worry if Armando is feeding her some of this junk she's reporting."

"I wouldn't rule that out."

"Well, Javier, I know you're an honest man, if not an encouraging one at this moment."

On the way home, Bea stopped at the supermarket near Shandley for some tamales for a quick dinner. When she left the market there was a cryptic note under her windshield wiper. On the reverse side of a flier about a community theater production entitled "Murder is Easy," someone had written, in big capital letters, "YOU SHOULD SEE THIS!" Surely it didn't mean anything. She was getting ridiculously jumpy. It sure wasn't anything like Lila's note, with all the letters cut out from a newspaper, so it wouldn't be the same person even if it was somebody threatening her. *Stop it. Take some deep breaths.*

That night, Bea talked to Frank about her new job, but she did not mention the flier.

"It looks like you're gonna do fine," Frank said. Was she imagining this, too, or was he not entirely happy about her competent handling of the board meeting? Her new job would surely keep her away from D.C.

"So, what's the deal with this Armando guy? Doesn't he have a job?"

"Yeah, he's on the plant sciences faculty at the university," Bea said. "I know he teaches a course on native plants. I don't think he has tenure. He was complaining about how hard it is to get *academic* grants, as if the ones we get here are all a piece of cake."

"Almost all grants are hard to get. That's part of why I took this job; too risky out there in the freelance world. So, watch out for that guy. He's gonna blame you now. You're an easy target for the woes he's brought on himself."

"Warning taken," Bea said. After that, the talk was much pleasanter. But it would have been better if she could have talked to Frank across the queen-sized bed, there in the master bedroom of the euphemistically named Palo Verde Acres. The phone screen grazing her cheek was a poor substitute for his touch.

She didn't go to sleep right after the call. She found herself searching for a review of "Murder is Easy." Apparently, it was a comedy about a guy who eliminated anyone who stood in his way, without ever being suspected. Not her kind of comedy, Bea reflected. But surely that note on the back of the flier had been written by somebody who simply enjoyed theater.

Chapter Fourteen

"**M**om, you never let us watch TV in the morning!" said her son, who was always ready to comment when his mother breached the rules. He was especially good at noticing this when *he'd* been called on something; he'd desperately wanted wheat squares for breakfast, and his mother had just pointed out that they were completely untouched and turning to thick brown milk mush.

"You're right, honey, but I'm making a TV exception because I need to watch this show for work."

It was Channel Two's *Wake Up, Tucson!* broadcast, and sure enough, the anchors were talking to Stephanie Shores. She was there in the studio with them, not at Shandley Gardens, but she was talking about Shandley, all right. "Yes, we've discovered that Alan Shandley employed the person whose bones were found on his property, a man named Crow Johnson. Police are not discussing whether there is a connection between Crow's death and that of Alan's wife, Liz, last summer, or whether there is a connection with the near-fatal bicycle accident suffered by Shandley's executive director, Ethan Preston," she announced triumphantly. "Or at least they're not discussing those things *publicly.*"

"That's a lot of mayhem for one peaceful little botanical garden," said the male anchor. His eagerness was all too apparent. The female anchor chortled at his witticism.

"Well, keep us posted!" she said.

How did she know about Crow? Bea turned off the TV.

Her son looked at her gravely. "This is trouble for you, huh, Mama?"

"Andy, please don't worry about it. It's just work, that's all." He looked doubtful and pulled his ear, but his sister bopped him on the head with her spoon, and the resulting tussle lessened the tension.

At work, there were calls from the newspaper, a rival TV station, and even a PBS reporter. Bea told them, with as much stoicism as she could muster, that she knew of no connections between the incidents and that she had no information for the reporters.

She spent a good part of her day going over everything that Joan Madsden would have to do in the next three months to cover what had been Bea's job. But Bea wouldn't have Saturday off, even with Joan taking her tours. She'd have to take on Ethan's VIP tour to a potential donor who'd said she was "vitally interested" in funding a children's garden adjacent to the Events Center. This sudden vital interest from an unknown person was unexpected, but certainly welcome. Bea had been wanting a children's garden ever since she'd visited a superb one in a L.A. botanical garden. It would be great to have a place where kids could interact with plants. Meanwhile, she'd bring her own children to work on Saturday. She'd just have to figure out how to keep them occupied. Ethan had let her do that when she needed to.

And Angus, the director of horticulture and her esteemed colleague, would be back tomorrow as well, relaxed from Caribbean margaritas, steel drums, and colorful fish, and ready to deal with the craziness at the Gardens. She'd have another sounding board. She wondered briefly again why he hadn't been chosen as acting director. Was it just that he was on vacation at a critical time? Well, they'd talk about it. It was true she didn't have the help she needed to be both an executive director and the mother of two young children, but, she thought, she had good people in her life she could trust, and that counted for a lot. It made up for the work she'd better get to in Ethan's "Grants Due" file, for sure.

Her mood changed when she saw what was outside her window. Armando Ramos was in the Mediterranean garden with a group of students. She'd seen him at the Gardens with students before, but this time was different. This time Stephanie Shores was here with the live remote truck. Bea watched as they filmed Armando sporting his expertise. As he held up a sprig of rosemary to the nose of a particularly blonde and particularly attractive female student, Bea looked at Stephanie, who stiffened her posture as well as her smile. They all moved out of her field of vision. Bea opened the tour files on her computer.

Of course, Armando's tour wasn't scheduled. And any feature story should have gone through the executive director's office, acting or not. Armando had improperly pulled his board rank in two ways. She couldn't let this pass. And no doubt he told Stephanie Shores about Crow and Alan. But she had no evidence of that.

She wasn't about to talk to Armando in front of his students. She sent him an email and said she would like to talk to him about the TV segment he'd just done.

Then she put her nose back into the grants file. When she looked up at the clock, she realized she had to hurry to get the kids from the after-school program. She was only two minutes late, and the teacher said they wouldn't charge her the $5 a minute per child overtime fee... this time.

***

On Friday morning, Angus bounced into her office with a fine gift: a woodcut of tropical flowers. "I've been blessedly internet-free for two whole weeks!" he exulted. "I'll bet I haven't missed anything of importance!" His wrinkled, tanned face looked so happy and open, Bea hated to enlighten him about what he'd missed.

"I beg to differ, Angus," Bea said. His tan began to fade as she hit him with one event after another. When she got to Ethan's accident, he began to twitch. His left foot had taken on a life of its own. "I'm not sure why I'm in this position instead of you," she said.

"You're welcome to it!" he said. "I'd rather help than be responsible for this whole place, especially in its present mess. So why didn't you move into the director's office?"

"Because Ethan will come back, we hope, and I don't want to be presumptuous."

"That's why you're a good choice. And he's still out cold?"

"Very much so. I haven't visited him yet, as a result"

"I expect you've had plenty to occupy you. I want to go back to my island."

"*I'm* glad you're here."

"Okay, I'd better go find Javier and see if the plants are in as bad a shape as the people of Shandley."

"I'll take any bet you offer me that they're not."

"No deal."

"Aren't there an awful lot of visitors for this early in the morning?" Angus asked, as he looked at three groups outside Bea's window.

"It's the looky-loos. There will be tons down by where they dug up Crow's bones, if we don't stop them. Javier's cordoned off that whole back section, because people were surging all over the desert to see the place where the bones were found. Yesterday, Javier said some of them went through his caution tape anyway. It looks like the crowds are already picking up."

"You're absolutely right, Bea. There are threatened plants out there. I'll get some warning signs going. Goodbye, hammock by the sea!" He threw his arm up in a farewell gesture as he exited.

Copperton seemed more than one state away. Bea was glad to leave the work on *that* investigation to the professionals. If she'd had plenty to deal with before, there was no question now; if Marcia asked her to, she couldn't take a workday to go to Copperton as she'd done only last week.

But then she got a call from Lila, and it turned out Bea was interested in Copperton events after all.

"Bea, I think Mac and Gert Curry are really losing it. I don't know if he wrote that evil note to me or not, but he's hopping mad about something. I ran into them at the bar where Eddy's playing, and Gert looked at me, held her nose, and said, "I smell a rat!" It'd be comical if I had some idea of what was going on. Then a friend at my table said when she was driving down the highway earlier that day, she saw a state trooper heading into their driveway."

Bea asked if she was sure it was the New Mexico cops, and not local ones.

"Yep. But Mack and Gert are definitely at large. I'm wondering if you'd be willing to satisfy my curiosity about something. Have you ever been to Mack's shop in Tucson?"

"No, I know as much about antiquities as I do about ceramics."

"Well, he knows you, so it's no good your checking the place out, but is there somebody you trust who might poke around there?"

Angus. "Very possibly. What would we be looking for?"

"Well, do they have something to hide? I mean, why

are they so up-tight about cops? Why were state troopers at their house?"

"Let me think about this, Lila."

Lila went on with other news. She hadn't heard about Rob's fight in the bar, but there was news about another member of what she was now calling the "doughnut trio."

"Tom Franzen's major property, the lodge he was building at the same time Alan was about to build his lodge? Well, the bank just took it over. He put too much money into modernizing it."

"No wonder he would rather not be questioned about Crow Johnson right now. He's had other things on his mind," Bea said.

"So, Lila, back to Mack Curry's store." Bea had been asking herself if she'd be interfering in an investigation if she asked Angus to check the store out. However, it was open to the public, and if she or Marcia went there, Mack would surely be on his guard. "I think I know somebody who'd love to check it out it, actually."

Of course, she was right. Over lunch, they planned it. Angus bore very little resemblance to a wealthy art collector, but he loved games. Angus would comb his long gray hair back, and borrow some Dockers, Top-Siders, and a polo shirt from his preppy brother-in-law. "I'll tell him I have to go to a funeral. He'll be delighted that I'm showing some respect, for once." Angus's deep tan, from years of outdoor work and enhanced by his recent Caribbean vacation, would be chalked up to leisurely days on his yacht, docked in San Carlos, Mexico, six hours away. Angus's singer-songwriter wife Jean had a few items in her closet that would turn her into a wealthy yachtie, as well, especially if she wore the simple emerald necklace she'd inherited from her mother.

"Don't worry! We won't be breaking any laws, and it'll

be fun!' Angus told her.

It was hard to be as enthused as he was. He hadn't been living with this story for several days now. Lila wasn't *his* friend, and although Lila was minimizing that threatening note, Bea couldn't help but be concerned for her, with hot-heads like Rob Chance and cranks like the Currys around. Then there was the question of whether Ethan's accident *had* been an accident. And the nagging worry, if she were honest with herself, that she was far too close to both of these incidents to feel entirely safe.

***

She talked it out with Frank on the phone that night.

"Mack and Gert have shown they didn't like to play by the rules, and Crow definitely liked to call people out on rule-breaking. Kind of like Andy."

"Do not equate your son with those people!" he said. She liked that.

"Well, let me talk this through with you, Frank. Rob Chance could be violent and had a history of being violent with Crow, and he also collected artifacts in ways Crow didn't approve of. Tom Franzen and Buzz have fewer motives."

"At this point," Frank said.

"Yes, at this point. And Alan actually seemed to like Crow."

"And then there's Liz."

"Who didn't much care for Crow, and who probably hated his self-righteousness about how she and Alan dealt with their archaeological site."

"Of course, Crow was so good at offending people that he could have brought someone down on him from some earlier epoch in his travels," Frank said.

"You're right about that. I should just leave all this to

Marcia. But Frank, I don't see how Ethan's accident could possibly have anything to do with archaeological looting in Copperton. But could there be anything to what Javier said? About Armando having something to do with Ethan's accident? Am I dealing with not just a jerk, but a felon on my board?"

"I know you can't stand that guy, but it does seem an extreme way to get a job that's not even that prestigious or well-paying. Not to mention certain."

"Yeah, I agree with you there. But if he's feeding all this garbage to Stephanie…"

"He already told you he's of the 'no publicity is bad publicity' school. Plus, maybe it makes him more interesting in her eyes, being so central to the Garden's existence, that is." This statement brought back the image of him holding up the rosemary to the camera. Bea sighed.

"Also, one of my board members—Margaret Rhodes— thinks Javier had something to do with Crow's murder just because Javier's family got kicked off their ranch here a hundred years ago."

"That sounds incredibly unlikely, and dare I say, possibly racist. I'd check that out with Marcia."

"I just wish it would all get cleared up and we could go back to being a public garden on our own merits."

"It'll happen."

They said goodnight but couldn't say they'd see each other soon. When would that happen?

Chapter Fifteen

Angus and Jean parked their old Subaru a couple of blocks from Mack's shop in downtown Tucson. "Too bad we don't have a BMW for this operation, Jeannie," Angus said.

"We have two blocks to find a confident stride. As if we can have whatever we want in this world, and furthermore, we're used to getting it," she said.

Angus reported all this to Bea later that evening. "Jeannie got into it. She painted her nails and put her hair up into a French twist, or something like that, and she had this dress and shoes she'd bought for a wedding. She was dynamite."

He and Jean had gotten to Mack's shop at 5:30, a half hour before closing time. They both took one look at Mack's beat-up old van—"Curry's Collectibles"—so faded that it could be read as "Cur... Collect....s," and both of them had trouble maintaining straight faces as Angus held the door for his trophy wife.

"It was dusty..."

"Their house was incredibly dusty," Bea said.

"And there was an old cider press, and some nineteenth-century farm tools were on display, like a hand-cranked ice-cream maker. It was hard to understand why we yachtie types would want to check the place out. But then we saw a shelf full of nice pots, over in the corner. 'Tell us about these,' I said. He got this sort of crafty look on his face, and he kind of checked me out a minute… first my face… I tried to show mild interest. Then my clothes. Then he said, 'This is some very fine Anasazi work.' There were some jars, and pitchers, and bowls with black geometric patterns on white. They ran from five-hundred to nine-hundred-ninety-five bucks or something. I told him they were nice, but I was looking for some really fine Mimbres work, depicting animals and plants and humans, like I'd seen at the Peabody Museum at Harvard."

"That was a nice touch."

"Jeannie googled that collection ahead of time. So, his eyes practically threw sparks at us seeing the money he was gonna get. He said he had a couple of pieces in mind that we might like. He asked for my card. I pretended to have lost it, but I gave him our home phone number on a piece of paper. Jean's gonna have to be careful answering the phone in the next couple of days. I told him we'd only be in Tucson for two nights, then back to our boat in San Carlos, that we were joining some friends and heading south. I asked if he would be able to call me before then, and could he ship to our home in California, and he said, 'Of course.' Then on the way out, I asked, as an afterthought, 'Of course you have all proper documentation of the legal status of this work?' He smiled. Kind of a creepy smile. Then he told us very formally that we would have everything we'd need."

"How do you mean, a 'creepy smile'?"

"Well, we could have been reading into it. But it wasn't sincere, and it wasn't matter-of-fact, either. It felt like, 'Of course we both know what you mean by asking me about *documentation*.' But maybe the cloak-and-dagger's getting to me. I admit that's entirely possible. In any case, I don't know where we go from here, because Jean and I sure can't be buying any multi-thousand-dollar bowls."

"You can always change your mind when he calls. But tell me if he does. Meanwhile, I'll tell all this to Marcia. She may want you to brief her in person."

"Glad to be of service, my lady."

"Oh, cut it out. I'll see you tomorrow."

Bea made it into work on time the next morning, left a message for Marcia about Angus and Jean's field trip, and managed to get some work done before accepting a call from Lila.

"Bea, I know you're busy. I just wanted to tell you that Ed and I had a great time with all three of you, so come back anytime. And bring Frank."

"He took a job in D.C."

"Oh. Well, in that case, you'd *better* visit us!"

"So. My friends impersonated wealthy collectors and went to Mack's shop." Bea recounted the story.

"How much do you want to bet that the pots he has aren't legal? And that that's why he was so pissed about your bringing cops to his house, and why he's pissed at me."

"And back to the problems here. Maybe Crow tried to expose him forty years ago and he killed Crow?"

"Maybe we should both take this more seriously."

"What a pleasant thought."

Angus found her with her head on her desk. "That bad, huh?"

"I feel like I'm in a footrace with my life and I can't keep up."

"I think you need some horticultural therapy." Bea started to shake her head, but he went on, "Bea, you know as well as I do that working in a garden reduces heart rate and blood pressure. The butterfly garden needs some more sprucing up. How about if I place the plants and you do the digging?"

"Well, maybe for half an hour or so."

"Ten-four, boss."

"Don't call me that!" She gave him a shove, but she put on the old sneakers in her closet and got out the gardening gloves that she kept under the bathroom sink.

"Angus," she said, looking up from digging a particularly rocky hole, "What do you know about comas?"

"They typically last no more than a few weeks, and then the person may take a while to get back up to speed. But they can take longer, and the person can be in something called a "permanent vegetative state.""

"Ethan wouldn't want that."

"If I had to bet on how long you're going to be in this job, I'd say two or three months. I'm counting on Ethan to pull through."

"That's pretty much where I am on the whole thing."

"Good. Feel better yet?"

"Yes."

Marcia and she finally made contact, after a day's worth of phone tag. As Bea expected, Marcia wanted to talk to Angus directly. She was a little curt about it.

Before Bea left work that night, Angus sauntered in with what she assumed was his new yachtie swagger.

"Looks like I have to practice this walk," he said.

"Why is that?"

"Well, I guess the Tucson Police Department and the Copperton cops weren't too happy about us doing this on our own, but since we've started, they want Jean and me to go back to look at whatever Mack especially wants us to see. I think that Lila's not the only one who suspects Mack's dabbling in the black market. So, Jean told me he called today and sure enough, he's got 'two very *lovely* pieces for you and your husband to view.'"

"Be careful, Angus."

"I will. I'm just going to ask him if I can take a look, then think about it. I doubt he wants me to take pictures. I'm going to ask him for provenance, you know, the records on where the pots came from." He suddenly grinned. "So, Jean and I have an appointment at three tomorrow afternoon. Do I have permission, boss?"

"I hardly think I have a choice."

"We can't wear the same disguises, but I guess we can rustle up some acceptable clothes." Angus seemed loathe to admit that he had anything that might be deemed "acceptable" in this circumstance.

On the way home that night, Bea *knew* she was getting paranoid. A tan Camry kept making the same turns she did, almost all the way home. It stayed a couple of cars back, so she couldn't see the driver, who seemed too tall for most women, but that's about all she could tell. She lost the car on Speedway Boulevard, but thought she saw it again right before she turned into Palo Verde Acres.

She sent Angus an email. "Do you happen to know what kind of car Armando drives?"

"A new bright red Toyota Tundra pickup. Why?"

"I'll tell you tomorrow. Did you happen to see what Mack Curry drives?"

"Well, he has that beat-up van. Remember, 'Cur Collects?' Why? You're worrying me, boss."

"Let's just talk tomorrow."

Chapter Sixteen

Since it was Saturday, there would be no Stephanie Shores broadcast. She was probably merrily trysting with Armando, Bea figured. Meanwhile, the kids wanted to watch cartoons. They weren't on all the non-cable stations as they'd been when Bea was little. She'd read that part of the reason networks had cancelled cartoons was because of divorced parents; the noncustodial one wanted to have 'quality time.' This was not happening in her family; the noncustodial parent rarely saw the kids on a Saturday. Well, she supposed Andy and Jessie could watch cartoons on the TV in the Shandley library, if Angus looked in on them during her tour with the donor.

They all headed to Shandley Gardens, which was fine with the kids, because they'd get to see Angus. He'd be at work before his next expedition to Mack Curry's shop. Angus had never had children, but he was superb with them; he was a surrogate grandfather for Andy and Jessie. Bea's own father was in California. He was a formal man uncomfortable with spontaneity, which made grandparenting mildly alien for him. Her ex-husband's father was long dead, probably from a surfeit of women and wine. So, Angus filled an essential role with Jessie and Andy.

Bea installed her children in the library with something on PBS about a cow that talked. She knew nothing about the woman who'd asked to meet with her about children's programs, other than the nugget that she was "collecting information for her family foundation." And that she was "vitally interested."

The potential donor's name was Lesley Land, and she was a kick. She arrived for their meeting in "pure hemp, we must promote it!" Bea thought she'd be a good backup singer in Ed and Rainbow's band in Copperton: her long gray hair splayed wildly over her shoulders, and she carried a purse decorated with orange and purple paisley and elephants. Unlike the older Copperton women Bea had seen, though, Lesley had clearly had quite a bit of work done on her fine-featured face, which was a good twenty years younger-looking than the rest of her body. "Let me see where you want to put this garden!" was her greeting.

Out on the grounds, on the way over to the open area designated for the future project, Lesley declared, "Let them plant plants, eat plants, draw plants, dance plants. Above all, let them smell plants! After all, if once you smell creosote bush, you'll never stop!"

When Bea gave her an amused smile, she said, "Pardon me, dear, I tend towards the dramatic." But then she went on without drawing a breath, "So tell me, have you chosen a landscape architect for this project?"

"Well, no, although we have some on a wish list."

"Would Marcos Chung be one of them?"

"Yes, indeed. I love the children's garden he designed in L.A., and so does the rest of our staff. We've all seen it. I'm sure the board would agree if they visited it."

"Oh, lovely! Let's schedule a Shandley field trip! Alan would so approve. Although I do have to convince my brother. You see there are only three of us on the foundation board. The Jemuel Land Foundation, you know. Two votes does it!"

Bea thought she'd simply nod and see what came next; this was a wise move, as Lesley continued, "You may be wondering why I told you of my 'vital interest' in this project."

"Well, I'd love to hear about it."

"My sister wants to donate to a big city opera house that shall remain nameless. But they have all kinds of restrictions on the gift. I thought we could make a much bigger difference in a younger, smaller organization like Shandley. And I've *almost* got my brother persuaded. If you'll all agree to the landscape architect we discussed, I'm pretty sure he'll be copasetic! My brother and I have a friend in Phoenix with a *private* Chung garden, and it's nearly as fanciful as the one in L.A.!"

Bea wasn't sure whether this whole conversation was the product of her imagination, or perhaps more likely, Lesley's imagination. But she had no time to contemplate this, because Lesley talked on. "And I will tell you, because you're a good listener, that there's a more personal reason that I'd like to make our foundation's mark at Shandley Gardens."

"Oh?"

"Like more than one woman, I loved Alan Shandley. This is partly for him. We almost built something together, but it was not to be. Certainly, he deserved better than the woman he married."

She didn't clarify what "love" meant. And Bea didn't know if "built something" meant more than bricks. It seemed best not to comment. Nothing about Alan, after last summer's events, could surprise her. So, she pretended not to notice the verbs and went on to describe her wish to include climate change as a theme of the garden.

"Of course, we have to include climate change! What's more important than that! My dear girl, I'm virtually certain we can cough up the money for Marcos to come up with some initial plans. Then all we'll have to do is sell everybody at Shandley on them, as well as my brother and sister!" Lesley gave Bea a huge enfolding hug, squeezing her melons against Bea's small breasts. "Well, I must be off! You'll be hearing from me!" She headed for the front door, swishing her long skirt. If it had been a little shorter, it would have worked as traditional square-dancing attire in Copperton.

Is that woman for real? Did she really have family money? Bea thought it was past time to do a little research on the Jemuel Land Foundation. Did Lesley just have some crush on Marcos Chung, as she seemed to have had on Alan Shandley?

Lo and behold, according to Google, Lesley Land and her siblings were the heirs to a major sausage company. Their family foundation donated to arts organizations, which botanical gardens were sometimes considered to be. Bea tried googling Lesley herself and discovered that she had had a brief acting career—somehow, this was no surprise—and that she was a noted "patron of the arts" with homes in Chicago and Phoenix. Also, she had "real estate interests" in southern Arizona and New Mexico.

Bea was all ready to leave work early, take the kids to the mall, and buy some clothes to ready herself for further executive pursuits, when she noticed that Marcia had called. Bea left the kids with a talking purple platypus on the screen and returned the call.

"Before we discuss anything else, Marcia, I have a board member who suspects Javier. He's not by any chance on your list, is he?"

"She called and discussed her suspicions with me. I was able to tell her that Javier was in Mexico getting a degree in horticulture in the late Sixties. We did some checking and he is *not* on our list, for several reasons. But let me get back to what we *are* investigating. We have a tip about the car that ran into Ethan on that backcountry road. It may not have been an accident. I'm hoping to know more soon. Meanwhile, Bea, I want to tell you, it's just possible that the driver of the car has a lot of hostility for Shandley Gardens rather than Ethan personally. Be careful."

"Oh, great. A benefit of being acting director. Is there any chance Armando Ramos has anything to do with this?"

"Why do you say that?"

"Well, he wants Ethan's job. I hesitated saying anything about this, but there it is, since you say Ethan's 'accident' might not be accidental." She didn't say anything about the tan Camry, because, well... she was obviously getting paranoid.

"Very interesting. We'll keep that in mind. We'll be in touch. Angus and Jean will be having their second visit to the shop this afternoon, by the way. Next time, check with me before you get something like this started, Bea."

Bea didn't answer right away.

"Okay, Bea?"

"Yeah. Sorry."

The rest of the afternoon went better than that phone call. The kids got yogurt and a Grow-Your-Own volcano. Bea bought a new brown suit that was appropriately serious, but with a swingy skirt that gave it a bit of flair. And Bea had a real day off to look forward to. Ex-husband Pat was scheduled to take the kids from about ten to four on Sunday, *if* he didn't cancel, pleading some urgent business engagement. She'd have time to entertain herself. After she'd cleaned the house, of course.

Angus called her that night. He was completely wired. He said Marcia had given him permission to tell her the story.

"You're not going to believe this, Bea. Mack has a *secret room.* He says it's quote, only for serious buyers, unquote, because he wouldn't want to get broken into. I mean, can you believe it, it's actually behind a bookcase full of antique junk. He presses a button and it moves open."

"And?"

"And there was a little room with a few more Anasazi-looking pieces and two Mimbres bowls. One of them had some men tending corn plants. It was beautiful. I wish I did have the money to buy it. If it's really legal, but more about that later. Mack was pointing out how fine the lines were, how delicate the artistry. The other pot was also cool, and it was huge, maybe almost two feet in diameter. It had all these bats, with like, rabbit-ears and turkey-tails. Super cool. Mack wanted ten grand for it. But I pretended to be interested in the other one, which went for a mere five grand. I asked for its provenance, and here's where it gets really interesting. Mack showed me papers that said that they were recently acquired from the private collection of a Thomas Franzen of Copperton, New Mexico. He dug them on his property in 1967, so the papers say. Thomas Franzen... that's one of your buddies back there, right?"

"He's hardly a buddy."

"But a doughnut shop guy? Which one?"

"Tom Franzen is the real estate guy. Chance is the angry former Ford dealer. Buzz is the radio voice. Tom's major property just got taken over by the bank."

"Wow. So, Marcia asked me to ask about any pots with fish on them. Not sure why, but since my new persona is a guy who boats around in Mexico, I guess it sort of fits. Anyway, Mack really screwed up his eyes and said he had access to another pot from a private collection, with astounding marine fishes on it, including some being spear-fished. I pretended to be all gung-ho about spear-fishing, which is the last thing I'd do, but anyway... we have another appointment to see it in a week. I said that would work for me, we'd decided not to sail back home to California but to mess around the Sea of Cortez some more. I said we'd be back in town in a week for a friend's sixtieth birthday party, and we'd make a decision about the corn gardening pot then, after we saw the fish pot. And back we went through the secret door. Jean was full of thanks and compliments on the quality of 'his' pieces, which softened Mack up a bit. I kind of doubt he's going to call me again, though. I gave him a false name—Yates Whitaker. Jeannie went googling around to find a nice preppy name. It seems like Mac's probably gonna check me out more thoroughly before I come back. Well, especially if he does have something illegal to hide. He said something about the fish pot being a 'very special piece, worth at least fifty thousand.' I managed not to blink, but still..."

Bea's brain was clicking. "So, the documents Mack showed you said that the pots had been found on Tom Franzen's private property in the 1967, before current laws about digging in grave sites on private property were in effect. So, unless these documents are proved to be false—in other words, that the artifacts came from federal or tribal property and not their own land—then Tom and the Currys are in the clear on this. And he may really need to hide his valuable stuff behind a secret door."

"On the other hand..."

"On the other hand, if those pots can be shown to be from public land in that period... if they came from an illegal pot-hunting expedition, then Tom at the very least is in violation of the law, and if Mack knew about it, so is he." She stopped for a moment.

"Bea, you still there?"

"Well, then there's a shred of a connection with the Crow Johnson case. Maybe Crow caught them digging on government land. The time period is right," Bea continued.

"So, we did okay, huh, boss?"

"Would you please stop that! What did Marcia say?"

"She said we did good."

"Let's have a relaxing Sunday, both of us."

Chapter Seventeen

Pat was only half an hour late to pick the kids up on Sunday. Jessie flew into his arms. Andy gave Bea a particularly hard hug goodbye. "I hope everything goes well, Mom," he said. Pat gave her a disapproving look.

And then Bea was alone. If she spent the morning cleaning house, she could reward herself with a hike on the far side of town, the Tucson Mountains side, far from Shandley. It was too late to ask anybody to go with her, and besides, once she got used to the lack of children, volunteers, board members, donors, and other sundry humans in her life, she enjoyed being by herself. She'd probably relax into it about the time the kids returned, assuming Pat didn't call and say something had come up, and he'd have to bring them back early.

It was a perfect winter day in the Tucson Mountains, the kind that brought tourists to town and made them stay and buy a condo. The temperature wouldn't climb above the upper sixties. There were a few cumulus clouds about, just enough to soften the skyline, but not enough to dim the sun. As Bea walked a familiar path to the top of a ridge, she caught sight of a roadrunner chasing a lizard. Tiny verdins seemed abundant this afternoon, their bright yellow heads flashing among the mesquite branches. They were so common, but apparently unrelated to most other birds in the western hemisphere. Bea was particularly partial to phainopeplas, crested birds that looked like black cardinals. They were munching on the mistletoe hanging in the mesquites, then they'd spread the seeds to another branch, after the berries had made it all the way through their digestive tracts. Bea thought for a minute that she'd have liked to bring some mistletoe to put in the doorway for Frank to see, but she quickly abandoned that thought. By the time he got to her place, the mistletoe would have disintegrated. He didn't have any Tucson visits planned.

She picked some mistletoe for Andy and Jessie instead. Scat and prints on the trail unmasked the recent path of a bobcat. The saguaros grew denser on the hillside, as she climbed to the ridge. On the top, she watched two red-tailed hawks riding the thermals. All was right with the world.

Back at her car, Bea felt ready for the week ahead. She could deal with Armando and the looky-loos and Stephanie Shores, and maybe even news that Liz and Alan had murdered a poor, lost, slightly unhinged gardener.

There was only one other car in the small lot by the trailhead, way over on the far end. It was surprising that more Tucsonans hadn't chosen this Sunday walk. As Bea pulled her old blue Toyota Corolla out of the lot, the other car started up as well. Bea's new-found relaxation seeped out of her muscles. Her hands tightened on the steering wheel. The car was a late-model tan Toyota Camry, like a million other cars in Tucson, but it was again making the same turns she made, and again it was back just far enough so that she couldn't really see the driver or the license plate. She sped through a yellow light and the car had to stop. She made a few turns that were unnecessary, not seeing the car, and decided she was way too anxious. If she saw the damned Camry again, she would memorize the license plate. As she turned into Palo Verde Acres, she saw a tan Camry down the block. It didn't turn in after her, and she reassured herself again.

She did send Marcia a short email about the incident, and the earlier Camry one, but then Bea was busy from four until nine, when she finally got the kids to bed. Jessie was wired on "way too much sugar," according to her older brother. Otherwise, Andy was uncharacteristically reticent with his mother.

"Anything you want to talk about?" she asked him, after tucking Jessie into bed for the third time.

He looked guilty. "No, Mom. I just don't really like going back and forth that much. Between you and Dad. But I know we have to. Don't worry about it." Once again, he was trying to reassure *her*.

"What would work better for you?"

"Oh, nothing. I don't like Dad's girlfriend that much, that's all. But she's okay, I mean, she's not mean or anything," he added hastily, seeing her alarmed expression. "I guess I'm just not used to her." He paused a moment. "And Frank's not coming back, is he?"

"He took a job in Washington. We won't see him that much. It's so far away."

"Yeah, I know. It's okay, Mom."

She wished she could make it so.

She put on a flannel nightgown although this February Tucson night wasn't all that cold. But her high-collared nightgown felt like childhood innocence, like a time when she didn't even have a boyfriend, much less worry about losing one. A time when the only car she thought about was her parents' banged-up station wagon, readied for a camping trip. A time when she had to be responsible for only one person, herself.

She went in to watch the children sleep. Jessie had gotten out of her bed and climbed into Andy's. She was lying on his arm, which he'd curled around her. Andy certainly worried about people other than himself, even at seven. There was something he wasn't saying, something he was trying to hide from her, and she was going to have to find out what it was.

She dreamed of a tan Camry crashing through her bedroom wall.

***

Mondays tended to be low-key at Shandley. Since the gardens were closed to visitors, the volunteers could get a lot done. So could the staff, if they were scheduled to come in.

The first thing Bea wanted to cross off her list was the call to Armando about breaches in procedure. She told herself to be diplomatic, no matter what he threw at her. He was, after all, one of her bosses.

"Armando, I saw you got us some publicity with Stephanie Shores. It's great that she was taping your class. Thanks. I just wanted to make sure that you know our policies and procedures. For the future, all tours need to be cleared through the education department, which is Joan Madsden right now, and all media needs to be cleared by the executive director." He didn't say anything, and she added, "Which is me right now."

"I'm all too aware of that fact."

"Armando, I hope we can work well together for the good of the Gardens. I just wanted to go over these rules in case you weren't familiar with them. We need to make sure that everything is on the master calendar."

"Do not forget, young lady, that board members have the ability to hire and fire the executive director."

"Yes, I certainly know that. And I hope and pray that Ethan will be able to get his job back very soon."

"That's rather disingenuous of you."

"I hope you're not implying that I want Ethan to stay incapacitated. Because that is not true."

"You did a fine job of outmaneuvering me at the last board meeting. But we'll see about that, young lady. We'll see. Goodbye." And he hung up.

What was with this 'young lady' b.s.? Armando was about her own age. She didn't mind the "my dears" from Lesley Land or Margaret Rhodes—they were older, and of a generation that spoke that way from courtesy. Courtesy was not in Armando's DNA. So, did he drive a tan Camry? She'd seen his macho red pickup truck. He couldn't be crazy enough to run into Ethan and try to do the same thing to her, could he? She'd better send Marcia an email describing her conversation with Armando.

As Bea was finishing the email, there was a knock on her door. Joan Madsden didn't wait for a "Come in!" before she pushed the door all the way open. She always had a determined presence, with her stocky build and severe grey bangs, but today her jaw jutted out farther than usual, and she sat down hard in the chair facing Bea's desk.

"It looks like there's nobody in here, and you're not on the phone. All's well with our instructors for the upcoming classes. Lisa Peace wants more A.V. equipment than we have, but I'll deal with it. The volunteers are in a state of *total gossip* about Ethan's accident and Crow Johnson's bones, but no harm done. What I want to ask you is: did you see that lovely bleached blonde Stephanie Shores, on the morning news?"

"No, I didn't turn it on. Bad habit in front of the kids. I don't want to show addictive behavior."

"I congratulate you. But you missed something crucial."

"Okay, tell me." Bea sat up straighter, her smile firmly and falsely affixed.

"Stephanie seems to feel that there is a connection between Ethan's accident, Crow's death forty years ago, and *you*."

Bea dropped the pencil she was holding and ran her fingers through her hair, realizing as she did it that she probably looked like her son. She lifted her head and said, in an even tone, she hoped, "Go on."

"Somehow, she got a 'scoop' that Liz and Alan owned property in Copperton, that their gardener, who was probably murdered, was from there, and that you took two recent trips to Copperton. And that you have 'benefited,' if you want to call it that, from Ethan's hospitalization. She says that 'all of the connections aren't yet clear,' but she seems to be implying that you're too big for your britches and may have been involved in a hit-and-run on your boss. And that 'there may be connections to the skeleton discovered on the Shandley Gardens' property.' She doesn't imply that you killed Crow forty years ago because you probably weren't born yet, or if you were, you were a wee thing, am I right?"

"Right. I'm thirty-eight. I hope somebody other than me can refute this nonsense." Her head jerked to her email to see if there was anything from Marcia about this. Just at that moment, Alicia called. Joan beat a hasty retreat as Bea picked up the phone to talk to the board president.

"Bea, I'm sure you're aware of Stephanie Shores' broadcast this morning."

"Joan Madsden just told me about it."

"I am sending out a press release saying that the board has full confidence in you as acting executive director of Shandley Gardens, and full confidence that you had nothing to do with Ethan's unfortunate accident. I don't know where she came up with this slander."

"I'm not sure either." Bea wasn't confident enough

of her relationship with the board president to mention her own suspicions about another board member. "But I appreciate the board's support."

"I'm just sending them all a copy. I don't need to contact them first with something this absurd."

"Thanks so much."

"I'm also sending a copy to all our staff and volunteers. I'm asking everyone at Shandley *not* to talk to the media about any of these issues. Normally, you would be the one to be our spokesperson, but given this ridiculous situation, I will be the *only* spokesperson on these issues. That is, Crow Johnson's bones and Ethan's accident."

"That's great with me. Thanks, Alicia." *What would this be like with a flaky board president?* Bea could think of several people on the board last summer, and at least one right now, whom she wouldn't trust in a public relations emergency. Alicia had pulled through both times.

After Bea hung up with Alicia, she checked her email. Marcia had written that she'd had several annoying media calls about Stephanie's report. Marcia had told them that Bea was definitely not a suspect in any case involving the Tucson Police Department, including the Crow Johnson murder and the Ethan Preston hit-and-run.

So maybe Bea could relax on this one. She was *not* going to watch Stephanie Shores tomorrow morning with the kids; she'd just have to find a story online. She took a deep breath. Then another. Could Armando really be crazy enough to leave that note on her windshield and to accuse her of all this stuff to Stephanie?

She tried to concentrate on a thank you card to Lesley Land, her possible angel-donor. She wanted to get a nice handwritten thank you in the mail before any foundation decisions were made. But she checked her email every couple of minutes, looking for an announcement from

Alicia that declared her innocence. How ridiculous to struggle with writing a simple thank you note—this was always something she enjoyed doing.

Then an email from Alicia entitled "PRESS RELEASE" popped up on Bea's computer, and she breathed a sigh of relief. Alicia had written exactly what she'd promised, calling Stephanie Shores' reporting "absurdly false and slanderous." A few minutes later, the only people who'd hit "reply all" were volunteers who were furious that Bea would be discussed in this way. She suspected most people would just hold their fire in public, but she knew Angus and Javier would be especially livid.

Just as she was thinking that, Javier came by with a bouquet of yellow brittlebush, one of the only flowers that had bloomed in February.

"Nobody in their right mind thinks you had anything to do with Ethan's accident," he said. "You got a lot more than you bargained for when you took on his job. Let me know how I can help."

"You're helping right now."

"Speaking of Ethan, I visited him again last night. He opened his eyes, but he's still not responsive. But the nurse was hopeful."

"Thank God! This is excellent news. Maybe it's time for me to visit, then."

"Soon, anyway. I just have a feeling he's turning the corner."

On her way home, racing to beat the kids who'd be dropped off by the after-school bus, Bea realized that she'd been a lot less stressed out when she'd been in charge of only education and volunteers. That had been just a few days ago. Her low-profile former job seemed particularly attractive when she thought she caught sight of a tan late-model Camry a few cars behind her. She was distracted enough to nearly hit a cyclist—*that's exactly what I need to do right now*—and by the time she'd swerved and gestured her apologies, the Camry was gone.

At dinner that night, Andy informed her that "some kids" had told him his mom might have tried to run over her boss, and he'd almost gotten into a fight about it, but his teacher had told the whole class that they needed to stop talking about this right away. "She told us the police said it was a dumb story, so that shut them up, Mom."

"Good job, kiddo," she said with a hug. But she was thinking how horrible it was that these controversies at Shandley leaked into her kids' lives. She hated to admit it, but her ex-husband Pat was right about that complaint.

On the other hand, Marcia was making a liar out of Stephanie Shores. Maybe Bea wouldn't have to deal with the consequences of Shores' grandstanding, at least after a few days. Maybe all she had to worry about was who was following her. If someone actually was. And if the person following her were one of her bosses, and if Armando were the one feeding Stephanie all this garbage.

Or if Mack or Gert Curry were at the wheel of a tan Camry.

Or if he were one of the doughnut boys. Maybe she should call Lila and ask her if they were all in Copperton right now.

Ed answered Lila's cell phone.

"How'd you hear?" he asked.

"Hear what?"

"Oh. Bea, Lila's been badly hurt."

"*What?*"

"She was out hiking. She was over in that country up north of here where there're lots of meadows, and where lots of people hunt elk. But we're past the season now. There were two shots. The first missed her, the second hit her leg. The cops are treating it like an assault, maybe even attempted murder.

"Any suspects?"

"Not that I've heard."

"Ed, this is a weird question, I know, but do you know if all the doughnut guys are in town right now?"

"Because you think they might've shot at her?"

"They might have done that, or if they were in Tucson, they might have been tailing me in a tan Camry."

"Well, I can tell you right now that none of those old boys drive Camrys. No Japanese sedans for them. I'm thinkin' the shooter here's some psycho guy who doesn't like Lila's op-eds. Or maybe some poacher who didn't want a witness to what they were trying to do. Course it could also be somebody who didn't like her helping the cops with that old Crow Johnson case. In which case you should watch it. Didn't your boss just get run off the road or something?"

"Yes."

"Honey, I'd be careful if I were you."

She was getting a little tired of people saying this to her.

Chapter Eighteen

The next morning, Angus blasted through her office door. He slammed his gloves down on her desk, and declared, with enthusiasm, "To think I complained about plant sales and home tours distracting us from gardening!"

"Now what?"

"You really don't know? Shandley's out of the news, thank God. And maybe Jeannie and my little acting job did some good. The Feds came and busted Mack Curry's store! They thought that fish pot he offered me sounded like something that's been missing from the Copperton Museum for forty years! Something somebody slipped out of there when there was basically no security. I guess that fifty-thousand-dollar price tag tipped them off.

"Why the Feds?"

"I'm guessing his provenance records may be a little fishy on some of that other stuff. Maybe your buddies from Copperton are in more trouble than we thought. Anyhow, this is part of a multi-city, multi-state bust. It was mostly Anasazi stuff... you know, the people who lived in the Four Corners Area, in Mesa Verde and Chaco Canyon and such. There were busts in Santa Fe and Albuquerque at the same time. But that's not all!"

"The suspense is killing me."

"Well, Jeannie and I weren't the only people playacting. Somebody gave the cops enough information to arrest a guy who supposedly forged lots of documents saying that stuff came from places it didn't come from, like from private property when it wasn't even close to being private. It was really from national forests or national parks or B.L.M. land or whatever, which you know is illegal."

"Right."

"So, the forger guy admitted his funny business to the informant guy, I guess because he thought they were buddy-buddy."

"Let me guess. The forger is Mack Curry."

"Nope. Guess again."

"It'd be a good job for his wife Gert."

"Keep guessing."

"Rob Chance?"

"Bingo! That guy's in federal custody right now. You met him in Copperton, right? Isn't he the one who blew up at you and Marcia? Handlebar mustache-guy?"

"He blew up at more people than me and Marcia. If somebody has to be arrested, I have to admit I'm not sorry it's Rob Chance. So did Mack know about these forgeries?"

"I'm sure they're talking to him about everything. I'd have liked to see where he said that fish pot came from. But I have to admit I was getting a little nervous about a third visit there. Glad the Feds did it instead."

"You know what I think, Angus? It would be great if somebody could find some evidence that Rob was the one who killed Crow. It seems like he's been on the wrong side of the law for a long time. I wonder if he stole that pot out of the museum?"

"I guess it's pretty tough figuring out who murdered somebody forty years ago."

"Well, the pot was stolen from the museum forty years ago, and they figured that out."

"Boss, I'd better get back to work!"

"Me, too. Would you quit calling me boss?"

"Nope," he said with a parting grin.

Bea did have trouble concentrating on the proposal she was writing to fund permeable pavement and retention basins in the parking lot, to better use rainwater when it came flooding through in the summer monsoons. What Stephanie Shores had been calling "The Events at Shandley" were considerably more absorbing.

Her mind wandered to the people she'd met in Copperton. It sure looked like Gert, Mack, Rob, and Tom could all have been involved in illegal activities, even up to the present time. Maybe even Buzz, although he kept emerging as the good guy who bailed Rob out of jail, or hauled him out of fights. Bea just didn't think Alan Shandley was a killer type, from everything she knew of him. Javier sure didn't think so. But she was a lot less certain about Liz. She could be a snob, for sure, and it seemed, according to Myron's and Eddie's and even Alicia's stories about her, that she had a temper. Plus, she hadn't liked Crow.

Bea thought, for the hundredth time, that unless there was some compelling piece of evidence, they might never figure out who was Crow's killer. Maybe all that mystery *could* increase their visitation long term. She'd prefer that people visited Shandley to learn about the beauty of desert plants, and how to save water, but maybe they would come to find out about the mystery and stay for the botany. Maybe that's what they were doing right now. Maybe Armando was right, perish the thought, about any media attention being good marketing. But Bea sure wished *her* reputation wasn't stirred into this witches' brew of a story.

As this worry, and all the others she'd been trying to corral into the far corners of her mind, began to overrun any thoughts about the work she was supposed to do, Bea decided to check out what people were saying on the grounds. Directors, even if they were only acting ones, were supposed to get the feel of the visitor experience, she told herself. The truth was that she mostly wanted to hear if they were saying awful things about her, based on Stephanie Shores' so-called scoops.

It was a lovely, clear February day. Bea put on her widest brimmed hat and largest sunglasses, which was as close to a disguise as she could muster. She wandered through the herb garden to the so-called Middle Eastern Garden, which consisted of an orchard of pomegranate, fig and quince trees and grape vines, all planted years ago by Alan Shandley. She now realized it had probably been planted by Crow, too, since these were his favorite kinds of plants. A large white woman dressed in sun visor, sunglasses, and plenty of Spandex was saying, "Let's go find out where the body was dug up!"

"Now I'm not sorry you dragged me out to this garden," her husband responded. He, too, was visor-clad and his high white socks reached nearly to his knees, almost touching his nylon shorts. His tee shirt proclaimed "I'm a Hoosier and Proud of It."

Javier had put up a plain wire fence, strung between metal posts—not barbed wire, which would be too un-public gardenlike—to cut off several acres of the back forty. Bea knew that visitors had been finding this spot ever since Crow's bones had made the news, which was now more than two weeks ago. She followed the visor people to see how they'd find the place. They asked some others, probably also tourists, given their February-white skins that were rapidly turning pink, if they knew "where the body was found."

"We're just following other people. We hear the garden doesn't want people over there."

Bea shadowed three couples to reach the path near

the fence. Angus had put a STAY ON GARDEN PATHS sign in a crucial spot, but the desert was heavily trampled from the path right up to the fence, where he'd placed some NO ENTRY signs. Bea stifled a laugh. She knew it was Angus who'd put the signs up; he'd sketched some heavily camera-clad tourists on them. They were over the top. Each tourist had at least three cameras, except for the woman checking something out with binoculars.

But there were footprints on the other side of the wire. She was glad the police were done with this site, but the desert would take quite a while to recover. She had to restrain herself from telling the four couples to stay on the path as they all headed for the fence. She was in disguise, after all, and trying to observe what visitors were thinking and doing.

"This is pretty high drama," said the visor man. "Does anybody know if there's a suspect?"

"I hear it could be the guy that founded this place," said a man holding a camera with a telephoto lens. He proceeded to snap a picture of the fenced-in area. Bea took another look at Angus's sketch and had a hard time suppressing her laugh. The resemblance was astonishing.

"Well, he was a heck of a gardener!" said a woman dressed all in pink, including pink sneakers.

"Yeah, he was. This place is pretty impressive. Honey, maybe we *could* take out our grass," said a woman whose tan indicated she might be a local.

Bea walked off. Silver linings, she thought.

The Garden's contract bookkeeper called her as soon as she got back to her desk. Pay checks would be coming out on Friday. "Ethan's vacation leave is almost gone, and he doesn't have much sick leave, either, because of that really bad flu he had. I just wanted you to know that if he's incapacitated for a long time, he'll have no pay."

"That's a horrible way to deal with a guy in a coma. I hear he may be coming out of it, but he'll still be in bad shape for a while. Let me talk to the board and get back with you."

Bea looked up the possibility of Ethan's getting Social Security disability benefits. He'd need to be in a coma for a month, and if he got better, but was significantly disabled, it could be complicated to apply for the benefits. She called Alicia. "I'd like to recommend that we give Ethan "emergency paid sick leave" for some defined period. Say, up to three months. The board can amend our personnel policies. We could say that emergency sick leave could be granted by the board on a case-by-case basis."

"You will need to show how this impacts our financials before I can try to sell this to the rest of the board. Let me know. And Bea, I appreciate your thinking on this."

As she worked over the numbers, she waved to Angus, who was staking some plants outside her window. Joan walked by with a herd of eager snowbirds. She thought about the pleasures of answering their ardent questions versus her current budgeting task. "Please recover soon, Ethan," she said aloud.

Bea got the numbers to work. The budget year would be over in a few months, and she had a pretty good idea about how things would turn out. She called Alicia.

"I'll be by in the morning, before work, if you can send something out for the board to look at tonight," Bea said. "We can vote electronically on this."

"What time will you be by?"

"Seven-thirty. Does that work?"

"Well..." She was going to have to level with Alicia. "I have to get the kids to the bus at seven-forty. I can't really get in before eight. I'm sorry. Can we work that out?"

"You're a single parent, aren't you, Bea?"

"Yes." She'd certainly never discussed this with Alicia.

"Okay," she said, and there was no indication in her tone whether or not it really was okay. "See you at eight in your office."

Bea thought once more that she could have had a very different board president, in which case she would be thinking about resigning if she had to do this job much longer. She sent her spreadsheet and reasoning about Ethan's sick pay to the whole board, all four of them. She realized they'd turned down hiring Armando for budgetary reasons. And maybe some other reasons. Would they agree to be compassionate now? It would look pretty bad for Armando if he didn't want to grant his jogging buddy emergency sick pay. If he'd actually had something to do with Ethan's accident, though, he'd do well to look compassionate.

Chapter Nineteen

Andy's second-grade accusers seemed to have quieted down; he didn't bring up any more of their taunts about his mom. So, Bea headed into work in a reasonably good mood. Angus was the first at her door, per usual. He leaned his shovel against the wall and asked, "Did you catch our dear friend Stephanie Shores this morning?"

"No, Angus, I'm counting on you to update me. She's not good for my children's health."

"Well, you didn't miss much. But Jean and I feel it's our civic duty to watch what she says these days. Stephanie had a quote from 'a source close to Shandley Gardens' that you 'allegedly' have always wanted the executive director job."

"I never even thought of it, and now that I have it, however temporary, I'm convinced it's no prize!" Bea exploded.

"Take it easy, my friend. Mr. Source has to be Armando. You already know you have more cred here than he does."

"Yeah, but this is my reputation with the public!"

"I can't help you there. Old Stephanie's really going with the fact that there is a "Copperton-Tucson connection" that may involve Shandley Gardens' founders, a dead gardener, an executive director who was the victim of a hit-and-run, an acting director with ties to all of the above, and an illegal antiquities bust that involves people from both Tucson and Copperton. That last thing's her newest 'scoop.' Hey, maybe Stephanie Shores will figure it all out for you!"

"It sounds like she has, and I'm the cause of it all."

"Bea, take it easy. Well, one thing's pretty clear. Our poor skeleton in the back yard seems to have been surrounded by unscrupulous characters. It was tough luck that he was inspired by God's righteousness, trying to bring them all to justice."

This was an interesting comment, given that Angus was an avowed atheist.

"He might have been crazy, but his feelings about how Native American burials should be treated was ahead of his time. I doubt that any of us would want our ancestors unearthed for profit."

"Point taken. Well, to work!" he said, picking up his shovel.

"Hello, Angus," said Alicia, replacing him in Bea's office. She'd barely missed being brained with the shovel, which was not an event that Shandley Gardens needed to repeat. "We certainly have a cast of characters here."

"Yes," Bea said, raising her hands in a "What can I do about that?" gesture, which she immediately felt guilty about. "So is the board okay with giving Ethan extended sick pay?"

"We have a tie. We do need to get an odd number on this board soon. John is with me—he had an employee out for some time with cancer treatments, and he covered the guy. But the only employees Margaret Rhodes has ever supervised are gardeners and cleaners employed by other companies. She wants to take a tough line so we don't establish precedent. I think you can talk to her and sway her, like you did about the Events Center." Alicia smiled, but then her expression turned serious. "I wouldn't bother with Armando."

"Why, what did he say?"

"I'd rather not tell you. Let me just say, Bea, that he has taken your appointment as e.d. rather to heart."

"Why does he even care about this job? It's not like it's a prestigious academic position!"

"Well, I suppose you should know this. It seems that he'll find out very soon if he's gotten tenure. He says he's been "fighting hard" for it. He implies that he's been treated very unfairly. If he doesn't get tenure, the way I understand it, he doesn't get fired immediately, but he needs to find another job."

I'm not surprised he's having trouble with tenure, if he treats his colleagues the way he treats people around here. Bea restrained herself from saying this aloud.

"So, he might be a bit desperate. At any rate, he feels that we can't afford to pay Ethan, you and Joan, no matter what the numbers say, because we couldn't afford to pay him. I didn't let on that pay was not *my* primary reason for my desire to appoint you. The only way Armando will agree to three months' sick pay for Ethan is if you go back to your old job, and Joan is let go."

"And we'd pay him to be executive director?" asked Bea incredulously.

"No, he'd do it for free, for three months. He says he can do it in concert with this semester's teaching responsibilities."

"He'd be a hero." *And he'll expect to be appointed director at the end of those three months, if Ethan hasn't fully recovered by then. Even if he hasn't. Horrible thought.*

"So," Alicia said, rising from her seat across from Bea, "concentrate on convincing Margaret. Your numbers look good."

As Bea turned to her computer, she found that Angus's

wife Jean, ever the sleuth, had sent her an article from the Copperton paper.

Federal Agents Arrest Local Businessmen

Missing Pot Returned to Copperton Museum After Forty Years' Absence

Copperton Museum Director Juana Jones is delighted to have recovered a Mimbres pot missing from the museum since 1969. The pot was discovered in the back room of a Tucson store owned by Copperton resident Mackenzie Curry, with a fifty-thousand-dollar price tag attached. Documents held by Mr. Curry state that the pot was found on the property of Grant County rancher Rufus Jones (no relation to the museum director) in 1937, and sold to Copperton resident Thomas Franzen ten years ago. Museum Director Jones says that the artifact, which features several Sea of Cortez marine fishes, was professionally excavated around 1937 by the University of New Mexico on Salvaje National Forest land.

Thomas Franzen, former President of the Copperton Chamber of Commerce and current owner of the financially troubled Copperton Inn and Spa, has been accused by the FBI of selling Mimbres pots with forged provenance, or origin papers, to Mackenzie Curry. The alleged forger is another Copperton resident, Robert Chance. Franzen and Chance are members of the "Monday Morning Coffee Club," and both men dispute the charges against them. Mr. Franzen has not been charged with theft of the museum pot at this time. Mr. Curry has not been charged.

The Copperton arrests are part of a larger operation that includes several dealers and buyers of Anasazi pottery in Santa Fe. According to the Federal indictment, Mr. Chance was allegedly involved in forgeries for some of those artifacts as well. The forgeries imply that pots were found on private property at a time when laws were more relaxed about excavating artifacts associated with burials. Some of the pots are alleged to come from government land instead, according to one or more federal informants whose identities have not been disclosed.

Gertrude Curry, wife of Mackenzie, told the *Copperton News:* "Those old boys ran a scam on Mack. They never gave him the time of day. Don't include him in with *them.* It's not the first time they've stung him. H***, they ran him out of town once before, so he had to set up shop in Tucson. He never should've done any business with them."

Museum Director Juana Jones summed up Copperton's momentous news this way: "We got our pot back. If others were taken from federal sites, they will need to be repatriated to tribes or donated to museums. This will all take a long time."

Director Jones has announced that rep-
resentatives of three northern New Mexico
pueblos will come to the museum to bless
the return of the pot to the Copperton
Museum and to talk about the sacred nature
of the Museum's artifacts.

Bea sat a while before she decided what she wanted to write to Jean. Finally, she typed: "Thanks for the clips. It looks like justice has been done."

After she sent the email, Jean replied almost imme-diately, "Isn't there a little too much going on to say that? Aren't there a few too many coincidences?"

Bea was not always a believer in the power of coin-cidence. That kind of thinking could be useful, but it also breathed life into conspiracy theories. Her own neigh-bor believed in "chemtrails", contrails thought to release gasses that control our thinking, citing the fact that her daughter switched her party registration to Republican during a day the Blue Angels had flown in the San Diego air show. But that didn't mean Bea was feeling comfort-able about things, even with the current arrests. She need-ed to find out how Lila was. Bea shut her office door and made the call.

Lila was home from the hospital and almost chat-ty, which was reassuring. "You remember Sandra in the police force here? She says that she thinks it was planned. Somebody drove in on another road about a mile from where I was hiking, stopped, and walked to where they could shoot me. Big boots. They probably could have done more damage, so it may be another warning like that damned note. It's not that bad a wound, Bea, no matter what Ed tells you. I was trying to think what might have set them off, and I remembered something. I told Beggie that I thought maybe her husband Rob or one of his bud-dies from the old days could have killed Crow over his haranguing them about stuff."

"You can't mean Beggie would shoot at you!"

"No, I don't mean that. But she really has it in for Rob. She might have taunted him with what I said. He might've guessed where she got the idea, even if he didn't mention me. I guess Sandra's looking into all that. Rob's in custody already. He's in big trouble because of all that pothunting stuff. I just hope whoever shot at me is already in jail and doesn't endanger anybody else."

"Or doesn't stalk them in a tan Camry." She explained that remark to Lila.

"My gut is that it's Rob and he's taken care of," Lila said. "Still, I'm going to be careful."

There wasn't much time to ponder all this. Joan Madsden was at the door, letting Bea know that the volun-teer who was scheduled to set up the table decorations at the Valentine's Day brunch had broken her hip. Joan had brought a card for Bea to sign.

"I can help with that," Bea said. She was going to have to be at the brunch anyway setting up, since it would be studded with donors and potential donors. But, other than her usual child care problems, why should she care about having to work on Valentine's Day? Frank was far, far, away, and there was certainly no one else she'd spend the day with.

Should she send Frank a card? At lunch, she popped into the Hallmark store next to the supermarket where she picked up a Caesar salad encased in plastic. What was the right sentiment to send Frank? Probably "Missing You." What else was there to say? She'd told Frank that she hadn't had time to think about missing him, but that was a lie. When she woke up at three a.m., she missed his gentle breathing. She even missed his snores. She'd bought papayas for breakfast, because he'd gotten her into that habit. She thought of him when she sliced the tiny *limones* she bought at the Mexican *tienda* not far from her house, and when she squeezed the juice onto the papaya the way he'd shown her. She should stop buying papayas. But she couldn't stop driving by the park where they'd shared a bottle of wine and counted constellations—it was on the way to Shandley. She could drive a different route; it would add only a minute or two. They hadn't talked in three nights. Was this a silent pact to begin a gentle process of weaning each other from their lives?

***

After the kids were in bed, Bea found that her hand was on her phone, scrolling to Frank's name, when he called her.

"I have a Valentine's Day present, if you want it," he said.

"What do you mean, if I want it?"

"I can be in Tucson for most of Valentine's Day weekend. I won't have the whole weekend off—I need to show a major donor around this potential preserve in central Arizona on Valentine's Day itself. Sorry about that."

She felt her voice catching in her throat. "Frank, I have to work that day, too."

"I can show up late on the fourteenth, that Saturday, and stay through Monday."

She caught herself hesitating but quickly said, "Yes."

"I'm very glad to hear that word."

They caught each other up on work news. Frank was working twelve-hour days, "which is par for the course in this city. The D.C. mantra is 'so much ambition, so little time.'" He was spending what few leisure hours he had with his mother, who had rallied when he moved to Washington. But she was sinking back into a depression. His visits, she said, "were like firefly lights in the huge dark of the day."

"That could be positive, Frank."

"I'd think so if she didn't emphasize *huge.*"

He talked a bit about the Trust. He was working on communications about a couple of purchases, including this one in central Arizona. "That might get me out there every so often, Bea."

"Better than nothing." *Maybe they* could *stay together.*

"Also..." There was a pause. "My mother would like to meet you. And I'd like that, too."

"I don't see a trip to D.C. anytime in the near future, Frank. For one thing, we have to see what happens with Ethan. And as you know, I hardly have reliable child care here."

"I know." Was it guilt she heard in his voice? "So, catch me up on things in the sunny Southwest."

He was pretty sanguine about everything she told him until she mentioned the tan Camry.

"Bea, you have to get that license plate. This is not something to trifle with."

"It may be coincidence or just my imagination."

"So, reassure yourself—and me—that it *is* just a coincidence. If it seems like the car is following you again, get the license plate number and give it to Marcia. You have no good reason to trust that Armando guy."

"Okay. I've got an idea how to do this. I'll ask Angus to follow me home a couple of times and see if he can get the license number. He'd probably love the derring-do."

"I'm glad to hear you're taking this seriously."

She was glad Frank hadn't bowed out of her life yet.

"I didn't call you because I didn't want to be clingy,"

she said.

"I know exactly what you mean. Same here."

That's cleared up. Things are going awfully well.

At work the next morning, she met first with Margaret Rhodes. Luckily, Bea kept good Irish breakfast tea in the kitchen. That gave her initial credibility with her board member, who was dressed, as usual, as if she were going to an afternoon tea. Bea had never seen her in anything but a skirt and pearls.

Bea managed to dispel Margaret's concerns about the precedent-setting nature of giving Ethan emergency sick leave. Bea told her, "It's unlikely that this kind of awful situation will come up again anytime soon, and if it does, the board would still review things on a case-by-case basis. If our finances tank, it wouldn't be an option."

"Perhaps we should insist on disability insurance for all staff members."

"That would have been great for him. Do you mean that the Gardens should offer that as a benefit?"

"I *mean* that perhaps you should buy it for yourselves." She took a look at Bea, who tried not to register any emotion. She just kept Margaret's gaze. "Well," Bea said, "perhaps the Gardens could fund *part* of it. After a year or two of employment." Margaret seemed unconvinced, but she clearly had no concept of how hard it would be to pull that sort of a payment out of everyone's minimal pay checks.

"Well," Bea said in an offhand way, "nobody is here because they're looking for a big salary." Margaret flared her nostrils, ever so slightly. Bea continued, "We have to start on next year's budget soon." Margaret dropped her gaze, but angled her head to look at Bea as she kept talking. "I hope Ethan's back to take charge by then. In any case, we can look at working something like this into the numbers. As an option."

Margaret gave her a long, cool look this time. "You're better at this than I expected. I'll tell Armando that, too, the next time he decries your youth and inexperience." She smiled and made her exit.

Next, Bea enlisted Angus in tracking the Camry. He took out his paper calendar and marked off five times that week that he could shadow Bea either to or from work. On Friday afternoon, they'd discuss the weekend. He put the pocket calendar back into his jeans pocket and extended his hand with a flourish. "At your service, boss."

She was about to settle back into the permeable pavement grant when she noticed that Jean had sent another email from the Copperton paper. She couldn't resist opening it. Another article was attached.

Begonia Chance Revealed as FBI Informant

Local resident Begonia Chance, known locally as Beggie, has been named as one of the sources for the recent raid on antiquities dealers in Tucson and Santa Fe. The raid revealed that her ex-husband, Robert Chance, was the alleged forger of several documents purporting that artifacts were legally obtained. In an exclusive interview with the *Copperton News,* Mrs. Chance said, "I know for a fact that Rob doesn't believe in the new laws where you can't dig up grave sites even if they're on your own property. He used to joyride out into the national forest and find stuff at night. Don't know if he still does." Mrs. Chance said she hadn't intended to do anything about her ex-husband's lawbreaking until she heard he'd asked a friend about his fee for "getting the kind of papers you need." She then contacted Copperton Police Officer Sandra Ramirez, who put her in touch with the federal authorities.

Mrs. Chance said that she "had no idea about all those folks up in Santa Fe. I'm sure I'm not the only one who gave the feds some clues."

When asked for a comment, Mr. Chance said only, "Should have known it was Beggie. My ex-wife has always had it in for me."

Mrs. Chance is a volunteer at the Copperton Museum, which has just had a valuable pot returned to its collection after it was seized during a raid of a Tucson antiquities shop. Museum Director Juana Jones said that "Beggie Chance has now truly carried out the museum's mission of preserving and educating the public about the cultures of the Southwest."

Okay, Bea thought. *Maybe Beggie had a big blow-up with Rob. And she taunted him with Lila's suspicions, too. And Rob went off the handle with a gun in the woods. I'm sure glad he's locked up. Although I'm surprised he didn't go after Beggie.*

Chapter Twenty

Angus followed Bea home that evening. As she pulled into the driveway of her Palo Verde Acres unit, Angus pulled alongside. "No tan Camry," he said. "Sleep well, all of you."

The kids were not interested in the idea of sleep that night, however, and it took three stories and four songs to get them to close their eyes. The last song was more of a Gregorian chant than a song. Bea was nearly asleep herself when she'd finished.

The phone rang the minute she crept out of their room. It was Pat. Her ex-husband wanted to have the kids over for dinner the next night, Wednesday, as he'd be "out of town" for the next two weekends.

"Where are you going?"

"Um... Kauai."

"A Valentine's Day trip?"

"Well, sort of."

"Gee, we never went to Kauai for Valentine's Day." *In fact, I've never even been to Hawaii.*

"That's an inappropriate comment, Bea." As always, he became preachy when he could be faulted. *Some things never change.*

"Sorry for being *inappropriate*. So will you be picking them up from school?"

"No, I have to work late. I thought I'd just pick them up at six and drop them off after dinner."

"Whatever, Pat. Have a good night." When she hung up, she reflected on a conversation she'd had with Lila in Copperton. She'd laughed when Bea explained her "joint custody."

"The guys may think it's joint custody, because they never did that much when you were together. 'Joint custody' is just more of the same." *True enough.*

That night, Bea was too tired to do much more than channel surf. She hit on an old Western that showed two lean lawmen galloping off towards saguaro-studded hills. She recognized the place; it was over on the west side of town, near the Old Tucson movie set in Saguaro National Park West. The movie didn't have much of a plot beyond the righteousness of the good guys, but the cinematography was pretty nice. The Visitors' Bureau had recently discovered that saguaros and sunsets, rather than golf, were what visitors remembered most about Tucson. The old Western moviemakers had known that long ago.

But one of the actors was familiar. Bea wasn't much of a Western movie fan; why had she noticed this? One of the lawmen, wearing a white hat, had stunning blue eyes and high cheek bones. Curly blonde hair crept over his ears. *Oh my God, it's him, a much younger him.*

She googled the movie. Gus Graves, *Buzz Winters*, Susan Defoe. Shot in Tucson in 1969. What was it with 1969? Everything kept coming back to that year. Alan pulled up stakes in Copperton, the Mimbres pot was stolen from the museum around then, and Crow died. There were, of course, events of greater moment—the moon walk, Woodstock, the Vietnam War grinding on and on. But in Bea's current world, 1969 kept turning up. Buzz Winters was shooting a movie in Tucson in 1969.

Channel surfing was *not* putting her to sleep. She gave up and googled the movie again. *Showdown at Tom's*

Tavern. Buzz played the good guy sheriff who brought the town ruffian tavern owner to justice. The bad guy was truly bad; he abused both ladies of the night and law-abiding settlers' wives. Bea scrolled through the list of actors, wondering if Liz had a bit part. She didn't, but—okay, this was too much—Lesley Land, her miracle donor, played one of the "ladies of the night."

Bea googled movies set in Copperton, New Mexico, and finally found one filmed in Hollywood and on location in Copperton that apparently bombed in 1965. Buzz was in it again, and Lesley Land and Doris Winters were listed as dancers.

Then she tried googling "Lesley Land Alan Shandley" and found a 1975 article in the *Tucson Post* about their business partnership in a Tucson office complex, after they'd 'worked on a great project that never got off the ground in Copperton, New Mexico,' according to Miss Land.

So now my new donor turns out to be part of the events in Copperton in 1969. Wonderful.

***

At work the next morning, Marcia called first thing.

"I'm just calling to check in with you. We're making a little bit of progress."

"On Crow's murder?"

"Nope. I prefer dealing with cases with more recent evidence. It's easier. The archaeology sting, for instance. The Feds were pleased with the results of our interviews over in Copperton, by the way. So even if they don't lead us to Crow's murderer, it was time well spent. Also, I have to say that your little scheme for Angus and Jean at Mack's store was useful in the federal investigation. But right now, I'm talking about Ethan's hit-and-run."

Bea exhaled quickly. "You found the guy who hit him?"

"Don't assume it's a guy. No, but we finally have a good lead. It's been difficult because Ethan was out riding his bike so early in the morning and it was still dark, in an area where there are so few houses. But one of the people in those houses said her husband was out for a sunrise walk that morning on the street where the accident took place. We can't get in touch with him, because he's on a backpacking trip and out of phone contact. But he'll be back in a few days. His wife said that she and her husband heard the ambulance, but they didn't know what the emergency was. They were afraid it was a health issue with their elderly neighbors. I guess the guy didn't cross paths with Ethan. Anyway, she thinks he may remember any vehicle traffic that morning. Also, it sounds like Ethan may be getting more cognizant, which is good on all sorts of counts, including identifying whoever hit him."

"That's all encouraging." She told Marcia about Angus's plan to follow her around. She also mentioned her late-night google searches.

"I'm glad you've got Angus on patrol. Now we just need to do a little detective work and get some things wrapped up, and the doctors need to get your boss back to work! Although you may have mixed feelings about that. I like seeing you as the director."

"Marcia, I'd be more than happy to give Ethan his job back."

"If you say so. Talk to you later."

Bea set out to find Javier, looking forward to a walk in the early spring sunshine. Maybe a couple of poppies had started to bloom in the wildflower garden. But she didn't even get out the door. Javier was fixing a broken toilet in the staff bathroom. So much for the romance of working in a botanical garden.

"Hey, boss!" he greeted her.

"Not you, too!" she said. "Angus is giving you bad habits. Can we talk out in the hall?" He followed her out.

"What's up, Bea?"

"How's Ethan? I heard from Marcia that he's doing better. I don't feel close enough to him to visit if he's still unconscious, but if that changes, I want to see him."

"I was going to tell you. He's opened his eyes a few more times. But he doesn't respond to anything; it's just kind of a blank look. His mother and father are here now."

"It's about time!"

"I talked to his mom, and she said she saw a tear once. But she says the doctors don't know if he's going to be in a 'persistent vegetative state,' or come out of it. They're saying they're hopeful because of his youth and good health, and the degree of brain damage. Also, it's only been ten days. It's unlikely he'll be able to return to work for at least several weeks, and that's a best-case scenario. I told his mom you are trying to get the board to vote on paid sick leave for him for three months. We both know our health insurance isn't Cadillac, right?"

Bea nodded vigorously.

"So, Ethan may need expensive rehab that's only partially covered. His mom's been worried about how long it takes to get government disability stuff. She said that she and her husband were 'hurting' financially. That's sure not my business. She kept going on about the possible costs."

Bea was surprised about how much the usually quiet Javier was "going on" about all this. And he had more to say.

"This is surprising. Did you know Ethan is a big donor to the Horticultural Therapy Training Center?"

"No, I didn't. But Javier, what's that have to do with anything?"

"It turns out he has hardly any savings. His mother does *not* approve of his generosity, let me tell you."

"Well, that's interesting. He has told me he wants to hire a horticultural therapist as soon as we can."

"And he's told me that plants are the best therapy in the world, that they've saved him from depression. Good for him, but this all means he's in a tight spot. So anyway, his mom is grateful you're working on this for him. Oh, and by the way, Bea, when's the vote on the paid sick leave?"

"It was a tie last time. Alicia's trying again today."

"Good. Is Armando voting for it, since he wants to join the staff?"

"Hardly."

"He'd change his tune the minute he got hired. Which I hope our board has the sense to prevent."

Back at her computer, Bea found a voice mail from Lila in Copperton asking her to call. *Oh God, I hope she's okay.*

Lila assured her that her leg was healing well. Sandra was interviewing someone who'd been seen poaching near where Lila had been shot, as well as everyone who lived near there, and she was confident that they'd find the shooter. Rob Chance was a suspect, as well.

They chatted a bit about the sting operation, and how it was the talk of the town. "Rob and Tom are popular old geezers. Some people are not at all happy about this. Federal overreach and all that. Mack Curry's not a town favorite… he never really integrated into the community. Gert has pissed tons of people off. She gave me the dirtiest look this morning when I saw her at Walgreen's! So, there's not much sympathy anywhere around here for them. But neither one has been charged with anything. Oh well, that's not why I called you, Bea. In the middle of the workday, too."

"Call anytime, Lila."

"Okay, do you remember Beggie Chance?"

"She's kind of unforgettable. And now we know she informed on her ex-husband!"

"Yup. Well, she and Doris Winters asked me to get together a 'gathering of the girls,' she called it. She said it was Doris's idea. They want to have dinner together at Beggie's house. They asked me if I could put you and the kids up again, and I told her Ed and I would have you here anytime you can get here. So, how's this weekend for you? I know it's Valentine's Day, but didn't you say Frank was in D.C.?"

"I did. But I have to work on Saturday, and he's coming here for the weekend."

"Okay. That's good. I'll tell Beggie that it will have to be another time. They really liked you... maybe they related to another divorced woman. And Doris, you, and I all know about single parenting, too. I'm guessing that's what's behind the invitation. Doris said you remind her of herself at that age. So I'm anticipating a nice, old-fashioned gossip session about men."

"Maybe they'd like to take a trip to Tucson. Hey, Lila, did you know Buzz Winters was in a movie in Tucson? In 1969, no less?"

"Well, I knew he acted in Westerns, and he was fairly well known for a while. He played one of those totally moral gun-totin', outlaw-killin' types. I'm not surprised he filmed in Tucson. Lots of Westerns were, right? I remember his career went downhill after the peak of the cowboy movie era. But we didn't see much of him until the past five or ten years, when he came back here to retire. He managed to make enough of a living to buy himself a nice spread out in Pretty Valley, so I guess he did all right."

"Thanks, Lila. I hope I see you soon. But unless you come this way, it won't be this weekend. Take care of yourself."

"You, too."

She might as well give in to her curiosity. Permeable pavement was not going to be able to keep her interest until she looked up Buzz online. She found an obscure site about Western Movies from 1950-2000, and Lila was right. Buzz's fame was almost entirely related to the "Sheriff Sam" movies, which were all filmed in the 1960s, some of them in Tucson. Before that, Buzz had been in a cancelled TV series with a western theme. He was described as having grown up in Copperton where he "worked in retail before moving to Hollywood in the Fifties." His post-film career consisted of advertising manly products like whiskey and after-shave, and playing some bit parts in some television series. He had one daughter, and had been married to the former Doris Martin, from a prominent Copperton family, from 1949 to 1969.

There it was, that year again.

An email from Alicia popped up on her computer. She'd held another vote on extending Ethan's paid sick leave for three months. It passed, three to one, with Armando as the nay vote, of course. Alicia chose not to comment on this.

Bea then headed out in an improved mood to meet the Valentine's Day caterer in the courtyard. The two of them figured out how to site all the tables and chairs they'd need for the reservations. On the way back, Bea heard Armando's authoritative voice pontificating in the cactus garden. She went over that way, and stood by the door to the greenhouse, watching. He shot her an annoyed look. He had a group of undergraduates in tow, the same group that Stephanie Shores had been filming before. They were not on their TV behavior now, and she saw a pocket of giggling girls near the back. Several had on Arizona Wildcats sweatshirts, and Bea thought they looked fit enough to be on the softball team, or maybe it was volleyball.

Of course, he hadn't cleared this field trip with her. She wondered if it was time to bring this up with the board president. He was deliberately refusing to follow Shandley Gardens policies.

"So, what is the purpose of cactus spines?" Armando asked.

Nobody raised a hand, until a pudgy girl in a jacket too heavy for the mild morning raised a hand partway up, parallel with her ear.

"Protection from predators?"

"Yes, and what else?" Armando's eyes roamed among the attractive giggling girls in the back. They didn't respond. A gangly young man at the front of the group raised his hand, holding it higher as Armando's eyes raked the class for another respondent. Finally, he called on the guy. "Edward?"

"Spines are modified leaves. The plant transpires through its stem instead of its leaves, reducing the total surface area for transpiration. Spines also shade the plant."

"Very good, Edward. Yes, spines are an excellent desert adaptation. It's hard to imagine that spines could really provide much shade, but all those little shadows add up. Speaking of shadows," he said, giving Bea a disgusted look, "meet Bea Rivers, the Garden's volunteer coordinator, suddenly turned acting director." The gaggle of athletic girls in the back stopped talking to each other and looked at her.

"Didn't the real director just die or something?" asked a freckled boy in gym shorts and a fleece pullover.

"Not at all," Bea countered. "He's recovering from a serious bicycle accident. Be sure to wear your bike helmets; it could have been worse if he didn't have one. Enjoy the Gardens!" She exited quickly before Armando could get in any more public jabs.

The day went almost normally for a change. Joan Madsden needed to talk strategy about a volunteer who was alienating several others. It was amazing how a once-annoying problem provided some welcome relief from her current woes. Also, Angus wanted her okay on removing some Alan Shandley-era plants that were no longer attractive enough for a public garden (yes, she'd take the flak from those who thought nothing should ever change from the original plantings until things actually died). Bea sighed and did what she'd been putting off thus far. She opened the file on next year's budget and studied it, trying to familiarize herself with the numbers enough to be able to make some projections. If Ethan wasn't back for another three months, she'd have to create next year's budget.

She and Angus walked out to the parking lot together at 5:15. "Where's your truck?" she asked. He drove a beat-up Datsun pickup. Angus's eyes flashed with the thrill of the game.

"I'm using Jean's car. So Tan Camry won't recognize me." He pointed to a blue Subaru wagon. "Armando drove a university carryall here today, by the way." Angus was loving this. Bea, not so much.

Angus followed her home and gave the heads-up as he had before. She arrived just before the kids piled in the door from the school bus. They had just enough time to show her their papers before she had to bundle them out again to have dinner with their father. They didn't even have time to take off their jackets. The three of them drove off, Pat gunning the motor as he headed out of Palo Verde Acres onto the wide city street.

Bea figured she now had about an hour and a half

to do whatever she wanted to do. She could have a salad with all her favorite things the kids had a current aversion to—arugula, beets, goat cheese. There was a decent little store nearby that stocked all those things and some good IPA, too. As she pulled out of the Palo Verde Acres main driveway, a few minutes after Pat's SUV had made the same turn, she spotted a tan Camry facing her in the YMCA parking lot across the street. She cursed the fact that Arizona did not require front license plates. There was no one visible in the car. Bea drove around the block and entered the parking lot from the other side, pulling up behind where the car should have been. But it was gone.

Considerably rattled, she still drove to the store, bought dinner, and edged back home. She knew how paranoid she'd become when she jerked her head to the rearview mirror, to check on a car that seemed to be following her, only to see the cloud of her elderly neighbor's white hair just above the steering wheel. There was no sign of the dreaded tan car. One thing was for sure. She wasn't going to tell Pat about this issue. It was certainly possible—likely, even—that she was obsessed with tan Camrys, which were a common enough car in Tucson. Pat already didn't like her working at Shandley because she didn't make much money, and because the kids had been briefly in danger during that business last summer. But she *was* going to mention the car in the YMCA lot to both Angus and Marcia.

She'd managed to settle into a semblance of calm— she was reading a novel and drinking chamomile tea— when the kids burst in the door with huge portions of leftover pasta. Jessie was excited about the "waiter with a black coat with a tail."

"It's a *tuxedo,* Jessie," her big brother informed her. "Dad's girlfriend wasn't there, so it was easier to talk."

"Why's she so hard to talk to?"

"Oh, I don't know. Suzie keeps telling us that we're so *cute.*"

Is that all it is? "That's not so bad, honey, is it really?"

"Kinda."

Jessie jumped in. "And when they go to Hawaii, Dad's going to ask her to marry him!"

"Jessie, you weren't supposed to tell! Dad said it was a *secret* only for us three!"

Bea sat down hard.

"How do you guys feel about this?" *How do I feel about this?*

Andy came over and hugged her. "I don't know, Mom. What do you think?"

"Honey, have you been worrying about this?"

"Well, I knew you guys wouldn't get back together, but still... well, he did kinda mention it before."

This makes more sense. This is what's been bothering Andy.

"This feels pretty fast to you, huh." *And to me.*

"Daddy said I could carry the rings in the wedding," said Jessie.

"Jessie, you are so *dumb!*" her brother retorted.

"You two need to get to bed. We can talk about all of this in the morning." *We can talk about this when I can figure out what to say. Which will have to be after I know what I really feel about this.*

She wrote an email to Marcia, telling her about the Camry following her. But she had to say something to somebody about Pat and Suzie, and she had known Marcia since they were in kindergarten. "Pat just dropped a bomb on the kids. He's going to ask his current sweetie to marry him in Hawaii."

Marcia shot an email back in three minutes. "You know

how I've always felt about your ex. I hope you're smart enough not to be hurting over this. As to what kind of step-mother 'Suzie' will make, I suppose that could be a matter of concern. Get some sleep. Given Pat's track record, he may tire of Suzie before the wedding bells sound. Besides, maybe she doesn't want to take on two kids!"

It was hard to say what she felt about Pat's getting remarried. She had definitely once loved the guy. But there was a wall in her head that cut off memories of their courting, the way they'd danced together, and hiked together, and... Sometimes she caught glimpses of Pat and Bea back there, in the back of her head, at their wedding, at the kids' births, but they were shadow figures.

It was like her hazy memories of the pain of child-birth. Forgetting such agony must be what allowed wom-en to keep having kids. But that wall in her head shielded her from something much deeper, the pain of humiliation and lost love. So how did she feel about this wedding? Well, her protective brain was telling her that she was well rid of him if he wanted to marry someone like Suzie. She had no trouble feeling anger; that didn't hurt one bit. Here's what was walled off: if he could marry Suzie so fast, had she deceived herself about what they'd had together once? Best to leave that in the shadows.

Could she be a dupe with Frank, as well? It might not be best to leave *that* in the shadows, but she was going to.

Oh, well, Marcia's probably right, I'm not so sure Suzie will even say yes to two kids. It was far more fruitful to deal with her job, her kids, and their safety, for God's sake. So, she emailed Angus about the Camry. He shot back a response saying he'd watch the YMCA parking lot like a hawk. He was so apologetic. It was good to have friends and colleagues who were looking out for her. Lord knew she needed it.

Chapter Twenty-One

At breakfast the next morning, Bea told the kids that they would probably grow to be better friends with Suzie, if she and their dad got married.

"But he said they *are* getting married, Mommy!" her daughter said.

"Okay. But he asked you to keep this a secret, and you need to do that. Okay?"

"Okay." Andy said this seriously, Jessie blithely. But then she asked, "Mom, are you going to marry Frank?'

"Good heavens, why do you say that?"

Jessie ducked her head. "I dunno."

Bea softened her tone. "We don't know each other well enough to even talk about getting married."

Jessie volunteered, "Well, Daddy doesn't know Suzie too well, either." Andy kicked his little sister.

"We need to get going! You'll be late for the bus!" This seemed like the best way to stop this discussion.

Bea thought Marcia was right; the Hawaiian getaway might not turn out the way Pat had planned. It was extraordinary that he'd mentioned the marriage to his kids before he'd popped the question. She could still be flabbergasted by his judgment.

She hadn't slept much and found herself slightly dazed when she sank into her office chair. Angus appeared in the door immediately. "Bad night, huh?"

"Is it that obvious?"

Angus ignored the question. "So. You know I'm friends with some of the plant sciences staff on campus, right?"

"I think you've mentioned that. Why?"

"Well, the word is that the dean talked to Armando yesterday. It's confirmed; he was denied tenure."

"I sure wouldn't be sorry if he moved on."

"The gossip is that what put the nail in his coffin wasn't his publication record, or his teaching, or his lack of collegiality, although my buddy says nobody could count on him to show up for committee meetings. I guess he wasn't so good at the service part of his job, which may be why he wanted to be on our board. Nope. I'll bet you can guess what the big issue is with him."

"Something to do with a student? Maybe a young one? A young, *pretty* one?"

"Bingo. But apparently it's not public knowledge yet, so don't mention it."

"That would be a major strategic error on my part."

"So, Bea, I think he's gonna make an even bigger play for your job now."

"You mean Ethan's job."

"You know what I mean. Watch your back. Also, did you hear the interview with him on the NPR station a few days ago? That gardening show?"

"God, no. He's supposed to run stuff by me if he's representing the Gardens."

"You can probably give up on that one. Maybe he was making a last-ditch effort to repair his community service record. Probably too late for that. I can't believe he did himself any favors with that interview, though. You should look it up."

"I can't wait. Meanwhile, we have an Events Center committee meeting this morning to go over the new architectural drawings."

"I doubt that Armando will want to miss that opportunity to show his superior knowledge."

Bea couldn't help herself. She looked up the NPR interview.

It turned out to be a panel discussion about "xeriscaping," or low-water-use landscaping. It was Armando, a guy named Bruce Beel from Turfin' Tucsonans, whose ad she had so deplored in *Tucson Trends*, and the third panel member was a friend of hers who ran the best nursery in town. Thank goodness for him, because the other two were giving the genteel moderator plenty of grief.

"There is really no place for turf in Tucson landscapes anymore," said her board member.

"Well, but Armando, the concept of xeriscaping encourages thoughtful use of turf. A small amount of a total landscape—about ten percent—is part of the idea. Some people want a bit of lawn for children and pets," said her nursery friend, who sold only low-water-use plants.

"Let's face it, ten percent is way too low for most people. This is just part of the political correctness of the lawn Nazis!" said Bruce Beel, who clearly had a financial stake in promoting lawns.

"Nazis!" yelled Armando. "I find that offensive! Apologize, please!"

"Let's take this down a notch," said the worried moderator's voice.

"Okay," said Armando, in his professorial mode. "I hope your listeners are aware that Arizona is facing huge problems with the old Colorado River Compact negotiated in 1922. It was based on much-higher-than-average rainfall years. As we face climate-changed-induced drought, we have no choice. We have to cut back to all but the most essential use of water."

"Climate change! That's what you people always use

to get your way! Yeah, the climate changes and then it changes back again! Things always change! There are wet years and dry years!" Bea could imagine Bruce Beel spitting as he said this.

"You're such a fool!" said Armando. "Haven't you seen the graphs about global warming? There is absolutely no question that the planet is getting warmer. And that does not bode well for the desert, which is already hot and dry! You clearly don't know the difference between *climate* and *weather.* I suggest you look it up."

"Who are you calling a fool?" said Bruce Beel. Bea imagined him rising to his feet with a raised fist.

"We need to cut to a break," said the moderator.

When they came back together, things were slightly more collegial, thanks in no small part to the nursery owner. Angus was right; Armando hadn't done himself any favors. The thing was, she agreed with almost everything he said. He just managed to deliver it in a supremely alienating way. Kind of like Crow, she thought, although she'd probably agree with a lot fewer of his lectures. Was there any connection between Armando and Crow?

Meanwhile, she had to go to a committee meeting with Armando very soon. She hoped he'd gone on a plant-collecting trip to salve his wounded ego about the tenure decision, but she had no such luck.

Bea was the first to sit down at the conference table in the board room. She laid out her papers at the head of the table. The architect was the next to arrive. He'd been selected by this committee, and Bea barely knew him, but she liked him. He had a wide smile and tended to pounce on ideas with exclamations of "Excellent!" He had wavy white hair that was a few weeks overdue for a cut, but she suspected he preferred to have it creeping over his ears and shirt collar. He wouldn't want to be mistaken for conventional.

Margaret Rhodes arrived next. She was, as always, the picture of propriety, with her ice-blue knee-length skirt, matching jacket, black silk blouse, and pearls. She'd warmed up to Bea considerably since the first Events Center meeting she'd attended just a few weeks ago. "Holding the fort, my dear?" she asked Bea.

"Keeping out the marauders," Bea said, and thought it had been a Freudian response, as just then Armando Ramos sauntered in, wearing a Hawaiian shirt popping with palm trees, which were revealed when he removed his fleece jacket. If Bea'd had a bad night, Armando's appeared to have been worse. His eyes were puffy, and she could smell whiskey even two seats away from him. Margaret stared at him, sniffed, and moved to the far side of her chair. Alicia slid into the seat across from Armando and gave him an appraising look. *She probably heard about the tenure.* Alicia had lived in Tucson all her life, and she knew people everywhere.

The architect launched into an explanation of his new drawings, but he hadn't gotten far when Armando called, "Wait a minute!" about twice as loud as made sense, given the size of the room and the committee. Margaret moved farther to the edge of her chair. Alicia said, in an even tone, "Is something bothering you, Armando?" Bea had to gulp down a laugh.

"Hell, yes, something's bothering me! This is a *botanical garden,* for God's sake, and I don't see any plantings on this drawing."

"The landscape architect is a different person from the same firm," Bea explained. "We'll see those drawings at another meeting. *These* drawings are to show us how the building looks now that we've asked to shrink the size."

"Damn it!" Armando thundered. "The landscape architecture should *never* be subsidiary to the building! If we had a 'director' who knew about anything besides teaching little kids, that would have been communicated."

The architect ran his hands through his shock of white hair, looking from one to another of the committee members.

Alicia spoke quietly and with very little inflection. "Armando, I have to ask you to leave, if you cannot be civil."

He seemed to realize then that he had gone too far. "Sorry, Alicia. I'm not feeling well."

"I believe your apology should go to Bea, young man," said Margaret. She was old enough to be able to call almost anyone "young man."

"Sorry." He was about as sincere as Jessie was after she'd eaten most of her brother's Halloween candy.

When the architect got to the part about a green roof, Armando cut him off. "I can come up with the plant list for that," he said.

"I believe that's part of the landscape architecture plan. Your comments will be welcome when we get to that," said Alicia.

"I could save us all a lot of money by creating those plans myself," Armando growled. "I guarantee you I would charge you less."

The architect hadn't even made a full pass through his hair when Bea explained, "We've told *Greenworks* we'd like them to propose both architectural and landscape architectural designs."

"I'm sure your ideas will be taken into account at the appropriate time," Alicia said.

Armando looked disgusted and suddenly had another meeting to attend. As he left, Margaret sniffed loudly and moved back to the center of her chair. The rest of the meeting went smoothly.

When Bea got back to her office, there was an email from Marcia. "The hiker/neighbor who lived near the place where Ethan had his accident is back now. He told us he never saw a tan Camry. He saw a van come by; he remembers it because it was speeding, and he wondered why somebody would drive like that so early in the morning."

Hadn't somebody mentioned something about a van recently?

When she headed out to her car in the Shandley parking lot, there was a note under her windshield wiper. It just said, in big, scrawled, capital letters on a pink half-sheet, "WATCH IT!" She turned the flier over and discovered an ad for a movie, this time. This was a documentary put on by the nonprofit Legacy of Torture, and it was called, "The Making of a Refugee." She couldn't ignore this one. It was too much like her other note. Also, it wasn't put there by Rob Chance, who was locked up. It was somebody local, who had access to these fliers. It was somebody pretty clever, too. She looked around. The only other vehicles left in the lot were Javier's and Angus's, and they didn't have fliers.

Bea sighed. She opened up her glove box and pulled out the winter gloves she'd last worn in Copperton. *Better to use them for making snowballs than to handle potential felons' handiwork.* She took the note inside and put it on her desk, and left Marcia a voice mail, adding a piece of information that could be important. "Marcia, I... well, I just have to tell you that Armando Ramos was at the Gardens this afternoon. During the time period when the note appeared. It wasn't there at lunchtime. And he left the Gardens in a lousy mood."

Marcia picked up partway through the message and said, "Thanks. I'll come by and get the note with the key that Ethan left our investigators. I think we have your prints on file; you had to get fingerprinted because you work with kids there, right?"

"Yes, but I was wearing gloves."

"That's good. Take care, my friend."

Nothing that evening calmed her sense of unease. Some anonymous note-leaver was telling her to "watch it" and her police officer buddy was telling her to "take care". Bea snapped at Andy when he pushed his beets to the side of the plate, although she knew perfectly well he'd hated them for at least two years. He gave her a wounded look. Jessie ate hers and his, too. Not for the first time, she thought that she and Andy should be more like her daughter.

Chapter Twenty-Two

Half an hour after Bea had tucked her children into bed, Jessie padded out in her long flannel nightgown decorated with unicorns. "There's a monster in the back yard, Mommy."

"No monsters out there. Let's go look out the window."

But when Bea went to Andy and Jessie's bedroom window, she heard the crunching sound of human footsteps on the gravel in the side yard.

She summoned her own mother's forced calm in an emergency and whispered, "It's just a dog, honey. I have to make a phone call, and then I'll stay here with you until you fall asleep." She hoped Andy wouldn't wake up, but he did have a disquieting sixth sense about trouble. Sure enough, when she turned from the window, he was sitting up in bed, watching her for cues.

"I don't think we need to worry, but I'll make a call just in case." The kids followed her into the living room, away from the window, and both half-sat in her lap as she called 911 from her cell phone.

She said that she was alone with two young children, that there were footsteps in the gravel in her side yard. Also that Detective Samuelson was aware that someone in a tan Camry could have been following her. Andy's eyes got ridiculously big at this last piece of news, which, of course, she'd kept from him. The dispatcher told her to stay on the phone while a police helicopter headed her way. Bea said to her kids, in the levelest tone she could manage, "There's a helicopter coming just to check things out." Jessie crawled fully onto her lap and Andy leaned against her, grabbing her free arm. The dispatcher was asking questions she didn't have answers to. Most of her mind was listening for footsteps, or a window opening.

She jumped up to check the window latches and door locks, causing a startled bleat from Jessie and another wide-eyed look from her son. He watched her at the windows with the phone in one hand and checked the kitchen windows himself. The helicopter still hadn't come. *At least it's winter, and the windows are all locked shut.*

"It's coming!" Andy yelled, just as she heard it, and the lights advanced on them. Brightness blared in all the windows on the side of the apartment. Andy winced. Jessie held on for dear life. The helicopter seemed to be right outside the kids' bedroom. Jessie put her hands on her ears, but Bea grabbed a hand. The 911 person was saying, "Stay on the line until we decide you are safe." They sat on Andy's bed, and the three of them looked out the window at an empty side yard. The lights illuminated the gray gravel where the intruder had been walking. They highlighted a picnic table with a few stray paper dolls, Andy's bike, Jessie's trike, and a seriously deflated soccer ball.

"This is kind of like a horror movie," Andy said in a flat tone. He had gotten off the bed and moved to the window. *How does he know about horror movies? I've never let him see one. Pat? I'll ask later.*

The helicopter circled their building. The elderly couple who lived across the side yard were standing out on the street, arms around each other. She could hear them yelling at the neighbors on the other side, who must have come outside, too. "No idea!" said her neighbor.

After another circle, the helicopter headed away from

the apartment. *Maybe they saw someone and they're chasing him.*

"I think they're way down the block, Mom," said Andy. His grip on her hand loosened just a tad. The dispatcher was still on the line, asking if Bea was okay, and if there was someone she could call to come over and stay with them. "We'll be fine," she lied. "But I need to talk to my children now," she told the dispatcher. "The person has run off." The noise and the lights were even farther away now, maybe not even over Palo Verde Acres. But then they headed back closer. Bea sighed.

"I'll stay on the line until you feel safe."

Bea put the phone down on Andy's bureau, leaving it on. *How am I going to calm us all down now?* She pulled them both to her. "Whoever was out there probably wasn't anybody to worry about, but the police are following him... or her... in the helicopter. I think he ran out to the street and is pretty far away right now." The helicopter noise was retreating again.

Andy pulled his ear. Jessie searched her face. They wanted to believe her, she knew. It would help if she believed herself. "I'll make us all some chamomile tea with honey." She carried the phone with her into the kitchen. "It sounds like the helicopter's moving on. I really think we're okay."

"I can hang on," the dispatcher insisted.

Andy was ready with questions when she got back in the room with tea. "Mom, why would somebody be in our back yard? Are they after you for something at the Gardens? Does it have to do with those bones?" He didn't touch the chamomile tea.

"I don't see how it could have to do with the bones since I have nothing to do with them. It could have been somebody looking to steal your bike, to be honest, Andy.

We're going to have to lock it up at night." This was scary, but not as scary as the alternatives, and it had the additional advantages of being possible and something that was easily fixed.

She couldn't hear the helicopter at all anymore. She told the dispatcher again that they were okay, and they hung up. She couldn't think of anyone she could call at this time of night to come and spend the night. If only her parents hadn't moved back to California. Well, Frank would be here soon. Angus and Jean would come if she asked them, but they'd have gone to sleep already.

Bea read the kids a couple of books. They nestled on Jessie's bed, and she fell back asleep after drinking all of her tea and half of Andy's. Andy finally dozed off, too, after Bea read him a story that he'd loved since toddlerhood. Bea doubted she'd ever sleep that night.

Her bike theory could have been right. On the other hand, she did seem to have gotten involved with some people who were unstable, to put it charitably. Including one on her own board. Maybe Pat was right, and she should quit her job at Shandley. If her job truly were endangering her kids, she'd do it, but wasn't that an overreaction?

A Benadryl didn't even make her yawn. She thought she heard something in the gravel in the side yard again, and rushed to the window in time to see a cat's tail flash by. She tried reading a book her dad had given her about bee pollination, but it wasn't making her drowsy, just annoyed that she had to read the same sentences four times before she got their meaning. She picked up *Tucson Trends,* and turned to the most boring article she could find, about the new highway construction. There was the damned ad about the virtues of turf and the deprivations of low-water-use landscaping. She threw the thing in the trash; it didn't even deserve the recycling pile.

Bea was more than ready for some pleasantness in her life. Frank's plane would arrive at 7:00 in the morning. She *might* get some sleep before then.

She was surprised to find herself in the middle of a dream when the alarm went off at six. She had been hiding her kids in a badger den. This was not good. Bea staggered to the kitchen to get some extra strong coffee going before she had to face her children's questions. Jessie had to be shaken a bit to wake, but her little girl wasn't worried about helicopters, she was just plain sleep-deprived. Andy was another story. Before he'd swung his feet to the floor, he asked his mother if they knew anything about what the helicopter saw. She hesitated. "I don't know yet. I'm sure I'll talk to Marcia about it this morning." He didn't say anything, but he scrutinized her face for several seconds after this statement. Then he dropped his eyes and said, "Don't we have to get going?"

On the way to the airport, Bea tried to rearrange her feelings. *Fear and trepidation, get in the trunk. Excitement about Frank's visit, sit up front with me.* She was pretty close to success by the time she parked the car.

Jessie started jumping up and down when she saw Frank heading down the airport escalator. Bea had to hold her back from a full-on attack. Andy looked down, and scraped his feet, but when Frank said, "Hey, Buddy," he looked up and suddenly all four of them were in a messy hug. It felt so good. But feeling good meant that there was more potential for hurt. More hurt, after the pain of divorce eighteen months ago. Bea detached herself from Frank, but Jessie held onto his hand.

Frank insisted on taking them out for breakfast at a pancake house near the airport "since I'm making the big money in D.C." Andy tried to match him pancake for pancake until Frank shouted, "Enough!"

All too soon, it was time for Frank to head north to the town of Pinedale on the Mogollon Rim to meet his potential donors. There hadn't been any opportunity to tell Frank about the night before, but Andy brought it up. "We had a helicopter chasing some guy away from our house last night."

"I'll send you an email about it," Bea told him, with more cheer than she felt. For the kids' sake.

"Please do that," Frank said, and kept his serious brown eyes on her for a moment longer than necessary. She met his gaze and he nodded. Then he turned to her son. "I'll be back tonight and you can tell me all about it, Andy."

Bea dropped Frank off at the rental car counter back at the airport. He was expected up on the Mogollon Rim in a couple of hours, but he'd be back as soon as he could. He said this lightly, to the kids, and then he levelled that concerned gaze on Bea again. She smiled and hugged him, knowing Andy was watching carefully.

Back on the freeway, Bea realized she needed to think about the donor breakfast. Not Frank's brown eyes. Not helicopters or footsteps in the gravel. Not Pat's wedding. Not tan Camrys. Not sinister notes about scary plays and movies. Not people in Copperton who might have shot her friend, and who might be angry at her role in an antiquities bust. And most assuredly not the fact that the real executive director of Shandley Gardens was the victim of a hit-and-run, that looked like it could be malicious, and possibly Shandley-related.

Actually, what she really needed to do was focus on driving. A car had just cut in front of her on the freeway and she hadn't braked as quickly as she should have. She'd almost made all of her worrying moot.

Chapter Twenty-Three

At Shandley, she pulled the television out of the closet for the kids to watch PBS. She installed them in a corner of her office and headed out to do the brunch setup. One of their most artistic volunteers had already put together some lovely red-and-white bouquets, and all Bea had to do was move a few name tags around. She moved Lesley Land next to some folks who needed a little warming up before they made a donation. She was just starting to think about how that might work—would Lesley mention her own potential gift?—when her phone dinged. Marcia's text said, simply, "Your intruder eluded us." How was Bea supposed to concentrate on work?

She tallied up her blessings. Her mother's Pollyanna-ness had its uses. Frank was back, Crow's death was fading from everybody's consciousness, Stephanie Shores didn't work on the weekends, and it was a beautiful February day for an outdoor event which should win Shandley Gardens new friends and high praises. But she felt massively uneasy.

A van.

She called Angus. "Hey, Angus, did you say Mack Curry drives a van?"

"Yeah. Now is there a van following you?"

"No, but one might have hit Ethan. As far as we know, Mack and Gert haven't been arrested."

"I don't know if I mentioned Mack's van to Marcia. I'll

tell her."

Bea managed to disguise her antsiness fairly well as she stopped at each table at the brunch, chatting about current films, grandchildren, and ideas for improving Gardens exhibits.

She made her way to Lesley Land's table. As she'd predicted, Lesley was holding forth. She was talking up a children's garden, where kids could "celebrate plants with all their senses!" The couple Bea had seated her with, a white-haired gentleman in a blue blazer with brass buttons, and his wife, a pale, frighteningly-thin woman with a stunning gold choker, were both looking amused. "Come on," said Lesley. "If you could pick a plant that kids should smell, what would it be?"

"Well, why not let them smell a corpse plant!" said George Blair of the blue blazer.

"Lavender, of course. And it's low-water-use," said his wife.

"*Fabulous* ideas!" Lesley cried. "Now all you'll need to do is to support Shandley Gardens so that they have the money to consider your ideas! No guarantees for anything except that the landscape architect will be *fabulous.*"

Bea knew who should fill that vacancy on the board. Lesley was cheering her up.

She managed to disconnect the kids from the television screen with the promise of a zoo visit. She was still jumpy. She counted two tan Camrys on the way to the zoo. One car was about ten years old, she told herself, not the late-model one that might have been stalking her. The other one had Iowa plates and was driven by an older couple who looked like textbook snowbirds fleeing a Minnesota winter. And neither one was following her.

At the zoo, Jessie, as usual, didn't want to leave the spider monkeys. Andy was more interested in the big cats.

"I'm curious... Why do you like them the best?" Bea asked. "They're just sleeping, like they usually do when we come."

"Because they're the biggest and the strongest." Bea remembered when he'd liked the monkeys best. Where was this "big and strong" thing coming from? His friends? School? Pat? It was hard to know what influenced your seven-year-old child.

Frank came in the door that evening with a smile. He'd had success with his donors, too. First thing, though, he wanted to hear about the helicopter.

Andy jumped in with the story. "It was so loud I thought the roof was gonna come off," he said.

"So did they catch anybody?"

"Nope! He probably hid in a trash can or something," Andy said in an offhand tone. His casualness didn't fool Bea, or Frank, for that matter.

After the kids went to bed, Frank asked if Rob Chance was still in jail.

"As far as I know," she said.

"Okay, one other question and then we can forget all of this."

"Yes?"

"How do you think this Mack guy, or this Rob guy, or this awful Armando guy, or some other unsavory character you've been around lately... how does he or she know where you live?"

"How should I know? I mean, if it's Armando, he could probably get that information on the staff emergency forms. Board members aren't normally given them, but he could have asked Ethan for one. Oh, my God." She shook her head as if to clear it.

"Did you just remember something?"

"Before Ethan's accident... remember? Somebody broke into the personnel files. He thought it was me or

Javier at first. *I* thought Ethan was just overstressed and imagining things."

"And I thought maybe somebody had broken in and wanted something on Ethan. Which is still a possibility. Did he ever report anything?"

"I don't know. I think he said he was going to. That's when we thought the only danger at Shandley was last summer's murder. And whatever happened forty years ago.

"Let's forget it all for the rest of tonight."

And they did, until Bea woke up, thinking, around five am. The phone rang an hour later.

"More breaking news?" asked Frank. "You certainly lead an eventful life."

"Maybe it's a wrong number." She could hope. But her phone showed that it was Lila calling from Copperton.

"Hey, Bea, there's some news here that you might want to know about."

"Yes?" She wasn't breathing.

"Buzz Winters bailed his buddy Rob out of jail pretty soon after he was arrested. Really high bail, too. So Beggie took out a restraining order on her ex. Also, Gert Curry told Beggie she had blood on her hands for whistleblowing, which she called 'ratting on people.'"

"Blood on her hands? Isn't that a little dramatic? And didn't she say something to you earlier about being a rat?"

"Yes to both. You know, I always thought Gert and Mack were just crusty old characters, but now I'm not so sure they're mentally balanced. I saw Beggie and Doris at the grocery store, and they both looked nervous. Well, Doris was looking nervous. Beggie told me she'd pulled out her old handgun, which she hadn't even taken out of her underwear drawer for thirty years. She told me to oil mine up, which I don't need to do. I keep it in good shape.

You probably don't sleep with a gun by your bed, right?"

"No, I don't."

"Well, this is just a word from one friend to another."

Bea was looking over at Frank, who'd heard most of the conversation. Lila was agitated, and her voice normally carried even when she wasn't. Frank threw up his hands.

"Thanks for calling. And thanks for keeping me in the loop."

"I hope I didn't get you into something dangerous."

"I was thinking the same thing about you."

As soon as Bea hung up, Frank said, "So Rob might have been out of jail night before last, the helicopter night, huh?"

"Well, I guess."

"I'm beginning to think you'd all be safer in D.C."

Bea sat up in the bed and moved so that her leg wasn't touching Frank's.

"That would need to be *my* call."

"Whoa. Of course..."

"Frank, I do my best thinking when I'm in motion. I'll just take a quick run. I won't be gone more than half an hour. The kids probably won't be up by the time I get back. Okay?"

"Yes, ma'am."

"Frank, thank you. Truly."

His half-nod probably only indicated minor mollification. She pulled on her jogging clothes and was out the door in three minutes. When she returned, everybody was in the kitchen, pouring cereal into bowls.

"Okay, Frank, you're not going to like this, and it's not fair to you... but I want to go to Copperton. I have some ideas about what happened, and I don't know any other way to do this. I really wanted to spend the whole weekend with you, but I just feel like I *have* to do this. It's not fair to ask you to watch the kids today. I'll ask Susan Rice to do it. I promise I'll be back tonight, and we can have a great dinner."

"You're kidding me. You know I have to fly out on the redeye tonight. Why do you have to go in person?"

"No, I'm not kidding. I know it seems irrational, but I have a hunch and I need to follow it."

He frowned. He was definitely dubious about her intuitive abilities.

"We'll have some of the afternoon and all the evening together. And I'm sure the Rices will watch the kids—"

"Can we talk about this in your room?"

The children were following this conversation closely, turning their heads from Bea to Frank and back again. Andy volunteered, "I think she really wants to go."

Bea and Frank sat on the still-unmade bed. "Bea, it's not that I mind watching the kids, but I'm worried about you."

"I appreciate that. I really do. It feels wonderful to have somebody worried about me. But I promise to be careful in Copperton and it'll be a short trip."

"Okay, you're obviously determined to go. Your son knows you well. When will you be back?"

"It's a three-hour drive each way. And I don't think I'm going to need more than a couple of hours there. I'll add one hour for good measure. It's 7:30 now, so… by 4:30? If I won't be back by then, I'll let you know. And I'll call as I'm leaving for home. Okay?" This morning she'd been all efficiency, and she hadn't touched him at all. Now she looked him straight in the eye. "I have to do this. For myself, for Lila, for… others." He grimaced, and she hugged him, and he held her for a long time. But then she pulled away and filled her daypack with energy bars and apples, as she talked to the kids.

"You'll have the only car. I can take them to that park that's pretty close," Frank said.

"We can play Legos," Andy interjected.

"I'll be back as fast as I can. PLEASE be nice to Frank. I'll be home before dinner."

Jessie pulled at Bea's sleeve, but Bea took away her small hand and held it. "Well, o*kay* Mom," was Andy's only response, but she hugged him anyway, kissed Frank quickly and was gone before she second-guessed herself.

She waited until she'd gotten all the way out of town, before she pulled off at an exit and made a call to Copperton. By 10:30, she was parked in Beggie's driveway. This house wasn't in town like Lila's; Bea found herself in a neighborhood of widely-spaced, comfortable ranch-style homes, with long, now-icy walkways and driveways. Beggie opened the door and met Bea halfway down the sidewalk. "Careful, honey. It's slippery," she said as she took Bea's arm.

"Well, sweetie, you and Doris have both surprised me. She seems to want this meeting as much as you do. I can't wait to find out what you're both so het up about. Sure hope ol' Rob doesn't decide to pay us a visit, but I'm ready for him, honey." She put her hands together, and Bea thought for a moment that she'd rub them together in anticipation of a visit from her ex.

They walked into a cheerful kitchen with a small breakfast nook. Doris was sitting in front of a cup of coffee, twisting her ring. Bea thought for a moment that it was a wedding band that she was fiddling with, but no, it was on her right hand. Doris looked up guiltily. "Can I get you some coffee, Bea?"

"That would be great."

"Now I'll bet you haven't had breakfast," Beggie said.

Bea shook her head. "Neither has Doris. There is no point in discussing all this secret stuff, whatever you two have in mind, on an empty stomach. I'll just whip up some scrambled eggs and toast. Doris, why don't you dice the onions? Bea, you can do the peppers and tomatoes. Rye toast okay?" They both nodded. Bea's resolve ebbed in the face of Beggie's immutable will. Another five minutes wouldn't make a difference.

Doris stopped twisting her ring, but it was hard to tell if her tears were caused only by the very pungent onion she was cutting. She was quick about it, though, and so was Bea, and the plates of steaming scrambled eggs and buttered toast had the settling effect that Beggie had known they would.

After a few spoonsful, Bea began. "Doris, I have an idea and I want to ask you about it."

Doris dropped her fork on the floor.

"Honey girl, Bea seems to have your number. What in the world is goin' on?"

Bea tried again. "Was there a reason you wanted to come over to Tucson to see me on Valentine's Day?"

"I hate that day. It makes me feel like a fool." Bea waited. "I wanted to show you something." Doris had been talking into her lap. Now she looked up. "I mean, I suppose I should show it to the police. But you're working with them, and you... you have kids, you're divorced, you love to dance. And you're helping to solve a crime. You're maybe like a younger me, except for that last part. And I know I should change that."

Doris's hands were shaking. She pulled an old black leather purse off the floor and into her lap. Bea's grandmother had had one like this. It had a brass clasp that Doris opened with some difficulty. She pulled out a yellowed paper, clearly torn from a spiral notebook. She smoothed it out and slid it across the table at Bea. "Here goes," she said, and Bea noticed that Doris was examining her lap again, but then all Bea could see was the paper. Beggie walked behind her and read over her shoulder.

The letter was dated in the right-hand corner. October 29, 1969. The script was messy, but legible, with long, looping letters.

> *Dear Mrs. Winters,*
> *I am very sorry to have to right this note to you, I have to. Your husband has been sinning, for how long I don't know, but I have seen it with my own eyes right here on the living room couch. I think you know what I am talking about. He has been fornicating with Mrs. Shandley. I came in and told them they must stop their sinning, but Mr. Winters told me to leave and he said he knew how to handle a gun. He took the Lord's name in vain and he also used a word that I wood not right to you. I told my imployer, Mr. Shandley about it, and he said, right on the living room couch? They used to be more discreat. I guess this means that he was not surprised, but it is my duty to tell you, as the wronged wife.*
> *Sincerely Yours, Crow Johnson*

Bea exhaled, and then exhaled longer, trying to give herself time to decide what to say. "Why did you decide to show this to me?"

"I think you know."

"Does it have to do with Crow's murder?"

"I knew Buzz had cheated on me before, in Hollywood. But it wasn't anything important, and he always told me. I loved him so."

"That was your mistake," Beggie said.

For once, Doris was defiant. "Not for me, not then." She turned back to Bea. "But this thing with Liz Shandley was different. I confronted him. I told him about Crow's letter. He didn't deny it. He said he cared about her. He said he wanted both of us. Imagine! Imagine him thinking I would do that! I wondered who knew about them. It was so humiliating; I almost didn't want to leave the house."

"She never even told me," said Beggie, shaking her head in amazement. "I never trusted Buzz. Too smooth talkin'." She stroked Doris's arm.

Bea said, "Oh, Doris. I'm so sorry. So he was angry at Crow."

"Well," said Doris, continuing on her own trajectory, "it turned out Liz and Buzz had been together since before Alan bought the property in town for his lodge. It was all Liz's idea, them buying property in Copperton. She came over here the first time when we were filming a movie. I guess she tried to get a part, but all she got was my *husband*." Doris spat out the word "husband," and swallowed a couple of times before she continued. "That was when Liz met Rob and that crowd," She threw Beggie a pursed-lips look. "And she thought there was money to be made in digging pots around New Mexico. I guess she was right, even if she was early for the big money." Doris took a deep breath. There was a silence.

Then Doris barreled on, in a voice that quavered with age, but even more with anger. "It had gone on too long between them. I felt so... I don't know, said it already. *Humiliated*. All the people in the movie probably knew. Rob and Tom, that gang knew. They had to know. And who knows who else. When Buzz had had those other affairs, the ones that I... I ignored. They were on locations somewhere else. Not in my *hometown*."

Beggie interrupted with, "You're exaggeratin', Doris. Not many people knew. *I* didn't."

Doris shook her head, her white curls loosening from

the hairspray that controlled them. "And he still wanted me to accept it!" She started to cry then, in long ragged sobs. Beggie pulled her friend's head to her shoulder, but Doris reared back.

"So, I asked for a divorce! He went on a trip to Tucson and when he came back I did it! And then he told me he was so sorry that I'd been hurt that he killed a man." Bea felt her eyes widening, but she stayed quiet.

"Buzz told me he killed Crow. He said he killed that kid for writing that letter and messing up our marriage. Did he think that murdering that poor boy would make me want to stay married? Sometimes men make no sense." She shook her head again.

"He said he did it out in the desert behind Alan's place, over in Tucson. He told me there was a park road and he just drove right down it and he was so mad he just killed Crow, out there at his tipi by the back fence. I guess he thought nobody would really care that the boy was gone, and maybe he was right, which is a terrible thing. Terrible!" She blew her nose.

"Well, at least you went through with the divorce," Beggie said.

"Not right away, I didn't. I told him I burned the letter. I said I wouldn't tell anybody about what happened to Crow if Buzz gave me a divorce. He was a Catholic, you know," she said. "Divorce was against his religion." Her eyes were wet.

Beggie said what Bea was thinking. "I would've thought that murder was a little bigger sin than divorce."

Doris ignored her. "But then I went back on it. On the divorce. Like a fool."

Bea took her hand. "What happened to change your mind?"

Doris was very focused. She talked quickly, looking

straight into Bea's eyes. "I always thought he shot Crow. Buzz was proud of being a quick draw and all that. He really was as good as he was in his movies. As good at shooting a gun, anyway." She opened her black handbag, and took out an embroidered handkerchief to wipe her eyes. "But I read that newspaper article that said Crow'd been hit on the back of the head with a blunt object, like a shovel. *Our* shovel went missing around the time of Crow's letter. I asked Buzz where it was. He made a show of looking for it—he really *was* a good actor—and then he bought me a fancy new one with a rose tied onto it. He even wrote me a poem. I told him I wouldn't divorce him if he gave Liz up. He agreed. For a few weeks it was just lovely between us, or so I thought." She lost her focus and blew her nose on the dainty handkerchief a few times. She got out a clean handkerchief to wipe her eyes. She took a deep breath, and the eyes that turned back to Bea were very red.

"But then I saw the phone bill, and there they were, long distance calls to the Shandleys' house in Tucson. After Buzz had sworn he wouldn't have anything more to do with her. He thought I wouldn't notice. He thought he could have her and me both and just keep it secret, if I wouldn't agree to that arrangement. And he really killed that poor boy just to keep it all possible. That's the worst part. Buzz didn't do it because he was so mad about Crow's letter, about it hurting me, not really. So..." She finally broke her gaze and looked out the window. "I divorced him, and I fully intended to let it all be buried, just like that poor boy's body."

"And I thought I'd done a good job of burying it. I thought we'd both done a good job of burying things. But then I saw the thing about the 'blunt object' in the paper. And I was just so mad at myself. It just made me so angry, even after all these years, that I had almost taken him back because of a rose he tied onto a shovel like the one he used to kill somebody. And that stupid little poem. It didn't even really rhyme. Damn it." She sobbed then, and Bea stroked her tiny, blue-veined hand with its thin fingers.

"Plus," she said, "when he confessed to me about... you know, Crow... he said Rob Chance knew. About the shovel. And what he did with it. I guess Buzz told him, thinking Rob would be glad not to have to deal with Crow and all his preaching about pot hunting. But it made me so damned—I mean darned—mad that he'd kept bailing Rob out of all his fights. I guess because Rob had something on him. I mean, he wasn't going to kill Rob off with a shovel, was he? People might care, they wouldn't just write Rob off, like they did that poor boy. And then Buzz bailed Rob out of jail just now, and that was the last straw. And Beggie had to take out a restraining order because you never know what that guy will do, although I should talk. My ex-husband killed somebody, and Rob never did that."

"We think," Beggie said.

"Right, we *think*. I don't know. It was all too much. And Beggie was so brave in talking to the FBI about Rob's forgeries, I just decided it was high time for me to be brave." She looked at Bea with a new ferocity. "So now you know. You're friends with that policewoman who made Rob so mad. I wouldn't have talked to her but now I've told you two, and it's out. So, if you think I should, I will meet with her or whoever."

"Thank you," Bea said, squeezing her hand. "You're a brave woman. And yeah, you should definitely talk to the police about this, and show them the letter. You probably want to talk to Sandra Ramirez here in town right away."

"Okay. This is why I wanted to tell you on Valentine's Day. It seemed right. I have still been carrying a torch for him like Beggie told you at the dance. It took me forty years, but that's over. I think the second time telling this story will be easier."

"This should put Rob away for concealin' that he knew about Buzz all these years. That would make us all breathe easier," Beggie said.

"You two, I have a weird question. Does either Buzz or Rob drive a Camry or a van?"

"Hell, no," Beggie said. "When Rob had the Ford dealership, they all bought trucks from him. They all still drive Ford pickups. All those ol' boys do. Tom, too. Why, for Heaven's sake?"

"Just a little thing going on in Tucson that's probably unrelated. Mack and Gert have a van, but not a Camry, right?"

"Far's I know," Beggie said. I think they've got a pickup, too. Why?"

"Nothing. Let's call Sandra."

Chapter Twenty-Four

Bea made it back to Tucson well before dinner time, much to Frank's relief. She told him Doris's tale with the bedroom door shut, while the kids happily watched cartoons.

"Good job, Bea. How'd you guess about Buzz?"

"He kept bailing Rob out. Plus, he was around Tucson *and* Copperton. And Doris went running out of the square dance when the subject of Buzz came up the first time I met her. I just had a hunch she had something to say about him. Also there's the fact that he was an actor... who knew what he was concealing? But I didn't know his motive. That did surprise me."

"Well, you've helped catch a murderer and his abettor, but I can't say I'm comfortable. I guess the Copperton police can figure out if those guys were behind your harassment here. That would make me feel a lot better about things. Maybe they employed surrogates over here or something. But Bea, I need a break. I have a guest gym pass from an old buddy here. How about if I use it, and then we can come back and make dinner?"

"Absolutely." Frank's taking a break eased a bit of Bea's guilt about laying so much on him.

As soon as he left, Marcia called. "It's a good thing Myron Shandley acceded to his father's wishes and held onto that poem Crow wrote. I can already tell you that he misspelled some of the same words," Marcia said. "And I'm sure a handwriting expert can verify the likenesses in his two pieces of writing. Also, it looks like Rob Chance will have a few more charges to deal with. Including sending that anonymous note to your friend Lila. He didn't throw out the magazine he cut the letters from! And it looks like we *may* have some evidence that he was behind Lila's shooting. So, thanks, Bea, from both Sandra and me."

"You aren't the only one who's glad this is clearing up. But what about the tan Camry and the van?"

"It sure would help if you could get a license number. These still could be random sightings of a very common car, Bea. Meanwhile, I can tell you this: Mack's van was not in Tucson the day of Ethan's injury. Neither the Currys nor your friend Armando own tan Camrys. Which doesn't mean they couldn't have borrowed one. And none of them has an alibi for the night your intruder came by."

"Oh, I'll bet Armando loved being asked about that."

"He did not. He did ask if you'd accused him of something, and I said that you hadn't. But Bea, lots of things have been falling into place. Have faith."

"I'll try." *Pot-hunting rings and forty-year-old murders don't affect me directly. This other stuff does.*

"Give us a license number, girl."

"Frank's got my car right now."

But she heard from Frank before he brought the car back. When she picked up the phone, he started in with, "So. A couple of things, Bea. First of all, I flipped to the local news when I was on the treadmill, and Channel Two had breaking news about a development in the 'old murder case at Shandley Gardens.' They mentioned Buzz Winters' arrest, and said that Stephanie Shores would have a special report in the morning."

"I look forward to that."

"Yeah, well, the next thing's more serious, and I'm

going to report it to Marcia, so please give me her number. I just found another note on your car, in the parking lot by the gym. It's in block letters again, and this time it says, 'QUIT YOUR MEDDLING!' No playbill on the back."

"Oh." *What else is there to say?* She gave him Marcia's number.

"I'll be back as soon as I get this to the police. God knows, I may have to get fingerprinted, since I touched the thing. The house doors and windows are locked, right?"

"Yes. I'm sorry, Frank." She was apologizing a lot.

"So am I! Let's just have a nice last night together, okay?" He didn't sound too happy. *Now both my ex-husband and my boyfriend are wishing I had a different job. Wonderful.*

They did indeed have a good dinner together that night. Roasted chicken and vegetables, plus a scrumptious chocolate cake that Frank had picked up on his way back from the police station. And they had a good couple of hours together after the children went to sleep.

"Tonight is why I want to stay together, Bea. All of it," Frank said.

"Yes."

They actually managed not to discuss "various nefarious engagements"—Frank's phrase—until a little before the cab came to take him to the airport. But Frank couldn't help himself.

"I was thinking," he began and then stopped.

"Well?" Bea asked. She was afraid he'd say something about the future of their relationship.

"Do you think Alan cut out of Copperton because he thought Liz had snookered him into investing there? And she did that because of her affair with Buzz?"

Bea sighed. "I know, I can't stop thinking about this stuff, either. So... Alan also didn't much like his wife's greed towards archaeological sites. But he didn't have much call to complain about an affair on his wife's part, as we found out last summer. Kind of hypocritical."

"Men often have a double standard about this stuff. Back then, even more so."

"I sure hope that doesn't apply to you." She said it with a smile, but he knew there was enough seriousness in the charge that he started to protest.

She cut him off. "So did Liz know that Buzz killed Crow, do you think?

"It's hard to say. He killed Crow, supposedly, to shut him up. Liz thought Crow was a blabbermouth, because she said as much to Alan, right? Didn't she tell Javier something about how 'Penguin' didn't mind his own business? But maybe both Shandleys thought he disappeared into the ether. A lot of people did in those days."

"They still do. Yeah, I kind of doubt Alan knew about the murder. He would have been happy to see Buzz in jail, probably. But as far as Liz goes, well, we'll probably never know. I'll bet she enjoyed having Crow out of the picture. Who knows, maybe something will emerge in the trial about her being an accomplice or covering things up."

"Well, Stephanie Shores is right about one thing. A lot happens at your pretty little public garden."

"So everyone says."

"So, Bea." *Here it comes.* "When will we see each other next?"

"I really don't see a trip East in my future at the moment. I'm afraid it'll be up to you. If you want to."

"If we both want me to." She nodded and they caught each other's eyes for a long moment before they fell together.

"Stay safe, Bea."

There were tears in both of their eyes when Frank got

into the cab.

Back in the house, as the clock announced the minutes and then the hours, her mind was ticking away in perfect time.

Why hadn't she been clearer about wanting Frank to visit in the future? Of course, she wanted him to. So, what was her hesitation about? Okay, maybe some of it was *sort* of altruistic. She'd be dragging him into a full-fledged life of major time and energy commitments to her kids. Was this really what he wanted, or would he find the single life in D.C. ultimately easier and more seductive? She hadn't even asked him about his old girlfriend there. But then D.C. *could* prove more seductive if she held him at arm's length. Who wants to keep taking red-eyes across the country for a "maybe" with children?

Am I being honest here? It's not just about his feelings. She'd been badly hurt once, and her kids were still feeling it. Or at least Andy was. Wasn't this long-distance relationship a bad risk for all of them?

It's more than that, though. Fear of hurt: that's what her hesitation had been, in the beginning. But now there was something else. *If I let him into my life completely, will he expect to dictate the terms? I already let that happen once. I don't want to do it again.*

She told herself she needed some time to get out from under all the mess at Shandley. She couldn't think straight about Frank when she was afraid for her family's safety. She found herself looking out the kids' window into the side yard, twice. Nothing there. The third time, it was the neighborhood cat.

This was no good. She had to get that license plate. Angus had some more Camry shadowing runs planned. She'd just drive and drive until he got that number from the rear plate. She wasn't making it up. Just like she hadn't been making up those unpleasant notes.

She went to sleep resolved. She'd figure out who was stalking her.

***

In the morning, Bea debated whether or not she should let the kids see Stephanie Shores' show. She decided that Andy, at least, would hear about the arrests at school in the morning—his friends' parents didn't seem to have many filters about this sort of thing. So they might as well watch it and she'd comment along the way. Andy and Bea settled onto the couch together. Jessie said she'd rather color the kids' page in *Tucson Trends*. "Good Luck, Mom," said her five-year-old-going-on-thirty daughter.

"Channel Two News has a scoop!" cried Stephanie. She was standing outside Shandley Gardens' locked gates.

"About the old bones found on the Shandley Gardens property?" prompted the well-coiffed male anchor, flashing a shiny, white-toothed smile at his female counterpart.

"Yes! It's murder number two on the Shandley property, counting the one last summer! Liz Shandley was murdered then, and now it turns out that her lover killed a gardener because the poor guy knew about their love affair!"

"Tell us, Steph, why does that little botanical garden keep showing up on the police blotter?"

"It's all flowers, love, and murder at Shandley Gardens! One thing's for sure… we don't have the whole story of everything that's going on over there. Not yet! News accounts state that the alleged murderer, Buzz Winters, has an ex-wife who says that *Shandley's acting executive director Bea Rivers* was key in exposing Mr. Winters as the murderer! Bea Rivers is involved again!"

Andy looked at his mother with despair.

"Andy, what I did was go over and talk with Doris Winters. That's exactly what I did, and you can tell anybody who asks about that. Period."

Andy pulled his ear and nodded, but there wasn't much enthusiasm in the nod. Jessie seemed absorbed with her coloring. The cheery anchors cut in at this point. "Do we know anything more about the connections between this murder and Bea Rivers' boss's near-fatal bicycle "accident"?

"Not yet!" said Stephanie with enthusiasm. "Here I am outside the gates of Shandley Gardens, the center of many recent stories. Shandley's not open for business today—it's closed on Mondays—but who knows what will happen next here? Staff and volunteers still work on Mondays, sources tell me."

Bea growled at this, prompting another concerned look from Andy.

Stephanie continued, "A reliable source has told Channel Two News that Ms. Rivers made two trips to Copperton, New Mexico, the home of several of the people involved in last week's antiquities bust, and that Ms. Rivers has worked with the Tucson Police Department to uncover this forty-year-old murder, also linked to Copperton! There may be more to this story than meets the eye! Watch this channel for more breaking news on Shandley Gardens, site of flowers, love, and murder!"

Maybe I can come up with a good class series with that title. Channel Two can promote it.

The perfectly turned-out female anchor had the last word. "Thanks to our roving reporter, Stephanie Shores, for another awesome story!"

Fortunately, that was the end of the Shandley coverage.

Bea and Andy wandered over to Jessie's coloring project.

"Jessie, ocotillo flowers are red, not blue!" Andy said.

"Mine are blue," she said with authority.

He continued his criticism. "Look, there's that stupid ad with the guys surfing on grass." He had recently become a fast reader, so he read Turfin' Tucsonans' copy:

Are you tired of being POLITICALLY CORRECT?
Are you tired of hearing about REMOVING YOUR GRASS?
Break Out!
PUT SOME GREEN BACK INTO YOUR LIFE!
YOUR KIDS (AND PETS) DESERVE IT!

Bea looked over his shoulder. It was a full quarter-page, color job, replete with two little kids rolling on a lawn, a bigger kid playing catch with his dad, and a puppy cavorting with a ball nearby.

"Wow, Mom, they sure don't like the kind of stuff you talk about," her son commented.

Bea suddenly exhaled, occasioning yet another concerned look from her son.

"Get everything ready for school. I'll be back in a sec."

Both children stared at her as she went into the bedroom and shut the door.

"Marcia? I think there's somebody you should check out. I'm pretty sure he has a van, and he doesn't like Shandley Gardens. Bruce Beel of Turfin' Tucsonans."

"Funny you should say that. He's here right now for questioning."

"There? For questioning?"

"He's gotten more careless, it seems. His prints were on that note Frank brought us. It turns out he has a record of petty thievery, so we've got his prints on file."

"Oh. Petty thievery? Could he have broken into our personnel files to get my home address? And Ethan's?"

"We'll look into it. Why do *you* think he's so angry at you? You, and Shandley Gardens?"

"His business is planting turf, which uses lots of water, and we promote alternatives because there's not enough water here. I guess it's not personal."

"Yes, that's pretty much what he said, in more colorful terms. I need to go. We'll be in touch."

"Okay. But Marcia, you might talk to one of our volunteers who interned with Turfin' Tucsonans. She did mention his beef with us."

Marcia thanked her for the volunteer's name and number and quickly hung up. Bea blew out a long breath, put on her mother's smile, and took her kids to the bus.

Chapter Twenty-Five

When Bea dropped the kids off, Andy asked her what they were doing for Rodeo Days. She barely managed to suppress a major expletive in front of several families at the bus stop. The school district had a four-day weekend just after Valentine's Day. It substituted Rodeo Days for Lincoln's and Washington's birthdays. School employees appreciated this relic of Tucson's Wild West past, but the break wasn't popular with many working parents, since every other employer celebrated the federal holidays instead. Bea had been so caught up in "The Events at Shandley" that she hadn't done anything about taking care of her kids for Rodeo Days.

Maybe she should just take some vacation time. What a radical thought. It looked like maybe things were wrapping up.

Marcia had a way of reading her mind. She called and said, "Well, Bea, I thought you'd like to know what we've found, ahead of your fans in the media."

"Please let it be good."

"Good for you. Not for Mr. Beel. Your high school intern is willing to testify that Beel continually blamed his business failures on Shandley Gardens, and its efforts to get people to replace their lawns."

"We're hardly the only ones he could blame. There are plenty of landscape designers and nursery people who've been fighting the good fight."

"Be that as it may, your intern says he ranted about Shandley Gardens all the time. Also, another of his diatribes has to do with what Beel insists on calling rich guys in Spandex.

"Like Ethan on a bike?"

"Like the executive director of Shandley Gardens in spandex on an expensive bike. Mr. Beel drives a 2003 Chevrolet Express, by the way."

"I take it that that's a van?"

"Yep. Also, Beel has a pair of cowboy boots that fit the footprints under Ethan's window when the personnel files were broken into. Too bad he didn't leave fingerprints then; we could have cleared this up much faster. So, when he was confronted with all this, Beel took off on one of his rants, and said Shandley deserved everything it had gotten. It's Shandley Gardens' fault that his business is so deep in debt. It's because of Shandley that he gets such negative reviews from customers. You and Ethan clearly spend a lot of time telling all your visitors never to patronize his business."

"We've never once mentioned his business. We don't knock people's livelihoods."

"Yeah, well, he said it was 'too bad Ethan didn't join the other people getting murdered around there.'"

"Wow, I'm glad he's not on the loose, Marcia."

"Yep. Things seem to be wrapping up. Also, you'll be interested to know that Bruce Beel's mother owns a tan Camry, which he borrows on occasion."

Bea felt the tension seeping out of her shoulders. "I hadn't realized how much that was worrying me."

"Do you think that board of yours will let you take some time off?"

"I've got to. Rodeo Days is almost here."

"Bueno."

Bea was thinking about whether she should interrupt Frank at his office with all the good news when she received her own work interruption. It was Lila.

"Bea, it sounds like you made a visit here and didn't stop in to see me."

"No time. Sorry, Lila. I had to get there and back in a short day."

"Well, listen, my friend, I was at the Native American blessing ceremony for that fish pot that was returned. Doris and Beggie were there, of course, since they're docents, and Ramona Alvarez, that Forest Service archaeologist—she says she knows you—she was there, too. Also, there were lots of folks in the Archaeology Society. Believe me, they were making it clear they do *not* do things the way that Rob Chance and Tom Franzen do. The museum and the archaeology folks are putting on some kids' programs this weekend. 'Living in Mimbres Times,' I think it's called. Anyway, we thought you should bring your kids. Doris and Beggie want to treat you to a bottle of champagne. And you're not going to believe this, but Gert was there, too, and she wants to raise a glass to you. Apparently, she always thought all the doughnut boys were bad news, and she told Mack to stay away from them. She thought they were just using him, and quote, 'didn't have no respect.' She thinks he may be able to show he didn't know what he was selling. Now that's pretty unlikely, but anyway, she's in the clear for now. And Ed wants you to come, too! So, come!"

"I think Andy, Jessie and I might just do that! We've got a long weekend coming up."

"Then it's settled."

Andy was in a surprisingly good mood that evening. Apparently, his teacher had said that his mom had "helped catch some bad guys," and Andy's status had risen. Bea had just told them that they could have whatever they wanted for dinner, and the kids were negotiating whether or not that meant a leftover chocolate cake exclusive, when the phone rang. All good things come to an end. It was Pat.

"Bea, I made the mistake of checking the news on my computer. Somebody sent me a clip of a Stephanie Shores' broadcast. I don't believe all that b.s. about you, but the important question is, are my children safe?"

He sounded genuinely concerned. Bea chose not to take the call as a scolding.

"Thanks for calling about it. Yes, Pat, things are wrapping up and it looks like we know who killed the guy whose bones were found on the back forty. Somebody from out of town. Plus, we also found the guy responsible for Ethan's hit-and-run. Another person entirely."

He'll find out the whole story soon enough.

"If the kids are safe, and you are too, Bea..." She reared her head back at his unfamiliar concern for her. "I can wait to find out the rest of this drama when I return. I'd like to talk to the kids."

"Of course." She handed Jessie the phone.

"Daddy, are you really getting married? When do I get to be the ringbearer?"

Andy smacked Jessie on the rear.

"Oh, okay."

"He doesn't know yet about them getting married," she stage-whispered.

Andy took the phone from her. "Fine," he answered. "No, I wasn't scared. Well, maybe for a little bit. But not anymore," he said, after another pause. Then he seemed to listen for a while, said goodbye and hung up.

"Dad says he's just glad all three of us are safe," he said.

Again, she was surprised by his concern for her. But if

their positions were reversed, she knew she would have been concerned about him.

How had she been married to him for so many years? Habit and responsibility were powerful motivators, but really, that wasn't all. She had cared for him. Especially before they had kids and he became scarcer. But there was something else too, that she was only just now realizing. She'd bought into his idea that she was just *less than*—less than him, less than a lot of people, particularly of the male sex.

She called Frank that night. She decided she wanted to have plenty of time to talk to him and didn't want to make any announcements when both of them were in the office. Like Pat, he was mostly glad that she and the kids were safe.

"So life can get back to normal," he said. "Maybe we can have a more normal relationship."

"What does that mean?"

"Oh, you know. No death threats, no unidentified bones, no fake accidents, just two people caring for each other and having a good time."

"Frank, I hope you can get here soon. We're all going to Copperton this weekend. Maybe sometime I can get to D.C., but I don't know when."

"Yes, I understand that many things still haven't changed."

"It's still complicated."

"Yes."

In the morning, Bea's computer was jammed with emails. Alicia wrote early in the morning, telling her she was deeply grateful for her part in getting Bruce Beel off the streets. "I hate to think what he might have done next," Alicia wrote. Bea had had vivid images of what he might have been planning, which she kept to herself. Instead, she replied to her boss's email by saying, "Do you want to meet so I can update you on what I know, and we can discuss how it affects the Gardens?"

"Sure, Bea," Alicia shot back in reply. "I must say I'm sorry I ever doubted your fitness for the job!"

Bea didn't think Alicia had ever told her she doubted her fitness. She'd take the compliment and not get stuck on the skepticism.

"It's more scandal for Shandley, which we didn't want, but maybe it will increase our visitation," Alicia's email continued. *That does seem to be our mantra.* "I'm guessing that it will spark some stories about why we should be conserving water! So, are you free in an hour?"

She's asking me if I'm free? This is a turnaround. "Yes. See you then!" *Maybe I can be a little more candid with her about Armando.*

An email popped up from Marcia. It seemed to contain a poem, which was out of character. The poem turned out to be the one that Alan had sent Myron, the one that could prove that Doris's letter was real. Marcia was right, the handwriting and spelling looked an awful lot like the ones in the letter to Doris.

For Alan Shandley
Nobody wood like it
If somebody dug up
Their great-great-grandma's bones
Stole her wedding ring,
And didn't even cover her back up.
I'm righting you this poem
Because you get it.

Poor Crow, Bea thought. *His heart really was in the right place. Between his family's ostracism and his violent end, the world hadn't been kind to him.*

This meditation on the inequities of life was interrupted by a call from Lesley Land, who wanted her to know just how big the check was from the Jemuel Land Foundation. It was more than she'd dared hope for. But Lesley didn't stop at this announcement. "I'm now totally convinced that Alan deserved better than Liz."

"What do you mean?"

"You know I met Alan over in Copperton. We were partners in this lovely project, a mountain lodge with extensive gardens. But Liz put the kibosh on it. I think she did it just to spite him. She went on and on about how they were too good for a two-bit town. She thought there were too many Mexicans, for God's sake. I think she just exhausted him. Plus, she accused him of sleeping with me. Would that it were true. As it was, she caused me to lose quite a bit of money in the deal. And then all the time *she* was sleeping with Buzz!" She sighed. "It's too bad Alan and I didn't meet earlier in our lives; something very lovely might have happened between us."

Bea was a little dazed by this soliloquy and managed something bland like, "Maybe so."

"Well, anyway, my dear, no time like the present. You'll be getting a check to honor the world's children. As well as Alan."

When she hung up the phone, Bea sat still for a moment. Lesley had carried this torch for so many years. Her theory about why Alan pulled out of the Copperton project was totally different from Frank's. Maybe both Shandleys wanted to get away from Copperton for their own reasons. It was impossible to know the secret rooms in any marriage.

Before Bea scheduled a celebratory staff luncheon with Angus and Javier, she picked up a voice mail from

Armando that jarred her out of her euphoria quite effectively.

"I have stayed out of your personal life. Why are you messing with mine? I don't know what you said to Stephanie, but she won't talk to me. You really have an exaggerated idea of your power, don't you? I've told you before not to overstep your authority, young lady."

Well, if Bruce Beel's animosity isn't personal, Armando's sure is. He just lost his job. Now maybe he's lost his girlfriend because she figured out he's an unreliable news source. He suggested all these crazy happenings were one connected story, and they weren't. Bruce Beel had nothing to do with the doughnut boys, and their criminal exploits had little to do with Buzz and Doris's marital problems, and even less to do with last summer's murder, no matter how much Stephanie and her salivating public want to believe in a huge conspiracy. And damn it, none of her innuendo about my complicity in all this nastiness had a shred of truth behind it! Good riddance to Stephanie's Shores' credibility and Armando's, too!

Bea had been feeling guilty that she'd imagined Armando hurting Ethan and stalking her, but she didn't feel so guilty anymore.

Angus came in and didn't say a thing. He just gave her a hug. Then he handed her a printout that Jean had forwarded. It was the latest story in the online *Copperton News.*

Local Hero May Be a Murderer
"Trust Not Too Much to Appearances." Virgil

Buzz Winters has been one of Copperton's biggest heroes, the star of ten popular Western movies shot between 1960 and 1973 in Hollywood, Tucson, Copperton, and Las Vegas. Winters was known for his rugged blond good looks, his image as a "good guy in a white hat," and his quick draw with a gun. Winters was married to the former Doris Martin, a movie star in her own right. She was a country western dancer in two musicals. Doris Winters notified police of evidence linking her ex-husband to the murder of Crow Johnson, a gardener for Alan Shandley, a Tucson resident with business interests in Copperton.

Rob Chance, an alleged forger, was also implicated in the murder, and is now alleged to have harassed Copperton resident Lila Mortenson. Mr. Chance is also implicated in a shooting involving Ms. Mortenson. **See page 3 for details on both cases.**

"Thanks, Angus. I'll read the rest of this later. That Virgil quote is an interesting choice, don't you think? I trusted too much in Buzz's good-guy image myself. His loving wife wasn't the only one. At first, I thought those good old boys from Copperton were just colorful characters who might bend the law a bit. I certainly didn't take them for guys in a crime ring. But I thought Armando might be a murderer and a stalker, and now I think he's just a frustrated, sexist academic."

"He may not be a murderer, but he's definitely not a nice person. You need to keep watching your back, boss."

"That's what I was just telling myself."

Angus folded his hands and looked at her for a moment. "So, Bea, what about Frank?"

"What about him?"

"Is he as good a guy as he appears to be?"

"Not sure. I can't afford to be wrong on that one."

"Well said. By the way, I'd suggest visiting Ethan, now that things have calmed down around here... sort of. He's making a remarkable recovery. He's talking, slowly, and making sense. His broken bones are healing well, too. They think he's a great candidate for rehab."

"That's good news." She meant it, of course. She wanted Ethan to get his life back. And her life would be a lot easier if she weren't sitting at the Shandley Gardens desk where the buck stopped. Also, having one boss was a lot easier than having all those bosses on the board, and Alicia wanted to add even more of them. But Bea realized, with surprise, that she had mixed feelings about being a volunteer coordinator/education director again.

Javier came in next, to congratulate her. But then he sat down hard in the chair facing her desk. "Bea, I'm getting too old for this kind of work."

"You mean physically?"

"That, but mostly mentally. It's been tough finding out all these old secrets of Alan and Liz's. I don't want to garden for them, or the nonprofit, or anybody else right now, except for me and Maria. And I want to spend time with my grandkids. It's time, Bea. I'll give you as much notice as you want."

"Javier, this is a shock! You're irreplaceable!"

"Nobody is, Bea. I'll help you and Angus find a replacement."

"Well, you certainly deserve retirement. But I'll miss you. We all will."

She decided to walk the grounds to settle her feelings before she went back to work on the budget. It was the kind of February day that made people sell their houses in

Wisconsin or Connecticut and move to the Sonoran Desert. They sometimes failed to visit in the summer before they made that move. But today wasn't a broiling summer day, it was comfortably warm. And now there were poppies, and not just in the wildflower garden where they'd been watered. There were a few small orange globes emerging in the wild desert area near the place where poor Crow had met his end. Small lupine leaves, scattered among the poppies, would be joined by beautiful purple flowers in a couple of weeks. The little spring annuals had gotten enough fall and winter rain to come up this spring; sometimes their seeds stayed buried for years until the rainfall pattern was right.

Something gleamed white under a catclaw acacia bush. Bea veered off the trail, hoping that no visitors would follow her footprints. This time the bone really did come from a deer, unlike those bones Javier had held out to her on the shovel, just a few weeks ago. It was an old pelvic bone, like many she'd seen in her desert rambles. Bones didn't disintegrate for hundreds or even thousands of years in dry lands. They helped maintain the history of a place, Bea realized, as they had in this incident at Shandley, and in the burials in the Salvaje National Forest—in spots that weren't paved over, and driven over, and littered over.

Next to the pelvic bone were brilliant clusters of poppies, interspersed with purple scorpion-weed. Unlike the bones, the wildflowers came and went in a short season.

Crow's bones, like all of the other secrets buried for the past forty years, had been unearthed. So had surprising moments of satisfaction in being in charge at Shandley. She wasn't sure what was emerging in her personal life. It was possible that the relationship with Frank was just a brief spring bloom. It was probable that her stint as executive director was exactly that.

It was best to let all of this go and enjoy the brilliant dabs of color this early spring. Bea's feelings about *their* emergence were clear.